SALLEY VICKERS is the author of the bestselling *Miss Garnet's Angel, Instances of the Number 3* and *Mr Golightly's Holiday*. She has worked as a university teacher of literature and a psychoanalyst. She now writes full time.

Visit Salley's website at www.salleyvickers.com

From the reviews of *The Other Side of You*:

'In *The Other Side of You* Vickers' talent reaches a new level. It is by far her most intricate and important book, brimming with understanding and insight. As a psychiatrist tries to help a suicidal patient, her story unfolds alongside his own haunted, harrowing journey to self-understanding'

GERALDINE BROOKS, *Sydney Morning Herald*

'A tender, wise and beautifully subtle narrative about the relationship between a psychiatrist and a woman patient. "There's no cure for being alive", remarks one character; yet despite its exploration of deep psychic damage, the book ends on an unfashionably hopeful note'

TERRY EAGLETON, *TLS* Books of the Year

'A moving and absorbing novel ... Vickers debates the nature of relationships with unusual clarity'   *Mail on Sunday*

'The lives of the characters in this gently absorbing novel continue to resonate with the failures, possibilities, regrets and redemptions – consoled and mirrored by art – that we all endure'   CAROL ANN DUFFY, *Daily Telegraph*

'A remarkable novel ... Love and pain, death and life, self knowledge and insensibility – all these big, vital themes converge in this moving, utterly engrossing novel'   *Guardian*

'Kindred spirits and soul mates are at the heart of Salley Vickers' new novel. This is a fine and multi-layered book, which suggests that suffering is necessary and that opportunities for happiness should be taken whenever offered'

Daily Mail

'There is something rare and special about Vickers as a novelist. In exploring the connections between faith and imagination, art and redemption, religion and science in an intelligent, unusual but very readable way, she manages to touch something buried deep in all of us. It gives her work a compelling quality'   PETER STANFORD, *Independent*

'This novel – a return to the scintillating form of her first, the bestselling *Miss Garnet's Angel* – is a sustained examination of love: the way, through timidity or lack of self worth, we allow it to elude us; the appalling role of bad timing in relationships and the redemptive power of understanding and acceptance'

The Times

'The writing is so good and the structure so skilful that Vickers manages to make delicate and difficult notions vivid. Her territory is the faultline along which memories of loss are experienced by an individual both as integral to their identity and as constraints on their engagement with the present. This may be true of a great deal of fiction, but it is rare for a novel to present it so directly and with such success'

JOHN DE FALBE, *Spectator*

'Vickers writes elegantly but romantically about the process of analysis. A good story, neatly and absorbingly told'

Sunday Times

'Deceptively simple in form, *The Other Side of You* tackles huge and troubling questions about human relationships. While Vickers is not afraid of challenging her readers with such knotty problems she is also an adept and often witty storyteller, who draws imaginatively on art and religion to illuminate her quest for human authenticity. *The Other Side of You* is a brave and unusual book, a gripping read that offers the tantalisations and rewards of a whodunit'

Literary Review

'Vickers portrays the therapeutic process in all its messy glory – its imperfections, conflicts and possibilities – and she delivers wrenching conflicts of love within and outside marriage'

Publishers Weekly

'Following in the footsteps of Iris Murdoch, Vickers is concerned with the spiritual dimensions of love and love's effect on the soul'

Kirkus Reviews

'Absorbing, intellectual, enjoyable'

Tablet

'Vickers' astute descriptions of jealousy, passion and grief shift seamlessly from one character to another in the present without faltering. In her experienced hands the characters are complex without being contrived. Vickers has turned a thwarted romance into a serious page-turner'

Time Out

'A bittersweet tale of love, loss, sacrifice and regret. With experience of working as a psychoanalyst, Vickers elegantly weaves her knowledge into an insightful examination of the human condition. Her prose flows effortlessly … a thoroughly engrossing novel'

Scotland on Sunday

Also by Salley Vickers

Mr Golightly's Holiday
Instances of the Number 3
Miss Garnet's Angel

SALLEY VICKERS

The Other Side of You

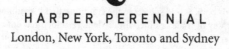

HARPER PERENNIAL
London, New York, Toronto and Sydney

Harper Perennial
An imprint of HarperCollins*Publishers*
1 London Bridge Street
London SE1 9GF

www.harperperennial.co.uk

This edition published by Harper Perennial 2007

First published in Great Britain by Fourth Estate in 2006

ISBN 978-0-00-716545-2

Set in Minion by Palimpsest Book Production Limited,
Falkirk, Sterlingshire

Printed by CPI Group (UK) Ltd, Croydon, CR0 4YY

MIX
Paper from
responsible sources
FSC FSC° C007454

FOR XOPHER

Who is the third who walks always beside you?
When I count, there are only you and I together
But when I look ahead up the white road
There is always another one walking beside you

. . .

—But who is that on the other side of you?

T. S. ELIOT, *The Waste Land*

PART I

When I count, there are only you and I together

1

She was a slight woman, pale, with two wings of dark hair which framed her face and gave it the faintly bird-like quality that characterised her person. Even at this distance of time, which has clarified much that was obscure to me, I find her essence hard to capture. She was youthful in appearance but there was also an air of something ambiguous about her which was both intriguing and daunting.

When we met she must have been in her forties, but in a certain light she could have been fourteen or four hundred – though when I say 'light' I perhaps mean that subtle light of the mind, which casts as many shadows as it illuminates but in the right conditions can reveal a person's being more accurately than the most powerful beam.

Once I would have known her age to the day, since it would have been part of the bald list of information on her medical file: name, sex, date of birth. Of the last detail I have a hazy recollection that her birthday was in September. She spoke of it once in connection with the commencement of the school year and a feeling that, in the coincidence of the month of her birth and a new term, she might begin some new life. 'You see, Doctor,' – when she used my title she did so in a tone that located it at a fine point between irony and intimacy – 'even as a child I must have been looking for a fresh start.'

Doctors are like parents: there should be no favourites. But doctors and parents are human beings first and it is impossible to escape altogether the very human fact that certain people count. Of course everyone must, or should, count. We oughtn't do what we do if that isn't a fundamental of our instincts as well as of our professional dealings. But the peculiar spark that directs us towards our profession will have its own particular shape. I have had colleagues who come alive at a certain kind of raving, who perceive in the voices of the incurable schizophrenic a cryptic language, a Linear B, awaiting their special aptitude for decoding. One of my formidably brilliant colleagues has spent her life attempting to unravel the twisted minds of the criminally insane. It's my opinion no one could ever disentangle that knot of evil and sickness, but for her it is the grail that infuses her work with the ardour of a mythic quest. My colleague Dan Buirski had a bee in his bonnet about eating disorders. I used to kid him, a long cadaver of a man himself, that he liked nothing more than a starving young woman to get his teeth into. I said once, 'You're no example, you're a mere cheese paring yourself,' and he laughed and said, 'That's why I understand them.' He's lucky with his metabolism, but his grandmother and his two uncles died in Treblinka. Starvation is in his blood and he's converted that inheritance into a consuming interest in humankind's relationship with food. It's a strange business, ours.

And what was my peculiar bent, the glimmer in my eye which has in it the capacity to lead me into dangerous swamps and mires? For me it was the denizens of that hinterland where life and death are sister and brother, the suicidally disposed, who beckoned. Like is drawn to like. Alter the biographical circumstances a fraction and my colleague who worked with psychopaths would make an expert serial killer: she had just the right streak of fanatical perfectionism and the necessary pane of ice in the heart. And for all his badinage, Dan had a hard time keeping a scrap of flesh on him. I saw him once, after he'd had a bad bout of flu, and I nearly crossed myself he looked so like a vampire's victim. But despite the concentration camps, death wasn't his particular lure. That was my province.

It was a landscape I knew with that innate sense which people call 'sixth,' with the invisible antennae that register the impalpable as no less real than a kick in the solar plexus from a startled horse. To some of us it can be more real. It is said that the dead tell no tales, but I wonder. When I was five, my brother, Jonathan, was killed by an articulated lorry. It was my third day of school and our mother was unwell; and because our school was close by, and my brother was advanced for his six and a half years, and was used to going to and from school alone, she allowed him to take me there unescorted. The one road we had to cross was a minor one, but the lorry driver had mistaken his way and was backing round the corner as a preliminary to turning round. Jonny had stepped off the pavement and had his back to the lorry to beckon me across. Although he was mature for his age he was small, too small to figure in the mirror's sight lines. I was on the pavement and I watched him vanish under the reversing lorry and I seem to remember – though this could be the construction of hindsight – that it was not until the vehicle started forward that I heard a thin, high scream, the sound I imagine a rabbit might make as a trap springs fatally on fragile bones.

I doubt there was a bone left unbroken in my brother's body when the lorry drove off, leaving the mess of shattered limbs and blood and skin which had been Jonny. I believe I saw what was left of him, before I was whirled away in the big, freckled arms of Mrs Whelan, who lived across the street and had heard the scream and rushed me into her house, which Jonny and I had never liked because it smelled of dismally cooked food, and terrified me by falling on her knees and dragging me down with a con-fused screech, 'Jesus, Mary, and Joseph, the blessed lamb, may he rest in peace.'

Afterwards, I didn't know where my brother was, but I was pretty sure it wasn't with Jesus, Mary, or Joseph. The belief I clung to was that Jonny was still in the pine tree he had assured me was 'magic,' on whose stately curving boughs we used to swing to-gether in Chiswick Park. I heard him more than once, when I was allowed back to play there. He was singing 'He'll be com-ing round the mountain when he comes,' which was the song our mother sang when we were fretful, the two of us, on long car journeys. Later, when Mother had my twin sisters, born one behind the other within the hour, she sang other songs to them.

From that time onwards, it was always 'the girls' and 'Davey.' I, Davey, was the wrong side of the unbridgeable fissure that had opened up in our family, and although I'm sure my parents loved me, I was a reminder of that small bloody mess they'd left behind. The lorry driver never recovered and had to be pensioned off, unfit for work. But my mother was made of sterner stuff. She had in her a fund of life that was not to be defeated even by life's only real enemy. She was not a woman who lived on easy terms with her emotions. She was the daughter of a judge, and her upbringing, though liberal, had not bred in her a place for the easy expression of the finer shades of feeling. And I knew, too, though nothing in her outward demeanour ever gave this away, that if she could have chosen which son she had to lose, it would not have been Jonny.

I didn't blame her. After that, I was never going to be right for her again. I was the living witness to a calamity, the deeper reaches of which she could not afford to acknowledge if she was to continue to hold herself, and our family, together. Very likely she blamed me for the catastrophe. Why wouldn't she? I blamed myself for it.

My mother, for my father's sake, for them to go on together, and for the family to survive, had to set her shoulders and turn her back on the disaster. She faced a choice, and she made it by abandoning me and jumping the ravine which had opened with Jonny's death to the other side. It was a leap to the side of life, and the proof of this came in the form of my twin sisters, apples of my father's eye and each other's best companion.

For a long time I was expecting my lost brother to come round that mountain, with all the confidence with which he had stepped off the kerb of the pavement and into the lorry's fatal path. He was my closest companion, my hero, my single most important attachment to life. And when he didn't come, and I heard only the echo of his voice in my ear, as I swung alone on the low pine branch, pretending, for my mother's sake, that I was enjoying myself, a part of me wanted to go after him, for company.

2

At the time I am speaking of I worked in two psychiatric hospitals in the south of England: a big red-brick, mock-Gothic pile in Haywards Heath, and a cosier, less oppressive place near Brighton on the south coast. In addition, I had a small private practice, where occasionally I saw some paying patients.

From her appearance Mrs Cruikshank might have been one of those. She had the voice and mannerisms of someone born middle class. But I came to learn that this was part of a well-crafted veneer – like a piece of good furniture, she had a discreet sheen which was far from ordinary. In fact, she was the child of two immigrants, her father an Italian communist, who had come to England before the war; her mother, a refugee from the pre-revolutionary Yugoslavia, the illegitimate daughter of one of those two-a-penny Eastern European counts, or so she claimed. When I got to know her better, my patient told me she thought this may have been a compensating fantasy for the fact that her mother worked for a time as a dinner lady in the local primary school, the one her own daughter attended. Possibly the idea had conferred on the child a tincture of the aristocratic. Fantasies, if they are convinced enough, are also an element in the reality which shapes us, and there was a tilt to my patient's narrow nose which might have given an impression of looking down it.

She was the only child of a marriage that, given the natural antagonism of the backgrounds, was bound to be somewhat rocky. The parents were ill-matched in character, as well as history. It was a pattern I recognised. The mother was pushy and ambitious; the father, though something of an intellectual, more passive, content to read about revolution in Marx and Lenin but to let his own life take its course without putting up much fight. They bickered constantly, and as a result my patient left home early, in order to escape an atmosphere which grew increasingly abrasive as her mother's insatiable discontent was left unassuaged.

My patient was of the type of whom a first impression suggests that they are either phenomenally bright or slightly deficient. When I established that it was the former – though the very bright are almost by definition always also somewhere deficient – I recognised it as the kind of intelligence which is unconscious of its own reach. In my experience this is more often a feature of mental illness than is commonly acknowledged. Living in the world is hard enough, but if you see through it, yet lack the resources to deal with that keener vision, it can be a whole lot harder. I concluded that the school my patient had attended could not have provided the nourishment necessary to feed her potential. There had been none of those inspirational teachers who rescue many hidden intelligences. I thought it likely that the habit of concealment she had perfected at home had acted as a more general camouflage.

The effects of an unhappy beginning are various: shame, rage, anxiety, inhibition, insecurity, self-doubt, a propensity for self-harm; but there is one common factor: a fundamental mistrust, an insidious feeling that the world is not a place where you are welcome or can be at home. It can take a long time to get over that feeling – if it ever can be got over.

My first meeting with Mrs Cruikshank followed her admission to St Christopher's, the smaller of the two hospitals I worked in.

She was a suicide case, a serious one, and it was clear from the start she was not one of your manipulative females trying to make a boyfriend or husband feel guilty with a fistful of painkillers and a bottle of wine. She was saved by one of those chances that make you believe in a beneficent providence. I don't know why there shouldn't be one: there's plenty of evidence of the baleful kind.

The man in the flat downstairs, whom she believed away on holiday, returned unexpectedly over some family crisis and, needing his spare key, rang my patient. Getting no reply, and assuming his upstairs neighbour was away, and his key being a matter of urgency, he let himself into her flat with a spare key with which he in turn had been entrusted. Having retrieved his own, hanging, as he knew it would be, by the front door, some instinct made him question the state of his neighbour's flat. He was ex-army, and thus trained in that vigilance which is alert to small disjunctions. Perhaps it was the unusually closed state of all the doors in the hallway, the absolute absence of lights, or notes, or those small signs of incompletion which we leave behind us to remind the world – or ourselves – that we have not wholly gone away. There is a peculiar silence which attends all finalities and maybe this is what Major Wilks noted without quite being aware of what he was sensing. In any event, he defied what I took to be an essentially conservative character and investigated the closed rooms, where he found my patient beneath the heaped blankets, grey-skinned and somnolent and at death's door.

Indeed, it seems she had all but crossed the threshold and had to be dragged back by medical main force. 'We nearly lost her,' Cath Maguire said, in the tone which indicated a suicide was the real McCoy and not a 'time-waster' (these were subject to Maguire's basilisk look, probably more of a deterrent to future episodes of self-harm than any stomach pump). Maguire made sure, if she could, that the suicides got to me. For the reasons I've outlined I had a certain success in that department.

My wife, Olivia, would say that I was poor at first impressions. At dinner parties, when people discovered that I was both a psychiatrist and a trained analyst – the two are not synonymous: a psychiatrist is medically qualified and attempts to cure principally with drugs, while an analyst's training, in Britain at least, is non-medical and the work is done entirely through words – they would often say something along the lines of 'I'd better watch what I say or you'll know all about me!' Irritating, and, as Olivia would be swift to point out, quite off the mark. My disposition prefers to see the best in people until faced with the worst. This is not especially commendable in me: I'm aware that a seeming good nature often stems from fear.

Olivia, however, was adept at picking up the more negative elements of character. 'A gold-digger,' she would say contemptuously, when I ventured that some woman we met at a party seemed 'awfully nice.' Or if I were to suggest that someone was 'frightfully clever': 'Oh, darling, he's just a stuffed shirt,' she'd sigh. 'I had the dullest conversation with him.' Driving home, as we often were during these exchanges, I would sometimes catch myself flushing in the dark. I've often thought it would be no bad plan to drive at night with the light on – people will so often speak their minds in the dark.

In any event, I would tend to spend the first session with any new patient asking pretty mundane questions, hoping I was absorbing the myriad clues which human beings give off even in the simplest transactions: the set of the head, or the jaw, or the shoulders, the arms folded or relaxed, the play of the hands, the flicker of the eyelids, the pallor of the skin, the way the feet make contact with the ground, the pitch of the voice – crucial, for me, I find – the choice of vocabulary, the pace and cadence of the words, how the eyes would meet yours or look away. I could go on: the way the shirt is tucked into the trousers or skirt, the colours and textures of the fabrics, the way the hair is worn, lipstick, nail varnish, earrings, aftershave, scent, shoes, the telltale signs of smoking and drinking, the timbre, and frequency, of the laugh, the moisture in the eye or on the skin, the posture in the chair, the poise of the head, the questions asked or not asked – particularly not asked.

These signs are all registered subliminally so I have no note of my first meeting with Mrs Cruikshank. Except that I am sure that I asked about her name. Her forename, as I read on her file, was Elizabeth. But when I asked her if she was 'Liz,' because it's important to get the name straight from the beginning, she said, in a tone which I can still hear across all the intervening years, 'No, Elizabeth.'

And there was another thing, though I can't say I noticed it at our first meeting. She must have had a bag with her, because once I had seen more of her, I observed she was never without it. A brown leather bag, not bulky, more like a small-sized music case. Although, necessarily, she had to put it down, she always made sure to keep it close by.

3

Olivia was right about my first impressions of people being at sea. But my second impressions, though I say it myself, are often spot on. I had a habit I'd picked up from Gus Galen, who supervised my analytic training. He told me that all he needed to know about a patient could be written down on a postcard. When a course of treatment finished, he said he often looked back and saw that everything that had been uncovered could be discerned in what he had noted there. 'It's all in how you interpret information,' he added. 'It can take years to understand in your head what your gut knows from the start.'

So I do have a record of the next occasion I met Elizabeth Cruikshank, since it was after that meeting that I made my notes. I no longer have access to any official files, and anyway I imagine the bulk of my case histories have either long gone through the shredder or are part of a disconnected account on some NHS database. But of my private postcard distillations there are a few I've chosen to retain.

Looking now at the card headed 'Cruikshank, Elizabeth,' I see handwriting which is recognisably mine but bears the marks of someone younger. The letters are more capacious and better formed, as if my script has shrunk in proportion to my person. Nowadays, I'm conscious that my five feet eleven inches has dwindled, but the worst thing about ageing is not the physical diminishment. My belief that I am equal to ordinary events and encounters is beginning to be eroded. I am apprehensive now over matters that would have been unimaginable to me then: of trains and timetables, major road junctions and mobile phones; that my plumbing will break down – and my bladder; that I will be locked out of my house; that along with my keys I may lose my mind. And, of course, my presence in the world has always had a touch of the provisional about it.

But then, as it seems to me now, from my present vantage point, I was in the thick of things. It is a commonplace that it is part of life's tragedy that while it must be lived forwards it can only be understood backwards; but maybe it can only be appreciated backwards as well. In any case, in those days I had some sort of notion that I knew what I was doing. Perhaps without that feeling we can't survive.

There's a party game in which someone goes out of the room and those left pick a member of the group whose identity is gradually revealed through answers to the ignorant interlocutor's questions: If X were a film, what film would he or she be? If a book, what book? If a colour, car, item of clothing, meal, country, dog, flower, painting . . . ? And so on. I don't know when it was that I found that this was a handy device for formulating an impression of the person whose essence I was in a sense trying to discern. After a couple of meetings I would jot down, for example, 'red, ferret, Jane Eyre,' or 'bulldog, jeep, Ian Fleming,' you get the idea. I used this as a kind of shorthand to myself, a way of setting in my mind the co-ordinates of the personality I would be sitting with.

The postcard I'm looking at is a little dog-eared and faded but the writing is firm. The comments are few:

Cruikshank, Elizabeth.
Suicide.

Elegant. Guarded.
Attractive voice. Quiet.
Azure blue. Swallow.
A hinterland person.

Beside the word 'Swallow' the initials 'JA' have been crossed out.

Another lesson I learned from Gus was to ask, 'What do I want to do with this patient?' Not, as he was at pains to point out, *should* or *may* I do, or even *can* I do, but what, in a world without consequences, do I *want* to do? In theory, this could produce some disturbing answers, though the number of shrinks who actually want to have sex with their patients is fewer than you might imagine. But it's not unusual to want to hold or hug or touch the hand or shoulder of those we feel for, even in circumstances where to feel for another's pain is not an inherent part of what is expected of us. Most doctors, if they permitted themselves, would admit to those normal, everyday human impulses which the nature of the work obliges us in practice to check.

Such inclinations take more intangible forms too. At that time, Jane Austen was my staple reading, a bulwark, I dare say, against my more disturbing professional encounters. For me to think of someone as a character in Jane Austen was a compliment. But, truth to tell, psychiatric patients are not really Jane Austen people. The Austen world has its quota of narcissists, hypochondriacs, low-grade psychotics, and the marginally depressed. But none would fetch up in a psychiatric unit. What the postcard, with the crossed-out initials of my favourite novelist, reveals to me now is that here was someone who, from the first, counted for me, and counted enough that I associated her with my own inner world.

My room at St Christopher's was a pleasant one, overlooking the back garden, and the chairs were arranged to ensure a view both for myself and my patients. In my mind's eye, I see Elizabeth Cruikshank looking out at a quince tree. This tree was a refugee from the days when this part of the hospital was a substantial private house, with the kind of garden that included orchards and well-stocked herbaceous borders. Most of this land had been sold off and was now taken up by the blocks of flats surrounding the hospital, whose inhabitants made occasional protesting petitions at being obliged to live cheek by jowl with the mentally disturbed. The beds at the front of the hospital had, by this time, acquired a municipal look: lobelias and scarlet salvias. But where a corner of the original gardens had been annexed, a couple of the old fruit trees had been preserved.

In spring, the quince was lit with a pale pink translucent blossom, but it wasn't spring when Elizabeth Cruikshank and I met. That autumn the south coast was experiencing unusually foul weather. She arrived regularly and on time, lowered herself, in a way which suggested extreme fragility, into the blue brocade chair which was once my mother's, and sat, as the wind whipped the branches of the old quince, saying nothing but staring out at the tree, which seemed to hold for her a persistent fascination.

There are different qualities to silences and in my job you learned to read them, like an old-style weatherman observing skies or an experienced fisherman reading surfaces of water for signs of imminent fish. I, for one, welcomed them. There are few jobs where you are paid to sit quietly, and in the silences ideas have come to me which voluble transactions would have scared away. My patient sat wrapped in her invisible mantle to protect the wounds which had brought her to me, while I sat, a little at a distance, at a discreet angle from her, saying nothing too. There was no antagonism in her demeanour. It conveyed only a lacklustre indifference, as if I were part of the furniture of a cell —

a nun's or prisoner's – an unregarded bystander to her pensive preoccupation.

I have no accurate recall of the number of meetings the two of us sat like this, and I became somewhat used to sitting, at my odd angle, alongside her. Her mute presence did not disturb me, other than through my growing sense of the extent of this uncharted pain.

But one day, when the weather was particularly violent, after staring a while at the tree outside, she volunteered, 'It could blow down in that wind.'

'Yes, it might,' I agreed, trying to conceal any off-putting excitement.

She made no follow-up to this, so after a decent pause I hazarded, 'Do you feel you might blow down too?' The grey eyes grazed mine and looked away. 'Or you mightn't survive a storm?'

She made a gesture, as if shrugging the invisible protective mantle closer round her, but we had made some sort of contact so I pressed on.

I first met Gus Galen at the big biennial conference on anxiety and depression. He would probably be either thrown out or not taken on at all by today's medical faculties. The son of an East End tailor, he was one of those annoying prodigies who won a scholarship to Oxford at sixteen, read Greats, became a classics don, gave that up and trained as a medic, specialised in neurology, and then found he took more interest in the impalpable than the substantive workings of the mind. By the time we met he'd had, I surmised, a fairly raffish past, but there was a childlike innocence in him, which shone in his mild, slightly protuberant hazel eyes. These eyes fixed you with a guileless stare which the susceptible found hard to resist. But he also had a talent for making the kind of simple-sounding observation which permanently affects the way you think and feel.

I met him pacing the pavement outside the hotel where the conference was held and which I'd left to stretch my legs and take a breath of air. He had gone outside to smoke one of the dreadful miniature cigars that I was to learn he was never without.

'Tell me, dear boy,' he said (everyone was either a 'dear girl' or 'dear boy' to Gus, unless they were a 'bitch' or a 'baboon'), darting over to catch my arm – he was a big man but with that nimbleness which big men, in defiance of gravity, sometimes display. 'What did you think of Collier's paper?' Steve Collier was a hard-line drugs psychiatrist.

'I thought it was pretty crude,' I risked. For all I knew, Gus was Collier's best friend.

'The man's a bloody baboon,' said Gus, and I felt I had passed some test. 'Fancy a stroll?'

We walked down to the Thames and alongside the grey-green river, then past the Tate and on up towards the Houses of Parliament, where we crossed the road to Westminster Abbey.

'The question,' Gus said, punching my upper arm in a gesture which I discovered was as much part of him as the disgusting little cheroots, 'the question is not how to cure or be cured but how to live.'

It was a comment which dropped like a diamond into the well of my being, where its simple brilliance never ceased to sparkle for me. The people we were treating were not so much looking for a remedy for anxiety or depression, they were looking for a reason to be alive. For the most part, the human race takes for granted that life if not a blessing is at least desirable enough to cling to. But for those for whom the business of being alive is a much more vexed question, the illness is the question, or, to put it another way, the illness is how the question may be posed.

For these hesitant souls it is life and not death that holds the terrors, and if I recognised the feeling, it was because I shared it. But it took Gus Galen to put it into words for me.

'See there,' he said, stabbing with a burly finger in the direction of the old church, as if he were about to accuse it of some serious misdemeanour, 'that's what places like that should be for. To help us live. There's no cure for being alive . . .'

'There's no cure for being alive,' I suggested into the autumnal silence to Elizabeth Cruikshank.

'There is.'

The ginger tomcat, against which I waged war, as it used the garden as a latrine and attacked the garden birds I liked to feed, was balancing nonchalantly on the fence outside. I waited a little longer. I wanted her to say it.

'There's death.'

She seemed a lot further from me across the three feet or so of space between us in the room than the cat outside.

'So you were attempting that cure? Rather a drastic one.' I allowed the smallest trace of irony into my tone.

Again she shrugged, looking not at me but out at the rain which had begun to drizzle down on the elderly tree.

'Not to me.'

'Not unwelcome, maybe, but drastic nonetheless.'

Something about her made me feel that the distinction might be one she would understand, but it produced nothing. I tried a different tack. 'I gather you've decided not to take any further medication while you're with us.'

'I prefer not.'

'I see. Any reason? I should say I shan't force anything on you but drugs can sometimes help.' It was in my mind that it was drugs which had failed to help her leave life, so I could appreciate her antipathy to having them help her endure it.

'I'd rather not.'

'Fair enough,' I said, deliberately brisk. 'Let's see how you go.'

I waited again in case she came out with anything more, and the silence thickened, hovered for a moment, as if she might relegate it a second time, hung in the air between us, and then attenuated and passed over. I felt there was no more to come from her, but I made an appointment to see her the following day.

The principal part of the hospital was located in a modern building across the garden from the old house where I had my room. I was about to make my way over there when I heard the unmistakable voice of Lennie, our office cleaner.

Lennie was a recovered schizophrenic. I say 'recovered' but more accurately I should say managed. He had stayed on after being brought in for the umpteenth time from under the pier, where he hung out, madder than the vexed sea and covered with sand and pee and some or other form of the more diabolical kind of alcoholic spirit he consumed, and talking wildly to the more other-worldly 'spirits' who, on such occasions, invited him to demonstrate his faith in them by committing his body to the deep. I was the duty consultant that night and, I don't know why, he took to me and I persuaded him that a regular Modecate injection might prove a sensible precaution against the spirits' more disruptive injunctions.

Lennie took to dropping by my room, where, if I was free, he would stand and smile and I would smile back. As Gus Galen will tell you, there are important conversations which have nothing to do with speech. One day, he pointed at the window which looked out on to the quince, then transfigured by pale pink flowers, and said, 'You see the blossom better, Doc, if I was to wash the window.' We had problems at the time getting cleaners and, with one of those brain waves which occasionally I act upon, I decided to make an advantage out of the fact that Lennie seemed to want to be useful. The inspiration paid off: Lennie took the job and was by now our longest-standing, and easily most efficient, cleaner, which arrangement allowed me to ensure that he kept up with his Modecate injections. In turn, he cleaned my office as painstakingly as if it were an emperor's palace.

He was a bulky man, never to be seen without a yellow woolly bobble hat, which sat, jammed on his black head, atop his six-feet-plus frame, like a baby's bonnet. He had become a popular figure around the hospital: his disposition was as benign as a baby's and he had only one enemy, Dr Mackie, who was my enemy too.

Mackie disapproved of the informality of my association with Lennie and disliked the way I worked in general with my patients. And Lennie, as is the way with many psychotics, without any tangible information to go on, had picked this up. It was ironic, because it was drugs, more than words or kindness, which had helped him in the end.

But now I heard Lennie's usually deep voice risen to a squeaky pitch and hurried down the corridor to find him upbraiding Mackie, who was standing in the hallway looking down at his feet.

'You dumb fucker,' Lennie was saying. 'That's my clean floor you've trod your fuckin' feet over! Get your fuckin' act together, man!'

From Mackie's reddening face I could tell he was about to round on Lennie, whose arm I now grasped, sternly saying, 'Stow it, Lennie. Dr Mackie didn't mean to muddy your floor. Apologise to him, please.'

I don't know why this public schoolboy style of address came to me when dealing with Lennie, but he responded to it. He quietened down, muttered a sullen 'Sorry, Doc,' and resumed his manic mopping of the hall floor.

I walked through the grounds to the main building conversing politely, and pointlessly, with a flustered Mackie. I knew he wouldn't easily forgive my witnessing his humiliation at the hands of my protégé.

Luckily, we met Maguire at the entrance, so I had an excuse to get away.

'Good,' I said, 'I wanted to catch you. Mrs Cruikshank. How d'you find her?'

'Always the same. Quiet as a mouse. No bother.'

'Do you like her?'

'What's to like? Haven't seen enough of her yet.'

'Well, keep me posted,' I said. 'You know how I rate the Maguire nose. And by the way, we can stop trying to push medication on her. She's safe enough under your beady eye, no need to force things.'

I had to go cautiously, especially with a suicide case, though in those days we had more leeway. God knows how the poor bastards who work in the NHS cope now. But my sixth sense suggested that, her effort to escape from some intolerable anguish having failed her, my patient was less likely to try that solution a second time.

4

After Jonny died, up to the time when I finished at university, I dreamed of him regularly, so that I now cannot swear which of my recollections are real-life memories and which remnants of the dreams. Nor can I judge how far my love of reading was a consequence of having lost my brother, but from as far back as I can recall, I have always found solace in immersing myself in others' lives, and worlds. It was therefore natural that my first degree should be in English literature. However, when I decided to go on to medical school, although I dreamed still, the dreams about Jonny seemed to stop.

I missed them – as I had missed him. But I retained the memory of them, and in one, which had seemed to recur, he would say, 'Eat this, go on!' and on a slender silver spoon was something I expected to be Milo's ice cream.

Milo's was the first soft ice cream I ever tasted, and it was a treat Jonny and I used to clamour for when we were out shopping with our mother on the Chiswick High Road. In those days Chiswick had a Lyons, where we ate buttered teacakes, and a draper's shop called Goodbands, where our mother bought buttons for our shirts and thin apricot satin ribbon for her petticoat straps. And it also boasted an up-to-the-minute ice cream bar. In the dream, I would shut my eyes and open my mouth and Jonny would carefully place something on my tongue, and

I knew, though I could never recapture the taste on waking, that it tasted remarkable: better than anything in life.

At the time, Olivia and I lived in a flat in one of Brighton's Regency squares, and on the days I worked at St Christopher's I sometimes took my exercise by walking to and from the hospital. As I walked home that evening, this dream came back to me. I knew it was death's allure I had tasted from Jonny's cold spoon and I wondered how it had tasted to Elizabeth Cruikshank.

We were due for dinner later at the home of a colleague, Denis Powell. On the whole, I tried to avoid social events during the working week, but the Powells hardly counted nor did Dan and Barbara Buirski, who were invited too.

Olivia was in the bath when I let myself in and she called out to come and find her. At forty-two she was still a pretty sight, and naked, and wet, and without make-up and in her shower cap, she looked about sixteen. I kissed her shoulder and went to pour us both a drink and came back and sat on the lavatory seat and chatted to her about her day. We hardly ever discussed mine.

Olivia and I were a mystery to me. We had next to nothing in common and there were many occasions when with good conscience I could have finished with her during our erratic courtship. In the end, I was always pulled back by something I could never quite put my finger on. It wasn't simply sex, though sex was part of it. I seemed unable to do without her, and yet we were never a fit.

It was a puzzlement, but I knew this much: the hook was inside me, not in her. She was – well, she was Olivia. Perhaps it was that she was so unequivocally herself that drew me to her. She was substantial, she was on the side of life, especially when that life was hers.

'No kids,' she said, when I asked her to marry me. 'I'll marry you but I don't want any brats.'

'Fine,' I said. Perhaps because of Jonny I wasn't sure I wanted any either.

In fact, she did fall pregnant and, after some debate, in which I took a pretty passive position – excusing myself with the alibi that it was for the woman to make the final decision – she had an abortion. Our sex life wasn't terrific afterwards. I suppose I thought it was the result of the termination, and assumed that eventually things would resume their previous pitch. They never did. And I never liked to enquire why. It seemed a pity, because it was one of the things which had been good between us.

But when we weren't sniping at each other, or more often she at me, we could be affectionate, and sipping my whisky I looked at her naked shoulders appreciatively in the bath.

'Shall I soap your back?'

'Would you, darling?'

'It would be a pleasure,' I said, and meant it. Olivia would have made a good artist's model. She had a long back and it was worth soaping.

It was worth seeing her dress too, and she scolded me a little, but not unpleasantly, for stopping to watch her put on her stockings. She had nice legs and good taste in shoes.

'People will think I'm a foot fetishist,' I complained once when she came back with yet another pair.

'Perhaps you are. Shrinks are always cagey about their own perversions. I wonder what yours really are?'

I wondered too. Perhaps a trace of masochism. Certainly if there was any masochism at play it was not in Olivia.

I was changed and wearing my silk and wool tweed jacket long before she was ready, and I waited while she did her face and sprayed herself with scent and changed her shoes a few times. She was more gregarious than me and liked dinner parties, and this evening she was in an unusually cheerful temper.

Driving to the Powells', she remained in a friendly mood, which had the effect of relaxing me. It bothered me that she was able to alter the atmosphere with one brief phrase, or word, and that in my domestic life I had fallen into a more or less permanently propitiatory position. It might have been masochism or it might have been the desire for a quiet life. The desire for a quiet life can be a dangerous ally, I'm afraid.

Chris was still in the kitchen when we arrived and Denis let us in with his usual exaggerated compliments over Olivia's appearance. This had once worried me, for Chris's sake, since she is one of the ugliest women I know. But she is also one of the most likeable and I had come to the conclusion that Denis was genuinely unaffected by physical charms. Or maybe he was just sensible enough to recognise that with Chris he had a gem and to hell with appearances. I admired him for this and it made me obscurely ashamed. Olivia's glamour had an undoubted appeal, though the appeal had more to do, I think, with how I wanted to be perceived than with a more personal response. Denis's gallantry was pure good manners: as a skilled diagnostician he recognised Olivia's need for adoration.

The Buirskis were already drinking wine in the Powells' untidily hospitable sitting room. Olivia was incapable of getting anywhere on time. I suspected that this was because she liked to make a conspicuous entrance but also because while she was keen on her own shoes she was not much of a one for putting herself in other people's.

In general Olivia's self-centredness was indulged. Dan, however, was an exception. He found my wife exasperating and didn't conceal the fact. And this meant there was often an edginess between them which I would have to smooth down. He made a comment now as we entered the sitting room.

'Sound the trumpets! The McBrides have graced us with their presence.'

'Belt up, Buirski,' I said, 'and budge up. I want to hold hands with your wife.'

Dan got up and went to poke the fire burning in the grate, which had been ripped out during a renovation of St Christopher's and would have been dumped for rubbish had not Chris, who had no eye for herself but a magpie's eye for useful household treasures, rescued it. Barbara Buirski moved along the chesterfield, bought by Chris for thirty quid in an auction, patting the place beside her for me to sit down. Bar was an ex of mine, someone I took up with during one of the 'off' periods with Olivia. She was characteristically good-tempered when I explained that Olivia was back, and Dan, when I told him, said, 'You're mad! Bar Blake is terrific. I'll have her if you don't want her.' And so far as I could tell, they'd been happy together. He was right about Bar, she was terrific, but she never got into my bloodstream the way Olivia had.

None of which prevented me from keeping up a flirtatious friendship with Bar. Dan seemed not to mind. In fact, he seemed to enjoy it. As for Olivia, I wondered sometimes if she would care if I slept with another woman. I couldn't say, as I'd not tested it, but certainly she was too secure in her own attractions to bother her head about my harmless flirting.

Bar was a dermatologist, a very able one; Denis was a consultant in geriatric psychiatry; and Chris, before she had the kids, had been a midwife. So when the six of us got together the conversation was often work-centred, which meant that Olivia, as the only one of us not medically qualified, sometimes played up. She'd been PA to, and mistress of, a high-powered MP when I met her. He'd dropped her like a hot brick when the press got wind of his extra-curricular activities and rapidly returned to the arms of his plain and uncomplicated Southampton wife. I imagine it was this jolt to her self-esteem which propelled Olivia into my unembarrassed arms.

We met over a medical delegation she'd organised to the House of Commons, where I sat beside her at lunch. The button on the sleeve of my jacket got caught in the lace of her blouse. I'm deft-fingered, and I disentangled it with the occasional flamboyance which can visit me when I am not trying too hard. The episode, conducted across the table from the treacherous MP, acted as a tonic to Olivia's wounded feelings. Looking back, I can see that her animated responses were designed to put the MP in his place, rather than to encourage me to take it. But she was attracted by my doctor's status, and maybe too by my patina of cultural sophistication, though as is often the way, she liked the idea of this more than its manifestations. When we got to know each other better, and she discovered that my flash of extroversion was atypical, I suspect she was shrewd enough to recognise that this had compensations: I was unlikely either to dump her or gainsay her.

Nowadays, Olivia ran a boutique in the smarter part of Brighton. It was a waste of her intelligence, but I'd long abandoned my earlier efforts to steer her career and the job seemed to suit her, mainly because much of the stock found its way on to her person.

'Livy, that's a fabulous frock. I'm green with envy.' Bar, the least envious woman alive, was generous with compliments. Privately, I preferred her outfit, which was a pair of well-cut black trousers and a silk shirt. Besides being good-tempered Bar had a good behind.

'Like it? It's Gina Fratini.' Olivia pirouetted, showing off the dress's elaborately ruffled skirt.

'I haven't a clue who Gina Fratini is,' said Chris, coming out of the kitchen in a pair of filthy trousers, 'but she's obviously posh. I'm afraid I'm as you see me, covered in dog hair as usual.' The Powells had four children and three rowdy dogs. It was debatable which they spoiled more.

'You've worried Dr McB about his trousers now!' Dan had observed me covertly brushing at them. It was a subject for badinage among the assembled company that I'm fussy about such things.

The dogs had been shut in the kitchen, but after a good deal of barking they were let out, until Cassius, an excitable Labrador, leapt at Olivia's dress and threatened to rip it, so, to my relief, they were banished again.

Dan, who showed an easy disregard for his clothes but disliked pets, remarked that 'Olivia's narcissism' had 'its uses,' which I was afraid might lead to one of their scratchy dialogues. I could see Olivia had gone the pink of her dress, and fearing she was preparing a retort, I lobbed a comment at Dan as a diversion. 'I saw someone unusual today at Kit's.'

'Man or woman?' asked Dan, who could be readily distracted by an interesting case.

'Woman. A suicide, but not one of your run-of-the-mill sort.'

'Darling,' said Olivia, 'you sound so blasé, poor creatures.' She hadn't a grain of true sympathy for anyone misguided enough to land up in a psychiatric hospital.

'Method?' asked Dan. 'D'you mind if I smoke, Chris?' Dan, who never ate much at the best of times, had left half his first course untouched. Chris wasn't the greatest cook, but sometimes I wished he would try harder.

'I mind,' interjected Denis.

'That's why I asked Chris and not you,' said Dan, lighting up. 'This is an inter-course break.' He always made that joke and I was surprised to hear Olivia laugh. We had all long ago given up laughing at it.

'She seems to have acquired some Soneryl from somewhere, so either she's a darned poor sleeper or she's clever.'

'Darling, no one says "darned" any more,' said Olivia.

'Insomniacs are often clever,' Denis interposed swiftly. 'There's nothing to say insomnia addles the wits. Mostly the sign of the sharp ones, in my experience. If you must smoke, Daniel, use an ashtray.' He removed the plate on to which Dan had been flicking his cigarette and fetched a Stella Artois ashtray, which one of their kids must have taken from the pub.

'Well, no, I mean, she must have talked someone into giving them to her with a view to bumping herself off. Soneryl's a barbiturate. Not easy to get,' I explained for Olivia's sake. She couldn't have cared less, but I always felt this need to include her in these conversations.

'She give any reason?'

'Not so far,' I said. 'I think the reasons may be existential.' I rather wished I hadn't brought up the subject of Elizabeth Cruikshank.

'Darling, don't be so pretentious,' Olivia said, smiling at Dan as if to say: Isn't he impossible?

'Things too much for her?' Dan pursued, ignoring Olivia.

'Spare me people who have to attract attention to themselves in that "look-at-me" sort of way.' Olivia finally succeeded in terminating the conversation.

For once I was grateful to her. It suddenly felt like a betrayal to be discussing Elizabeth Cruikshank round a dinner-party table.

5

When I saw Elizabeth Cruikshank next, the late-afternoon sun was streaming through the window and lighting up my room. It was a big room, with high ceilings, and one weekend, when Olivia had a friend staying, I'd gone in and painted it white because I couldn't look a day longer at the existing institutional pale blue and cream. I'd also brought from home some paintings which I'd acquired before Olivia and I lived together. 'Horrible gloomy thing,' she'd said of the Orpen, a portrait of a sad-faced clown, I'd picked up at Kettle's Yard.

I have a bee in my bonnet about pictures being crooked on the wall and one thing Lennie failed at was setting them straight. More often than not, his big presence disrupted the paintings so, as my patient was settling in the chair, I walked across and adjusted the clown. I felt her eyes on my back, and when I returned to my seat she asked, 'Who is it?'

'The painter or the portrait?'

'The clown.'

I could have responded with 'Do you feel like that yourself?' or something equally alienating, but more by luck than judgement I chose to answer the question.

'I've always felt it must be an aspect of the artist. What do you think?' I never told Olivia this, but I'd bought the painting because it reminded me of Jonny.

'You'd need to know sadness to paint that.'

Something I'd picked up from Dan was that he almost never mentioned food to his anorexic patients. 'Drives them nuts,' he used to say. 'They've been questioned till they're blue in the face about their eating habits, having their food weighed to the last ounce, and God knows what, and when I don't broach the subject at all they get confused. Breaks their control, see.'

'Do you like art?' I enquired.

I didn't want to confuse Elizabeth Cruikshank or break her control, but I didn't want to go head on again into what had brought her to me. The strategy worked, because something rigid about her shoulders relaxed.

'Some.'

'Any special artist?' She appeared to frown so I added, 'It's not a trick question.'

'It's not that.'

'Oh yes,' I said, imagining she didn't know how to choose. 'For me, some days it's Rembrandt, some days Cézanne, or sometimes, you know, it's Titian.'

The light was partly obscuring her face – I should really have had blinds but I hate to keep out the sun.

'I used to like Caravaggio.'

That was a coincidence, though nowadays, of course, plenty of people admire the Italian painter. He was Gus Galen's favourite. In fact, it was Gus who introduced me to Caravaggio that time when we first met.

'Come, dear boy,' he said, pushing me along with his hand on my elbow, after a session on anxiety, 'I need to walk off some of my own anxiety after hearing those baboons.'

Gus walked faster than any man I knew and he was a terror with traffic. Why his life hadn't ended under somebody's wheels I'll never know. He stepped off the pavement without a thought for the oncoming cars, so that to accompany him on the streets was like a cue in a comic film for vehicles filled with swearing drivers to come to a screeching halt. A walk with Gus was a definition of a mixed blessing – his company was to die for, and there was always the possibility that one might.

By the time we got to Trafalgar Square I felt that had I been at all of a religious disposition I might have slipped into St Martin-in-the-Fields to light a candle in gratitude for having reached it in one piece. But Gus, still insistently shoving my elbow, steered me up the steep stone steps of the gallery and navigated us rapidly through its rooms, till we stopped in front of a painting I'd not seen before.

Here Gus let out an explosive snort, so that the drowsing attendant's head started up, fearful that this might herald some act of vandalism. But if the sigh expressed violence it was violence of a harmless sort – that of the innate passion which in Gus was always searching for a suitable object.

The picture he showed me was of a young beardless man, seated in darkness, at a table laid with food. Framing him, on either side, their backs half turned to us, were two seated companions. You could see from their posture that the central figure had just revealed something remarkable. The big-boned man to the left of him was caught, dramatically, in the act of rising to his feet, and his astonished elbow was poking through the torn sleeve of his green jerkin. His raw-nosed companion, to the right, had flung his spread arms wide, so that the large left hand seemed to shoot dangerously out of the frame and almost to poke me in the eye.

'Who are they?' I asked, though it was clear who the man at the centre of the table was. As I say, I wasn't too keen on religion, or its art.

Gus stood looking at the painting as if too preoccupied to have heard me, so I read the inscription aloud: '*The Supper at Emmaus*.'

'What d'you think?' asked Gus, as if he'd produced a gold coin from my nose or a pair of doves from my ears. 'Marvellous, isn't it? Beats having to listen to the babble of those baboons.'

At the time, I didn't marvel. But it would have been rude to say so, especially at a first meeting. But also something of Gus's passion rubbed off on me. I didn't like the painting – I didn't understand it – but what I did like was Gus's liking for it. His passion bred passion: that he could so openly avow his own love for it made me love him. And now this painting, which I had encountered so many years earlier, gave me my first glimmer of insight into Elizabeth Cruikshank. Beneath that pallid exterior there must be passion too, however carefully concealed. But all I said was 'A dear friend of mine, Dr Galen, loves Caravaggio's work. He's an analyst too. A very original one. It's he who says there's no cure for being alive.'

'That's what you said last time.'

So she had taken it in. 'Yes. Gus's words. I'm afraid I'm not original. He feels that people aren't ill so much as lacking meaning to live. He thinks our job is to help them to find it.'

'That might be rather a tall order.' There was the ghost of a smile in her voice.

'Yes. And possibly arrogant, you may be thinking?'

'No, I wasn't thinking that.'

She lapsed back into silence and I dropped into a reverie.

Some patients, however little they say, keep your attention tied to them so that the silence is an effort. I've learned that this is anger. Angry people press on you, hold you down to keep you with them. But it was easy to drift off with Elizabeth Cruikshank. She didn't mug you with her presence; she let you go as lightly as a dandelion seed.

I was contemplating this when she spoke again. 'Why on earth would anyone want to bother with people like us?'

For a second I supposed she was referring to the two of us. Then, with a sense of slight shock, I recovered myself and recognised her allusion was to me as doctor and herself as patient.

'What are people like "us" like?'

She gave one of her little dismissive shrugs. 'People like me, then.'

'And what would you say you were like?'

The ginger tom was back balancing on the fence outside. It had an air of entitlement which in a human would be psychopathic. Perhaps that was why I so disliked it. It took for granted something I could never take.

'Oh, I don't know,' she said listlessly. 'Not very interesting.'

'Well,' I said, 'I don't know that anyone is uninteresting once you get to know them.'

'Really?'

'Yes, I believe so.'

'You have to say that.'

'I don't, in fact. And I don't, knowingly anyway, lie to my patients.' Deliberately, I introduced a note of coolness into my voice.

'I'm sure you don't.'

'There are as many misconceptions about shrinks as there are about –'

'Their patients? What are the "misconceptions" about your patients, Dr McBride?'

'That because they have had the misfortune to end up somewhere like this hospital they cannot therefore also be rather bright, for one, Mrs Cruikshank. That they aren't able to give us the run-around!'

We stared at each other.

'Do you think I'm giving you "the run-around," Dr McBride?'

'I think you are giving yourself the run-around, if you really want to know,' I said. And then, more gently, after another longish pause, 'But that's all right. It's your prerogative.'

The people who landed up with me were mostly in a state of terror, and one element in it was the fear that I possessed some professional means forcibly to overcome the complex safeguards erected to protect their secret worlds. I didn't want anyone imagining that, especially not this patient.

'You don't, you know, with me, anyway, have to say or do anything you don't want to say or do.'

6

The first dream I had when I started my analytical training took place by the sea and I can recall it as if it were yesterday.

I was walking on a pebbled beach when a man dressed in a loud turquoise shirt accosted me. He had in his hand a lump of sea-smoothed stone and he was shoving it in my face demanding to know what it was. I said, 'You should ask the archaeologist fellow.' Then the scene moved inland and I found myself on a steep hillside, by a small church or chapel, cut out of the rock face. But when I entered the building it proved not to be a church at all but a zoo. There was a skinny-looking puma restlessly prowling up and down the cage, its paces marking the limits of its confinement. In the same enclosure, a huge white barn owl was flying against the high fence, beating its wings frantically on the restraining wires.

When I mentioned the dream to Gus Galen he said that if he had a tenner for every dream he'd heard that began 'I was walking by the sea,' he would be able to reduce substantially his charges. He was fond of quoting 'God cures; and the physician takes the fee,' but as with everything about Gus in practice, his billing methods were eccentric. A woman I sent him once, the wife of a colleague, said she had to stop seeing Dr Galen because he never sent her a bill and it made her feel guilty. 'I went to see him because I felt guilty in the first place,' she pointed out. I sent her, finally, to a less unworldly colleague, who charged a king's ransom.

Anyhow, in those days I was glad to have the sea on my doorstep so that when I needed to mull anything I could walk along the beach and listen to the tread of the waves, and puzzle over my thoughts by puzzling out, at the same time, what principle enables you to tell where the water ends and the horizon begins, and observe the dark shapes of boats against the sky. Or if I'd got my rubber boots out of the boot of the car, wade through the dirty-cream foam.

Walking is a famous loosener of thoughts. Although I had many other patients in my charge, as I look back now it seems it was always Elizabeth Cruikshank I was thinking about when I walked by the sea's edge, and her story I kept trying to piece together in my mind.

Perhaps it was the reassurance that there would be no compulsion on her to disclose, or perhaps it was the tincture of chilliness with which I prefaced my absolving words, because after that last meeting my patient did yield up a few grudging facts.

After leaving school, with reasonable but unremarkable O levels, she took a job at a local library. From her father she had acquired an appetite for reading, and in those days there wasn't the current mania for formal qualifications, so she went quite a way up the librarianship ladder before deciding to get herself some proper qualifications. By this time, she'd cut loose from her parents and taken a flat in Camden Town.

'Any boyfriends?' I asked.

'I don't care for the word.'

'Did you go out with anyone?'

'I don't like that phrase much either.'

'Fine,' I said, cheerily refusing to be diverted. 'How about lovers? Are you happy with that term?'

She touched the leather bag she always had beside her in the chair and said, vaguely, 'Oh, you know, I never really expected anyone to want me.'

I pictured her, as she might have looked then, underweight, unfashionably dressed, a pale young woman. When I met her she still gave an impression of pallor and plainness, though no one looks their best in the aftermath of a suicide attempt, and it was a while before I saw Elizabeth Cruikshank smile. When she did I was reminded of an expression of my mother's: 'It was as if the moon had taken off her clothes and gone dancing.'

'But you married?'

'I married,' she assented. She gave an impression that if she could she would have denied it.

To augment her library studies, she explained, she enrolled on an art history course, which in those days was run at the old North London Poly. She met her future husband in the polytechnic canteen, where she was in the habit of going for a supper before the evening lectures. She'd queued up for her usual soup and bread roll, being economical with her rations, and, searching in her bag for her purse, accidentally tipped the tray so that the plate slid, spilling soup over the man before her in the queue.

'He was nice about it, though it ruined his jacket. It was light-coloured and the soup was tomato and I was mortified. But he laughed, and when I asked how I could make it up to him he said I could come to the pub. So I went. He seemed to like me.' She sounded apologetic.

'And you liked that?'

'I liked being the centre of someone's attention.'

Up till now, she'd barely held my glance, her eyes always flickering off to the quince tree, or to some point in her imagination projected on to the glass. But now she looked at me with a fierce directness that almost made me smile.

'Not everyone wants attention,' I said, and regretted it because she took it as criticism, which I should have foreseen.

'Yes, wishing to die is seen as attention-seeking, I know.' Her voice was low and she hardly raised it, but at moments of tension I noticed that her diction became precise.

'I didn't mean that,' I said. 'I'm sorry.'

It bothers me how infrequently people in my profession apologise. Everyone makes mistakes, why would a psychiatrist or an analyst be different? We should learn to make the mistakes as fast as possible, Gus says. It's mistakes that let the light in.

'I'm sorry,' I said again. 'That was stupid of me. Of course everyone wants attention, provided it's the right kind.'

She laughed, none too cheerfully. 'Who knows if this was the "right kind"? It was enough that I was paid any attention by anyone, let alone a man.'

While I was a medical student, I took this tall, thin girl called Wanda Williams out on a date. Because it seemed expected of me, I put my arm round her at the cinema and afterwards she invited me back to her room, in a dismal part of London. When we got in, she put on the kettle and then excused herself to go to the bathroom. I was sitting on the bed, leafing through a magazine and wondering when I could decently say I was leaving, when she came back into the room. She'd taken off all her clothes and there was a line round the middle of her waist where the elastic from her knickers had left a red mark, and another higher up where her bra had cut. I remember that the sight of these cruel-looking red impressions dividing up her pale flesh filled me with pity and dismay. I couldn't leave after that, so I went to bed with her and watched my unenthusiastic but polite performance with the inner imager I rarely manage to switch off. It would have seemed rude to do otherwise but it depressed me no end.

Several men to whom I've confided this story have revealed

that they've found themselves in similar situations. There was desperation about Wanda Williams and I found myself hoping that it had not been like that for Elizabeth Cruikshank. Somehow I didn't think it had been. Her despair felt of a different order.

Neil Cruikshank, it turned out, was an engineer, with a research fellowship at Imperial College, employed by the polytechnic to do some external examining. A stocky, square-shouldered, fair-haired man, with a moustache.

'I should never have married a moustache, Doctor. I might have guessed I wouldn't get on with one.'

She gave me my title with that faint edge, which seemed to imply: Yes, I know you are a doctor, but somewhere I know too that underneath all this, the hospital, the consulting room, the professional qualifications, you are no different from me.

We are most of us badly cracked and afraid that if we do not guard them with our lives the cracks will show, and show us up, which is why we are all more or less in a state of vigilance against one another. Although I paid lip-service to this idea, I hadn't properly acknowledged it in those days. It was Elizabeth Cruikshank who showed me the truth of it. She had a faculty of divination which is not uncommon among psychiatric patients, but in her case it was developed to a degree which enabled her to see through to the back of one's mind. But that was a recognition I had yet to reach, so when she added, 'You know, don't you, in advance, I mean, when you do something you'll regret, like marry someone you shouldn't?' I took refuge in a doctorly 'Go on,' that being one of many such mindless phrases I hid behind.

'But you do, don't you?' she persisted, and made a quizzical movement with her hands, which made me think of the wings of a wounded bird.

'I'm not sure I do,' I said, being a practised coward.

A few haphazard fruits, which had ripened on the quince, were still hanging, gold and knobbly, on the branches outside.

My mother was brought up in India and she used to tell us how if a mango tree didn't bear fruit they would pierce the trunk with a nail to make it fructify.

'You could make jelly with those,' Elizabeth Cruikshank suggested, looking away from me to the garden. 'It makes good jelly, quince.'

I dropped by Cath Maguire's office later on my way home.

Maguire was a lesbian but not the sort that doesn't get on with men. I had occasionally speculated what had made Maguire prefer her own sex. She was an attractive, sparky woman and, while not my type exactly, certainly could have been many men's. But when I once tentatively started on this line, she shut me up by saying, 'You're not suggesting that women are second best or anything, are you, Dr McBride?'

But one lucky consequence of Maguire's preference was that we had the kind of good-natured intimacy which is only possible between a man and a woman where sex will never be a factor. And I'd long given over questioning the whys and wherefores of Maguire's sexuality. What mattered to me was that I trusted her instincts and depended on them to fill out my own.

'How're you getting on with Mrs Cruikshank?' I asked.

'Elizabeth? I like her. Quiet, like I said. Doesn't make demands. Probably doesn't make enough. Always very polite.'

'Any visitors?'

'None I've seen, anyway. A couple of phone enquiries from her children, but so far as I know they haven't visited.'

So she had children. I wouldn't have guessed this and there was no mention of them on her record. She looked almost too girlish to have given birth. 'How many?'

'Two, I gather. A boy and a girl. The girl was a bit, you know, stand-offish, but the boy sounded nice.'

By the phone in her room was a book squashed face down. Maguire read two or three books a week.

'Does she read?'

'She's got a couple of books out of the library, but now you come to mention it, I've not seen her read them, unless she keeps them for nights.'

'What are they? Did you see?'

Maguire screwed up her face as she did when trying to concentrate. It gave her the look of a small girl, which always made me feel warm towards her.

'Not fiction, anyway.'

Maguire devoured fiction. Her favourite author was Ruth Rendell, but I'd noticed some surprising ones too. For a time she seemed to be reading her way through Proust.

'She used to be a librarian.'

'Really? I wouldn't mind that job myself.'

'Too late,' I said. 'I need your help here.'

'You know, I don't know if in the long run a really great story isn't more help.'

7

That autumn, Olivia had decided to enrol in some evening classes and she was out at one of them when I got home. She had a tendency to these sudden enthusiasms. They rarely lasted, and I therefore hadn't bothered to ask much about this latest. I was never quite abreast of which class was when, partly because I was glad to have an hour or two to myself. Olivia never forbade me anything openly but it's not so agreeable to listen to Schubert, or Bach, when the person with you would rather hear *The Archers*. Not that I've anything against *The Archers* – it was more that Olivia had something against Schubert: she assumed respect for my tastes but somehow it had the discouraging effect of dislike.

I had a deadline for a paper I was reviewing for a clinical journal, which was an added reason for preferring my own thoughts. So when the phone rang and interrupted them, I was put out till I heard Gus Galen's voice.

'Can you beat it?' Gus was one of those people who never announce themselves, as if one spent one's time simply waiting to hear from them alone. 'They've got that baboon Jeffries giving the keynote address. What the hell is a "keynote" anyway, when it's at home?'

'I don't know,' I said. 'A musical metaphor maybe?'

Gus was referring to the international conference on anxiety and depression which was to take place the following year.

'Nothing melodious about Jeffries's approach. It wasn't so long ago he was advocating bloody lobotomies.'

Lobotomy, or leucotomy, the surgical severance of the frontal lobe of the brain from the subcortical area, became fashionable as a remedy for intractable depression in the late thirties, and during the forties and fifties something like 80,000 such surgical operations were performed before it dropped out of style again. But since 1970 there had been a revival of interest in the procedure.

Gus was one of the first modern neurological experts to query the wisdom of this, which, as with everything else, he did vociferously.

'They claim it worked on monkeys, but I wonder what the poor beasts would say about it if they could speak,' he said, not long after our first encounter. 'Those baboons haven't a bloody clue how it works on humans, if it works at all, which I doubt. Monkeying about with the brain like that as if they were God All Bloody Mighty, though God would have more sense than to be so interfering.' As with many of his other associations, Gus appeared to have some informal access to the mind of God.

There was, and still is, a political division in our profession between an interventionist approach, which roughly speaking means drugs and ECT, and the so-called talking cure. Most psychiatrists practised a largely unconsidered mixture of the two, but Gus was passionately against the hard-line attitude and his training in neurology combined with his forceful personality gave him clout.

There's a place for drugs, and with schizophrenia or bipolar states only a fool or a miracle worker would attempt to manage without them. But, by and large, I was of Gus's mind. In fact – and of course he knew this – it was as a result of seeing the consequences of a lobotomy that I began my analytic training.

Mr Beet was a retired bank manager, a man with a large florid face gone blurred around the edges. He was neat as a guardsman, always in a pressed shirt and jacket and tie, but in the way that a small child is turned out, when the impression matters more to the dresser than the dressed. It was his wife who kept him trim. Her hobby was making padded coat hangers, a distraction, I surmised, from the sight of her husband's motionless misery. He had been an active man once, she told me with remembered pride, though overactive when the anxiety dominated. By the time it was my job to monitor her husband, he sat with his mouth never properly closed. You couldn't say he stared out of the window – his eyes were too horribly devoid of any directed interest.

Mrs Beet had soft English skin and fine hair and delft-blue eyes and seemed always to be holding on to some part of her husband, his hand, his elbow, his knee, patting it to remind him – or perhaps herself – that she was there. Despair, and loyalty, had taught her to make the hangers, when she came with him to the hospital for his occupational therapy. I imagine he simply sat there and she, like a mother with an awkward child, covered the hangers for him. One Christmas, she gave me three as a present. 'I don't suppose you'll have any use for them, Dr McBride, but maybe your wife would like them, that is if . . .' I reassured her that I had a wife. She was a sensitive woman and would have hated to make a mistake about my marital status, or my sexuality. Olivia, unusually, welcomed the gift: the padded contours, it turned out, were useful for her evening clothes.

I speculated sometimes about Mrs Beet and where she had ended up. It was unlikely that her husband lived long in that condition. 'He was depressed before, yes, Doctor,' she told me in her deferential yet subtly assertive tone, 'and anxious. But anxiety and depression aren't the worst things. They never told us how it would be afterwards. Nothing's as bad as seeing him like this, with all the light, and with all the sorrow too, gone from his eyes.'

'I agreed to do the response,' Gus said, 'but I've got this prostate problem hanging over me and there seems to be a feeling I shouldn't push my luck for the next month or two afterwards. All right if I get you to take my place?'

Mrs Beet appeared unassuming but she had a certain tenacious force which had a way of ensuring that the apparition of her mutilated husband stayed somewhere in the back rooms of my mind. It made one of its haunting reappearances now.

'Oh, God, Gus,' I pleaded, trying to dodge the reproachful recollection, 'I'd much rather not.'

This was a major colloquium and I was reluctant to take on Jeffries, who regarded intellectual opposition as tantamount to a declaration of war. He could block the career of those who were hostile to his views, and although I wasn't ambitious I was cautious. As I say, I liked a quiet life.

'Why not?' I was aware the tone was being made deliberately peevish. Gus had a whim of iron and didn't scruple to bend you to it. 'Time someone other than me made a noise.'

'I haven't your enthusiasm for mud-stirring, Gus.'

'Don't need to say anything startling. Just say how you might treat a serious-seeming case without zapping their brain cells to smithereens with drugs we don't understand or bloody electrical impulses ditto. You must have someone you're seeing who fills the bill.'

When I next saw Elizabeth Cruikshank, the year had crossed the shadow line when the clocks change and the late-afternoon light, an hour further from the sun, had begun to fail.

'Spring forward, fall back' was how my mother taught us to remember which way the clocks moved at the spring and autumnal equinoxes, and as with many of her proverbial sayings, the words stayed in my mind. They stayed my mind too, those familiar phrases, providing some kind of outposts of reassurance. Perhaps it was her way of mothering me, or perhaps – more fairly – it was an element of her mothering I was able to accept.

Poor Mother. I rejected her as much as she rejected me – and for the same reason. Neither of us could bear the other with Jonny gone – or, rather, neither of us could bear that he had gone, and we were, each of us, the reminder that he had. It was years before it occurred to me that my mother believed I blamed her for Jonny's death every bit as much as I believed she blamed me. After all, it was she who had been uncharacteristically ill that fatal morning and allowed her two small sons to go off unsupervised.

Maybe I did blame her. I can't be sure. There's so little I am sure of now, but I was surer in the St Christopher days. I was sure, for example, that the business of Elizabeth Cruikshank's marriage was unimportant. It wasn't, I would have bet my pension on it, the relationship with Neil which had left her knocking at death's door.

As we spoke that afternoon, I was aware that I had come to associate his name with the onset of lethargy. Drowsiness stole through me, and I began to feel impatience over the man whose impression remained too nebulous to be the centre of the mystery which had brought his wife to me. As we sat with the room darkening round us, I had an acute sense of her feeding me titbits of trivia.

'We lived in Hampstead at first. But we moved to be near Neil's parents.'

'Did you miss Hampstead?'

'I missed the Heath.'

None of this told me more than that she was still unwilling to let me into the circumstances of her concealed catastrophe. And, indeed, I had no right to any inroad into it. Besides, there's a rhythm to all nature, including human nature, and like a good naturalist a prudent analyst knows how to wait.

'How long were you and Neil together before you married?'

'A few months? I can't remember.'

'He doesn't seem to have left much impression on your memory.'

'Neil was all right. It was me that was wrong.'

'In what way "wrong"?' I tried to keep the note of curiosity out of my voice, but by now I longed to know.

It had grown too dark to see her distinctly, and reluctantly, as I try to avoid artificial light as long as possible, I switched on the bronze lamp, in the figure of Hermes, which I had on the table by my chair.

I'm fond of this lamp. I bought it in Paris when I once took Bar Buirski there, while she was still Bar Blake.

Outside, I made out the shape of the ginger tom poised on the fence and beside him, in weird juxtaposition, I could see a reflection of my lamp and my patient in the blue armchair, the few feet between us expanded into an unnavigable mirage of air.

At that moment she began to speak, and as she did so, the cat dropped down to merge with her image in the glass in an action so swift I almost jumped up in protest. It was as if a bird was being targeted with that intent feline spring. I can still see the orange shape leaping into the reflection of Elizabeth Cruikshank, as I can hear her near inaudible words.

'I was faithless.'

'Can you say more?'

'Another time. It's not possible now.'

8

Gus rang me that evening while Olivia was beside me in her dressing gown, her toes, like twin neat rows of glossy rubies, resting on my mother's embroidered footstool. She'd asked my help in varnishing her nails. I sometimes think my mother was right and I'd have made a better career as a surgeon: I've a remarkably steady hand.

When I spoke of work in front of Olivia I was always conscious of a slight awkwardness, and there were times, more than made me quite comfortable, when I wished I could leave the room, or ask her to leave. I conducted the conversation with Gus in the shorthand I'd developed for such occasions.

'I've been thinking,' I said, 'I'll do that thing for you.'

'Great stuff.' I could tell he was delighted. 'Got someone up your sleeve?'

'Exactly how long have I got?'

'The back end of May. No need for any earth-shattering stuff. Just your natural sweetness and light will do.'

'Thanks a million. I'll be crucified by Jeffries & Co. if I go on about "sweetness and light."'

'Better men than you have been crucified. I'll be at your side to fend off the baboons if the bloody medics let me.'

A patient who might have fitted Gus's purpose for the confer-ence paper was a young Pakistani student studying maths and physics at Sussex University. He'd been found wandering in the early hours on a trunk road outside Brighton. The police patrol that had picked him up reported him 'disoriented and appar-ently praying.' He was brought into St Kit's, where a diagnosis of schizophrenia had finally been applied.

Pages of a notebook covered with seemingly bizarre thoughts and disconnected prose, and an inability to name the current British prime minister, had formed the basis of this diagnosis. Later, when the confused young man had been formally admit-ted, and I was present at his case conference, I pointed out that precious few of us, in a state of distress, would be able to name the prime minister of Pakistan and that the seemingly deranged sentences in the boy's notebooks were attempts at formal logic. As a result of this intervention he was given over to my care.

He was agitated, desperately homesick, distraught, but not, I concluded, psychotic. I took him off the Modecate injections and tried to restore some sort of equilibrium. They don't say so in the textbooks but a lot can be effected through patience and calm. Maguire and I were in agreement that if this commodity were available on the NHS there would be far fewer admissions to psy-chiatric hospitals.

I'm not sure why there is something shaming about having no one to confide in, but in my view a good deal of aberrant behaviour stems from unbearable isolation and the socially un-acceptable sense of being quite alone. Hassid, I concluded, was suffering not so much a nervous as a social breakdown. Away from his close-knit Karachi family, his religion, his customary diet (food plays a much larger part in emotional stability than is usually acknowledged), and the regular ritual practices he had been raised in, he had lost his bearings.

I can't pretend to have liked all my patients, but those I did like tended to be the ones I found I was able to help most. I could never decide if it was gratitude at having some positive effect on their lives that made me like them, or if liking makes some significant therapeutic difference. In any case, I liked Hassid. I understood that he was lonely, but his character also caught my curiosity and I established his trust through an indistinct memory that grew to a clear recollection, which enabled me to identify the repeated appearance of 'iff' in his notebooks, not as some schizophrenic misspelling, as had been supposed, but as the correct logical term for 'if and only if.' As a result of this lucky strike, he confided to me the sad account of what had occurred.

He had gone, nervously, on account of the new and strange environment, to a student party, where towards the end of an already confusing evening he'd been slipped a tidy slug of vodka in his soft drink. The unaccustomed alcohol, together with the discovery of what he had innocently imbibed – I gather the idiot who performed this gross act was crass enough also to brag about it – combined to destabilise the poor young man's mind. His family, he told me, were strict Muslims, and the shame and guilt, along with the physical effects of the alcohol, precipitated a mental crisis. The university suddenly seemed to him a place of evil and satanic darkness, from which he felt an understandable need to flee; which is why the police patrol picked him up shoeless, beating his head and reciting, to them incomprehensible, verses from the Koran.

In those days doctors had more licence. Hassid was patently terrified of returning to his student quarters. I decided the best I could do for him was to keep him with us for a spell. I judged that what he needed most was rest in sympathetic surroundings while he found his feet.

But also there was something in it for me. I enjoyed our sessions together because I discovered that what Hassid wanted, once he had recovered his centre of gravity, was to talk about his passion.

It is a feature of our profession that you are exposed to others' interests and concerns. Thus, in the course of my duties, I have learned something of seamanship, sheep breeding, tax inspection (and tax avoidance), domestic science, the Petrarchan sonnet, horticulture, dentistry, astrology, astronomy, bell-ringing, and the rudiments of how to fly a helicopter.

Hassid's ruling passion, I discovered, was quantum mechanics. He was mad for Schrödinger's cat, he idolised Dirac, he worshipped Niels Bohr. What intrigued me most, so far as my limited scientific intelligence was able to comprehend it, was Hassid's account of their account of the nature of reality.

The structure of existence, which he attempted to convey to me – though often his words flowed by too fast for me properly to grasp them – was a thrilling and disturbing one, a tentative world of ambiguous possibilities rather than things or facts. Electrons, he explained, existed as a sort of misty potential, occupying no physical space in the material world but summoned into being only when a human measurement was made to determine their location.

'You see, Doctor,' Hassid said, 'it is not that electrons are here waiting, like invisible germs, to be discovered under the microscope –'

'Or black swans waiting to be discovered in Australia?' I interjected in an effort to show I was following.

But Hassid politely dismissed this. 'Not swans, no, Doctor, not even black ones, because, you see, this is not a question of induction. Electrons are not, in the sense we mean it generally, here at all.' His expression became sage.

I've always thought it remarkable that, while our bodies stand in the visible world, we ourselves are not in the world of three dimensions and our inner life has no position in space. And, equally, how little of another person's reality is visible to us. We see their form, their features, their shifts of expression, but all that constitutes their sense of self remains unseen. And yet this invisible self is what to the individual constitutes their real identity. I wondered, as I limped behind his explanations, if Hassid's electrons were somewhat similar.

'It is like a thought before one performs an action. The electron is no place and then' – he waved his elegant hand like a graceful conjuror – 'presto! Suddenly it is here, coming into existence out of seeming nothingness – but it is we' – excitedly he gestured at his chest – 'who bring it out. By what *we* do to it, you see, we give its state reality.' His face glowed with intense pleasure at the arcane mystery he was initiating me into.

It wasn't so surprising, I reflected after one of Hassid's 'seminars,' that he'd been mistaken for psychotic. The reality he described had its mad element. For one thing, it seemed to place human understanding at a central place in the universe. But then, great wits are oft to madness near allied. He was an engaging boy. And I warmed to him. But I worried that my feeble scientific understanding was insufficient to aid his adjustment to the ordinary world.

The day after Elizabeth Cruikshank had uttered those cryptic words to me I called by Maguire's office and found her chatting to Hassid over the library trolley.

'What's going on here?'

'Hassid's helping us out.' Making people useful was one of Maguire's rehabilitation principles.

'Sister wants me to look after the book trolley, you see, Doctor.'

The greater part of the library collection was the dud end of the old county library supply. Other books had been donated or left behind by patients or their visitors. Most of these were crime novels and thrillers, there were a predictable number of romantic novels and blockbusters, some out-of-date travel books, an old restaurant guide, and a few uninspiring-looking classics. Wondering who would nowadays read *The Swiss Family Robinson*, I picked out a tatty copy of *Pride and Prejudice*.

'Here you are, Hassid. This is a piece of Englishness which I guarantee won't corrupt you.'

Hassid looked eager, and remembering his tendency to bestow on any light-hearted remark of mine the status of a logical truth, I put the book back. 'Don't worry, it's not doctor's orders!'

'Bet you wish it was, though, don't you, Dr McBride?' Maguire was aware of my partiality for Jane Austen.

Hassid changed the subject. 'Doctor, Lennie has asked me to go with him to the match on Saturday.'

'Lennie the cleaner?'

'Yes, Doctor.'

I glanced at Maguire, who nodded.

'Sure,' I said. 'I'll let it be known you'll be out for the day. I hope the home team wins.'

Hassid made off, presumably to find Lennie and deliver the news of my official blessing, and Maguire remarked that Hassid was 'a nice kid.' 'Nothing much wrong there that a few friends wouldn't put right. He's been chatting with your Mrs Cruikshank.'

'They've something in common now. As I said, she was a librarian too.'

'Might she want to help with the books, then?'

I thought this unlikely, but I didn't want to quash Maguire, who had a knack of getting recalcitrant patients out of themselves. I could tell she was longing to know how I was doing with this particular recalcitrant. 'She's clever, our Mrs Cruikshank. But she keeps her cards pretty close to her chest.'

'The bright ones do. What's in that bag she carries about with her all the time?'

'I don't know. How did she get it, do you know? Was it with her when she was brought in?'

'Must have been. Unless it came with her other things. That army man who found her brought some of her bits over for her. Poor fellow. He was ever so distressed.'

'Did you talk to him?' Maguire was a conduit for information.

'Not really. To be honest with you, he couldn't wait to get away.'

'I'm glad Hassid's made her into a friend.'

'I wouldn't go that far,' Maguire said. 'Like you say, she keeps herself to herself.'

'Funny, Lennie taking him up.' I wondered how our cleaner would respond to Hassid's learned dissertations. It was possible that Lennie's less conventional mental processes would grasp Hassid's quantum 'reality' more ably than mine.

'Well, you know,' said Maguire, 'Lennie's an outsider too. To my way of thinking, he'll do the boy more good than that idle lot up at the university.'

Dan Buirski and I were booked to play squash that evening. He had a late clinic so I caught up with some admin for my secretary, Trish, while I waited for him to ring when he was ready.

I enjoyed my squash evenings with Dan. The exercise, for both of us, was an antidote to the tensions of work. He was a year or two my junior, better toned and fitter than I was, and his nature was more competitive. But I could usually give him a hard game and even occasionally beat him.

The phone rang, and expecting it to be Dan I answered, 'Ready when you are.'

'Darling,' said Olivia's voice, 'are you still squashing tonight?'

Olivia rarely rang me at work unless over some domestic crisis. 'What's up?'

'Nothing's "up." I thought you might like me to collect you.'

'That would be nice.'

She must have detected surprise in my voice, because she said, a shade defensively, 'My French class is just round the corner.'

Dan said Bar was out that evening so he and I had a drink while we waited for Olivia. She was flushed when she arrived and explained she'd had some difficulty parking and seemed genuinely bothered over keeping us waiting.

'It's all right,' I said, 'it gave this man a chance to buy me a consolation drink.' I was aware my defeats at Dan's hands might disappoint Olivia.

'All's fair in love and war,' said Dan. 'Olive Oyl, since you're driving, I don't suppose you'll want anything, will you?'

Dan's teasing often had an edge to it and I expected this to annoy Olivia, but she appeared to be in one of her accommodating moods and invited him back to our place with the suggestion that there at least we could have a decent drink.

While I was hunting for a corkscrew the phone rang and it was Bar. 'Is my husband there, by any chance?'

'He's next door boozing with my wife. You'd better come over and keep me company.'

'I'd love to but I'm exhausted,' Bar said. 'Tell him I'm home, will you, there's a lamb. I'm going to take a drink into a hot bath.'

Olivia and Dan were laughing when I came back into the sitting room. I was glad to see them getting on for once.

'That was Barbara. She says she's too tired to peel out again to fetch you.'

I was going to add that I'd take Dan home myself when Olivia said, 'I need to drop something off at the shop. I can give Dan a lift.' She was trying hard that evening. It was nice of her to offer to go out again when I knew she must be tired.

'It's all right,' I said, 'I'll run him home and drop whatever it is off for you,' but then the phone rang again and it was Gus, fussing about the conference, and then Olivia came into the study and mimed that it was late by pointing at her watch and indicated that she would give Dan a lift after all.

She was a while returning, and when she did I was engrossed in *Mansfield Park*. She went off to have a bath and I read on in my chair for a while, so that by the time I came to bed she was apparently asleep and didn't hear me thanking her for running Dan home.

9

Circumstances arose which meant that I was obliged to postpone my next appointment with Elizabeth Cruikshank.

In the days when social policy over the treatment of the mentally ill was more conservative, many hundreds of men and women in Britain had been confined to 'care' for the bulk of their adult lives. One of my duties at St Stephen's, the hospital in Haywards Heath, was to monitor the patients who had been inmates so long that the hospital had become their only home. Among those whom it was my melancholy business to oversee, one case especially troubled me: a man who suffered from the unshakeable conviction that he had a wolf lodged in the upper portion of his skull. His behaviour was always perfectly docile, but to his perturbed mind this phantom, to which he was the unwilling host, was a threat not to himself but to the world at large. In fact, as I had said in my report when he first became my responsibility, in my view he was now too institutionalised for the world to be anything but a far more serious menace to him.

Not long after my first encounter with this unfortunate, I found myself, due to some delayed appointment, killing time by visiting Whipsnade Zoo. It was a filthy November day, and walking briskly to keep my circulation moving, I landed up at the far corner of the zoo, by the enclosure which houses the wolves.

I was at once drawn by their lean shadowy forms and their

long-legged stilted gait. But what held my attention most was the way their narrow, vigilant muzzles and haunted eyes put me in mind of this man, so much so that I began to speculate whether the captive creatures mightn't suffer from the fantasy that they had a desperate human being trapped inside their skulls. Whenever I saw this patient now, I thought of those penned-in wolves. I could never decide whether it was the influence of the delusion or being confined like a beast which had rendered him so visibly lupine.

But that he was a harmless, docile wolf, I was convinced, and for more years than I could bear to calculate, he had been stashed away in the upper storeys of the hospital, which had originally served as one of the big Victorian asylums.

St Stephen's had retained in its running a remnant of the asylum policy wherein the madder the inmate, the higher up in the large mock-Gothic pile they were placed; and, in the cases of the potentially violent, in locked wards, with confining cells, and with nurses trained to deal with any dangerous outbreaks. We even had restraining jackets, based on the old 'strait' kind, though as Gus once said, why a 'restraining' jacket was deemed to be less offensive than a 'strait' one beat him. He and I agreed one evening, over a whisky or two, that if we were ever forcibly confined we would rather be straitened than restrained. ('And while we're at it,' Gus had added, 'what in God's name is wrong with the old word "asylum"?')

My purpose in visiting St Stephen's was to conduct the long-term patients' annual review, which had been scheduled for the following day. For the most part, this meeting was a mere routine of briefly reviewing, and then renewing, existing measures – security levels, medication, treatment plans – but when the wolf man's name came up I found myself asking, 'Why, as a matter of interest, do we keep him on level five?' Five was St Stephen's top security ward.

I was the consultant and the person who'd known the wolf man longest, and as I had expected, no one had any answer to this question.

'Have we any evidence of violence?'

Level five's charge nurse, an Irishman with bad skin and reddish hair, said that, as far as he knew, we didn't.

'Has he been any trouble at all, Sean? Anything not on the record we should know about?'

'Nothing, Dr McBride, so far as I'm aware. Though . . .'

'What?'

'He's always saying he *might* do something. Or so I'm led to believe. Can't say he lets on to any of us.'

'But that's his delusion, isn't it? My point is, why are we pandering to it? We've never had the smallest peep out of him in all the time I've been here. I think we should try him out on level four, or even three, see how he goes. Anyone got any objections?'

I knew they wouldn't have. And I caught the train to London with the self-satisfied feeling that I'd performed at least one valuable action that day.

The reason the meeting at St Stephen's had had to be brought forward was because I was obliged to be in London the following day. I was to appear as an expert witness in a medical case, which gave me an opportunity to visit Gus.

Gus lived in prodigal squalor in a cramped, snuff-coloured flat on Marylebone High Street. I'd never had much clue about Gus's private life. I gathered from some source, not Gus himself, that he had been married. Signs of various involvements were occasionally discernible, though I never met Gus in the company of a woman with whom, so far as I could judge, he had any close tie. I saw him once coming down Shaftesbury Avenue with a tall, elegantly dressed, striking-looking older woman. There was

a Russian air about her – she had a dancer's bones and deport-
ment – but if Gus noticed me he concealed the fact, and something in his manner kept me from making my presence known.
I thought afterwards that he had looked vulnerable with the
woman on his arm.

But no woman I've ever known could have managed more
than a night or two at Gus's flat. To this day, I couldn't say whether
the nicotine-coloured walls were that shade to blend in with or
as a result of his addiction. I removed a plate of what looked to
have been egg and beans and brown sauce, and settled into a
peeling leather armchair that put me in mind of a rhinoceros
with dermatitis.

Gus poured me a whisky, picked up a half-smoked cheroot
from the ashtray, stubbed it out absent-mindedly, lit a fresh one,
and stretched out a leg on the sofa. Watching him, I was aware
of a sensation which often visited me when I saw Gus, which
was that with him I was safe from harm.

I don't know when I first began to ask myself, at some point
in any association, whether or not this person would be likely to
shop me to the Nazis. I'm not even sure what this question means
since I'm not a Jew, a Gypsy, nor, so far as I know, homosexual.
I dare say it has something to do with losing my mother's un-
questioning support. If push came to shove, my mother would
probably have shopped me, because she would have judged it
right to save her own skin for the girls' sake, or my father's. Perhaps I'm being mean, but Olivia, I often felt, might shop me for
a couple of pretty dresses. I couldn't have told you how Dan
would stand this test. He might have proved the staunchest of allies, but I wouldn't be sure until an occasion to test it arose,
which summed up some crucial element in my relationship with
Dan. Bar – I didn't have even to consider it – would never betray me, however I might have betrayed her – and I was never
too sure about my own potential behaviour in this hypothetical

situation – and Gus, I was entirely confident, without a thought to his own safety, would lead a Resistance force to rescue me.

For Gus the fearful things which lurk for most of us at the ragged edges of consciousness were mere flimflam rubbish and piffle before the wind. With an agile innocence, he simply stepped over them or swept them aside. This, it came to me, in an access of gratitude – as I drank a generous measure of his excellent single malt, in the smoky, familiar room, and felt the muscles in my neck and shoulders begin to ease – was why I loved him. It was also why it was easy to tell him when I was afraid.

The court case that had brought me to London concerned a twenty-year-old female student's suicide. The family was attributing the tragedy to the negligence of the consultant, a Dr Hannan, and I was an expert witness for the defence. From what I could tell, the case had been conducted with due professional propriety, but it brought up inevitable anxieties. There but for the grace of some god or other went I. Any of us who did this work could find ourselves in poor Hannan's shoes.

Elizabeth Cruikshank was more than usually on my mind because of the postponement of our appointment, and the relaxing effect of the whisky, and the sense of security which Gus induced, prompted me to ask, 'Would you mind if I talk to you about somebody?'

Gus, the most voluble of men, had also the gift of listening deeply. He listened now, getting up only to refill my glass as I struggled to summarise the state of affairs with Elizabeth Cruikshank.

One asset of an analyst's training is that it teaches you pretty effective recall. Not that in this case there was much to remember. What, when you came down to it, did I really know about my contained, grey-eyed patient after all these weeks, apart from a succession of refractory silences? That she had been a librarian; that she had married; that she had two children who, so far as I

was aware, were not close enough to have visited; that she refused medication; that she always had with her a brown leather
bag; that she appeared fascinated by the quince tree in the hospital garden; these, and my sense of some mortally dangerous secret squirrelled away beneath that politely occluding veneer,
were the sum of what I had to report.

'She's got under your skin,' Gus observed when my sketchy
account petered out. 'Is she a burden? That you mind about her
is obvious, but does she weigh on you, get you down?'

I considered this. 'No, to a surprising extent she doesn't. I
rather enjoy her presence.'

'That's good. When all bets are off, theoretical statements
about "therapeutic commitment" are daylight rubbish. You might
as well lean on air.'

'For what it's worth, I do mind about her. I mind rather a
lot.' For the first time, it struck me that I was anxious about this.

'Yes, you do,' said Gus firmly. 'Thank goodness.' Probably he
had sensed my unease. One of the things I liked in Gus was that
he could pick up one's state of mind without the need to comment on it. 'Have you noticed how no one thanks "goodness"
any more? Goodness is out of fashion. So is minding. Minding's
considered bad form. God knows why. You must mind. You
have to love them – I don't mean go to bed with them, I don't
have to tell you that, but need them, need them to live, for your
sake too.'

' "It's in giving yourself that you possess yourself"?'

'Who said that?'

'Lou Andreas-Salomé.' One of Freud's first disciples.

'Don't know that one,' said Gus. 'But she's right. The thing
is, Freud never intended his ideas to be taken as a recipe for
bogus detachment. You know, the Greek potters could tell the
very second at which a glaze turned in a kiln from red to black.
They didn't need a thermometer. They trusted the blink of an

eye. The same's true of the heart. The heart can register true or fake before the theorist can say "knife!" Freud, for all his other nonsense, knew that. Naturally, others'll tell you otherwise.'

'Oh, "others" . . . !' I said. 'You mean like Jeffries?'

'Jeffries wouldn't save his own mother if she were drowning in her bath. The only reason he'd cite the Oedipus complex is as a valid excuse for refusing to see her naked. You must plunge into it with them. You have to – stand or sit, splash your feet in it – it doesn't matter as long as you're there too. Show them you can bear it, and you're willing to bear it with them.'

'But can you bear anything for anyone else, really?'

'No,' said Gus. 'You can't. But you can let them know you'll try. And that, very likely, you can't bear it either but –'

'In saying so, show you are bearing it?'

'Exactly,' said Gus again, approvingly, and poured me another large Scotch presumably as a reward. I'd drunk the first one pretty rapidly. It tended to be like that with Gus, I'm afraid.

'The Stoics had the right idea,' Gus resumed. 'Trouble with this age is it's got hold of the crackpot notion you can do away with suffering. Jeffries and his type are responsible for that kind of babyish attitude. Someone says, "Help, help, it hurts," and they hand out a bloody drug and say, "There, there, this'll make it better." That's sticking-plaster mentality. It doesn't make the bloody awfulness go away. It just covers it up. Pathology. The logos of suffering, or the word on suffering. Well, the "word" on suffering is, it has to be bloody well suffered, not covered up.'

I thought of Mrs Beet saying to me they had taken all the sorrow as well as the joy out of her husband when they lobotomised him.

'So how do we help the suffering suffer bearably?'

'The word "patient" comes from the same root as suffer. Patient: one who suffers patiently.'

'It's rather a tall order,' I suggested, nursing my whisky glass.

I wasn't unaware that I used alcohol to make the unbearable bearable.

'Yes, it is,' Gus agreed. He sounded mournful. I'd never fathomed what his own brand of suffering consisted of. 'And of course some can't take it. Like your patient. They want to bail out. You can't blame them.'

We sat awhile consumed with our own thoughts. I was reflecting how frequently I wanted to bail out myself.

'What is suicide, Gus? What are people up to, really, when they seriously try to kill themselves?' You'd be surprised how little my profession generally considers these questions. I suppose it's because we are kept so busy dealing with the consequences.

Gus lit another cheroot. 'Acceleration of life, perhaps? A suicide is someone who wants to take a short cut to one of the only certainties: death and taxes. Only taxes aren't as sexy as death. You could argue that a suicide is getting straight to the point: it's a fast-track method of transportation from one realm to another.'

'But there isn't a place you can be transported to behind the scenes, is there? Another country called "Death"?'

'The ancients thought so,' Gus said. 'I trust them. They'd a feel for the mysteries. Hades, for instance. Mind you, it was a pale sort of a place. Achilles hated it. When Odysseus visited Hades, Achilles told him he would rather be the meanest ploughboy alive than the great Achilles deprived of life.'

'But there was Socrates,' I said. 'What about him? He chose suicide, didn't he?'

'Yes, but for the Greeks suicide was always linked with courage. It takes courage not to be defined by life and courage consciously to enter the biggest of all unknowns. Socrates was using his life, sacrificing it, you could say, to make a point to the Athenians about their law. He was insisting that they act rationally, put their money where their mouth was and apply the law's sentence for the crime he had not been acquitted of committing. It wasn't that he wasn't able to bear life. Quite the contrary. He was so unfussed about it he knew how to play with it! He could have escaped the sentence, and it was clear they were keen as mustard that he should. That was the correct form: you applied the death sentence, the culprit made appropriate arrangements with his chums and tactfully buggered off. The last thing the authorities wanted was Socrates' death on their hands. But he wasn't having it. He put the frighteners on them by not caring enough about saving his own skin. You see, Socrates knew something else. His last request before he downed the hemlock, which incidentally wasn't such a jolly way to depart as people suggest – it would have given him shocking stomach pains – was that a cock be sacrificed to Asclepius. One of his better jokes.'

'Why is it a joke?' Another thing I liked about Gus was that he never made you feel that what you didn't know or understand mattered a straw.

'Asclepius was the god of healing. If you think about it, Socrates pays his last respects to a healer at the point when there was about to be nothing left of him to heal. I reckon he was saying, life is a sickness and death is a welcome recovery from it. Remember, there's no cure for being alive!'

'I told her that,' I said. 'I told my patient it was you who told me. It was one of the few things I've said which seemed to get through.' Which was when I remembered the conversation we'd had about painting. 'Actually, there's another thing. She shares your taste for Caravaggio.'

'Does she indeed?' said Gus. 'You know, I'd follow that up if I were you. Caravaggio knew about suffering. And passion. And death. There was nothing babyish or covered up about Caravaggio!'

10

My appointment with Dr Hannan's counsel was not till eleven so I had time, the following morning, to drop by the National Gallery.

I renewed my acquaintance with Titian's *Man with a Blue Sleeve*. I like that blue. And I adore Titian's supreme confidence. You can see it reflected in his nobleman, who's so clearly a bastard, but one of those bastards you can't help but admire.

It was almost twelve years since I'd looked at the Caravaggio and I'd forgotten, if I'd ever registered, how young the risen Christ looks. His cheek is almost childishly smooth, the rounded curves defying the recent experience of death, as if in dying his bloom has been renewed. Poor Jesus. I'd never considered it before, but how appalling to undergo that agonising death, and have all the relief of its being over, and then have to endure the redoubled torment of coming back.

I looked again at the stupefied pair receiving the news of this unlooked-for return. The hand of the disciple to the right, which comes springing out of the frame, as if the third dimension has been given literal shape, is the left hand, the sinister side, the hand of the unconscious, plucking life and flinging it at us out of the dark.

I'd not taken in the painting properly when Gus showed it to me first, inspecting it only out of politeness, and curiosity –

mostly about my new acquaintance. Now it hit me with the delayed force that the revelation they were witnessing plainly hit the two amazed fishermen, when the friend and colleague they had loved – and walked and talked and lain down and slept with, on lousy straw and rocky, inhospitable soil, and starved with, and eaten supper with the night before he died, and believed dead and gone for ever – rematerialised out of the blue to share this other supper with them and knock them back to life.

I doubt you can know until you have someone close to you die how unnatural the loss feels. I, who had lived with that absence from childhood, had a problem understanding the degree to which the dead are dead to most of the living. When I finally accepted that Jonny had gone, I began to believe I could bring him back by willing it. I used to invent elaborate rituals with my toys, toys we had shared. We had a jam jar filled with cowrie shells, a legacy from our mother's childhood, and Jonny used to form patterns with them on our bedroom lino. He would lay the shells out on the diamond-patterned floor and stand us both inside and speak spells and transport us to China, to India, to Arabia, to Timbuktu.

Those lands he transported us to were as real to me as the rocky Cornish seascapes where we spent our holidays, and where Jonny's inventiveness presided over rock pools and shrimping nets and fantasies of smuggling. In important ways more real.

At dawn and dusk, at teatime, breakfast, schooldays and holidays, and those isolated days I persuaded my mother I was sick and she let me off school – no easy feat, since she was rarely susceptible to pleading – I cast the cowrie shells. I also made potions from dock and dew, which I sneaked out early in the morning to gather in a cracked doll's cup, another relic from our mother's childhood, and drew blood from my arm with the pin of an old Thomas the Tank Engine badge and tried to furnish my mind with words whose precise meaning I didn't comprehend but whose obscurities I hoped might provide the necessary summoning power. But for all my dedicated efforts, and all my willing suspension of disbelief, Jonny never returned.

But Jesus did. According to the story. The story must have had the same impact on Caravaggio as he envisaged it had on the two disciples for him to have painted the shock of it with such electrifying intensity. An intensity which reached through time and space and penetrated my inhibited English breast as I stood in the particular quiet of an unpeopled gallery. There's a sense in which I fell in love with Gus the day he took me to see the Caravaggio. But it wasn't until that moment that I fell in love with the painting he had showed me.

I lingered, as lovers do, over this discovery, and my dislike of being unpunctual meant that I raced down the Strand and was sweating into my carefully chosen white shirt by the time I reached the court.

I needn't have worried. The young counsel was later still. As we went through my testimony again, I remarked, conversationally, that there was no way of stopping someone bent on doing themselves in, any more than you could halt the progress of a wild horse.

'Let's skip the horse ref, yah?' suggested the counsel, whose hair resembled the tail feathers of a bedraggled mallard duck. I wasn't fooled; these draggled young men are eagles when they fasten on their prey.

The image was purely for private communication, I assured him. In my testimony I would stick to medical principles of the purely conventional kind.

As I entered the windowless room where witnesses are asked to kick their heels, a garrulous-seeming woman started up at me.

'You a witness? I'm here for the bodily violence.'

She sounded as if she might be. The over-talkative have something of the terrorist about them. I organised my expression into what I hoped was a politely repelling aspect and withdrew into my thoughts.

Waiting is no hardship for me. Even today, when I am less oppressed by claims on my time, I am content to wait for hours at airports. It gives me a break from the perpetual feeling that I ought to be doing something – a licensed rest from the overactive sense of duty which my upbringing induced. The garrulous woman was called and I was left thankful for no further interruption. I tried to dredge from memory the story behind the Caravaggio painting. But it wouldn't come. My knowledge of such subjects is hazy, but no doctor could fail to have a soft spot for Jesus. Whatever else, he was a virtuoso healer, a colleague, in fact, though if you were to believe the story, one with rather superior credentials.

But your average doctor is not a god and shouldn't fall into the trap of feeling that is what is required. 'Stay awake, do your best, and don't expect results,' Gus would say. But those who suffer, and those close to them, expect results, and when these go awry the doctor can be crucified.

I've appeared, several times, as an expert witness, and each time the gravity of the occasion catches me. A glance at the judge revealed a narrow-featured man with serious spectacles whose wig had been thrown rakishly over his head like a dishcloth. It took me some years to work out that the greater the authority in court, the greater the licence with the wig.

I steadied myself to tell, if not the absolute truth – for how can any of us fairly do that? – at least to give my considered opinion, which was that on the available information Dr Hannan could not reasonably be said to have erred. Across the room I observed him repeatedly wiping with a large white handkerchief his hands, the back of his neck, his broad shiny forehead, even his plump trousered knees, and my heart went out to him.

Dr Hannan, it had been established, had discussed the attempted suicide's case with appropriate care, had requested that his patient be closely observed by the nursing staff and that all medication be strictly supervised. It was the girl's perseverant cunning which had contrived to steal enough from a hospital drugs trolley, left carelessly by no one could establish whom, to finish the job she had started. There was something awesome about this executive efficiency. It was a disturbing affair, not only because of the girl's youth, but because from her actions you could tell that she might have amounted to something. It takes a special kind of determined will to accomplish your own death.

I pronounced, and under questioning reiterated, my view that there had been no deficiencies in the treatment of Melanie Hope Claybourne, whose life had been taken by her own hand. 'And you remain convinced,' the prosecuting counsel pressed, 'that everything reasonable was done by Dr Hannan to prevent any further attempts by his patient on her own life?' Beneath his professional obligations I got the sense that no more than I did he want to condemn the sweating doctor.

'Completely convinced' was my honest answer.

But inwardly I wondered a little about that name 'Hope,' which seemed to hint at some ungrasped opportunity. The question which I had half anticipated never arrived, though I detected a shade of its possibility flicker in the eyes of our draggled counsel. What the other counsel might have asked was whether, in the circumstances, I would have followed the same procedures as Dr Hannan. The unspoken question had a certain validity. It was not that Dr Hannan had not done everything 'reasonable' for his patient's well-being; it was that he had neglected to consider the 'unreasonable.' And as Gus would say, in such cases it is often the unreasonable which is required.

Perhaps it was as well for Hannan that the unreasonable doesn't make convincing testimony in court. Nor is it yet a recognised prophylactic in psychiatric procedure. No one in any official position would consider saying, 'The girl was called "Hope," maybe you should have asked her, and yourself, what that unfashionable yet suggestive name might represent?' Nor did I have any way of knowing whether I could have succeeded where Hannan had failed. So much depends, I reflected on the train home, dog-tired at the effort of truth-telling, on how far one can gain access to the secret mind. As far as her physical person went, Hannan had behaved irreproachably, but the balance of the girl's life might have hung on whether he could find in her the 'Hope' for which she was named.

My mind darted anxiously to Elizabeth Cruikshank, whom it was my duty to try to perceive. How far did she want me to see her? But then, how far do any of us want to be seen? On the one hand, it is what we fear most, that our shamefulnesses, disloyalties, meannesses, cruelties, miseries, the sum of our hopeless, abject, creeping failures be finally laid bare. But the very opposite is also the case. I believed – or believed I believed – that we are in anguish until someone finally finds us out. And the deeper truth is that human consciousness can hold two contradictory states at once, and all our unmet longings wear an overcoat of fear.

To my annoyance I found I had left my scarf, cashmere, and a present from Olivia, in the railway carriage, and had to walk home from the station pursued by a wind screaming 'All is futile' around my naked neck and ears.

The lights in the flat were out when I reached it and I went round turning on more than I needed. It would have been consoling to find Olivia at home, and even to have her scold me a little over the scarf. I poured myself a whisky and switched an extra heater on, though the temperature was warm enough.

There was a note on the kitchen counter: *Back late. Ham, toms, etc in fridge. O.* Sometimes Olivia decorated her initial with a smile, which could irk me, but I missed it now.

I helped myself to a cold supper of ham and tomatoes and plenty of chutney and, in an act of defiance, because Olivia was fussy about the smell, three pickled onions. It was late, and I was too tired to work, so I settled down with a whisky and *Mansfield Park*. Getting up to refill my glass, and check the answerphone, in case Olivia might have left a message, I thought that when I had a moment I must remember to look up the story of that other supper.

11

The year was dropping fast towards the winter solstice so I had already switched on the lights in my room when I saw Elizabeth Cruikshank the following afternoon. From my chair I watched her enter the room with the awkward, faintly hesitant gait which betrayed uncertainty about her welcome.

As she settled into the blue chair I registered a glance at my clown. Perhaps it was a trick of the light, but the planes of her half-averted face looked even more pale and prominent than usual. She had about her that bird-like look which evoked painful images of cats, or cages.

I expected to begin with one of our familiar silences. I had had to cancel her previous session and I feared she might mind this dereliction, and my hunch was that she would mind that she minded. So I decided to tackle the subject right away.

'I'm sorry I had to miss our last meeting.'

'It doesn't matter.'

'If you say not.'

'It's not important.' This time I held my peace. 'I don't make the mistake of assuming I matter to you!' she broke out suddenly again, with more than a glint of sharpness.

Ah, my bird, I thought, a little more of that and I've caught you! But aloud I said, 'You think you are the only one to whom our meetings matter?'

The silence passed to her. Under her sway it deepened, chilled, iced over, and then, as rapidly, shifted temperature and melted as her neck and face flushed a violent red. Good, I thought. Time you showed your colours.

'How do I know what you think?'

'You might allow me to mind that I have possibly let you down.'

I'm not someone who plays games. Nor have I ever been of the view that games of any kind are what should be played in my business, or indeed in any human transaction. But it is not only in love affairs that there is a kind of dance, a stepping forward and a stepping back, a taking hold and a letting go, and I suppose I was banking on my studied politeness to provide a space for her to step out of where she was hiding.

'I didn't say you had,' she murmured angrily.

'But you would be entitled to think so,' I said, deliberately maintaining my tone.

I wondered if she would risk asking what had kept me from seeing her, and if she did, how I would answer her: that I had been releasing a patient who believed a wolf was trapped in his skull from years of being unnecessarily confined; that I had to appear as an expert witness in a London court on behalf of a doctor whose patient had committed suicide? It was with a mixture of regret and relief that I recognised she was going to stick with silence.

For the first time since I had begun to see her, I found myself becoming bored. I had spent more time and attention on this case than by any official reckoning I should have done and I had other, equally pressing, claims. And had I been asked to justify myself, I would have been hard put to give grounds for the amount of time I'd spent, or the level of my concern. There was nothing untoward in it, other than, by now, a well-kindled interest. But I was growing tired. Maybe I was too tired to continue trying to get blood out of this stone.

And then two things happened. That wretched cat appeared on the fence again and looked at me. Nothing more. It just looked, with its vile psychopathic stare, and clear as a bell I heard my mother's voice, which, perhaps unfairly, I always heard cutting me down to size. 'A cat may look at a king, you know, Davey.' And, as was often the way when I recalled my mother's familiar discouragements, I saw an image of Jonny standing in the road, smiling and beckoning me to cross. And then my mind flickered to Gus, and myself drinking whisky in his snug, untidy room, in the atmosphere of comfortable masculine intimacy, and then that image dissolved too, and reconfigured itself into the sweating bulk of the terrified Dr Hannan. Whatever the judgement of the court, poor Hannan would not escape his own judgement and the unspoken judgement of the dead Melanie Claybourne. Melanie Hope Claybourne, in whom, and for whom, all hope was now dead, dead as a doornail.

Something moved in me as palpably as if an old weathervane, which had stuck fast pointing north, had, through the aid of some invisible force, unjammed and careered round to the south.

'I had to attend a meeting to assess some patients at another hospital and then I was called to London to act as a witness on behalf of a colleague whose patient succeeded in killing herself,' I heard myself enunciate, and as I did so, I had the impression that I was delivering this statement up to someone, or some thing, over and above the woman in my room. Her head shot up but I couldn't read the look in her eyes. It might have been fear or anger. Possibly both. Whatever it was, it didn't deter me.

'I thought a lot about you while I was away. I thought that although it is your right to choose to die, I would be glad if you didn't. Very glad, in fact.'

'To save your own skin?' It was not quite a jeer.

'Yes, if you like. But for other reasons too.'

She said nothing so I pressed on. I'd got the bit between my teeth now.

'I looked in on a painting of Caravaggio's at the National Gallery yesterday. *The Supper at Emmaus*. I remembered you said that you liked him.'

'Yes?'

'My friend Gus Galen, as I think I mentioned to you once, likes him too. It was Gus who showed me the painting first. And the evening of the day I missed seeing you, when we should have been meeting here, I saw Gus and we spoke about you' – anticipating a protest I hurried on – 'or rather I spoke. He listened. Forgive me, but I've been worried for you. Worried about you. I told him you liked Caravaggio and he sent me back to look at this one. Or' – again I struggled to be accurate: it seemed more than usually urgent – 'I went back myself, off my own bat. Because of what he said, what Gus said. Gus is someone I trust. I hadn't really looked at that painting before, but I did yesterday. I rather fell in love with it. In my profession, the business of falling in love is often dismissed as fantasy, neurotic wishful thinking. But there are ways of falling in love which are, I would say, important. Crucial. And real.' I believe I might have been sweating though the temperature was December chill.

The quince's blossomless, lichen-covered branches were tracing a silver-grey pattern behind the glass and my mother's wounded mango tree came to mind.

'And painful,' I added, pushing myself over a further threshold. I was conscious of slightly raising my voice. 'Love is painful. Isn't it? It forces change upon you. It forces you – I should say us – to change. Or have a shot at changing, anyway,' I more lamely concluded.

There followed a very long silence during which I didn't allow myself to consider the odds on this gamble. Perhaps to counter a heightened sense of precariousness, my thoughts reverted to Lady Bertram on her sofa, with her pug, and her basket of cut flowers from the beds at Mansfield Park. There had grown in me a sneaking liking for idle Lady Bertram. She had no conscience whatsoever and I suspected that, for similar reasons, Jane Austen liked her too. Lady Bertram wouldn't have had the whisker of a notion of what I was on about. The only change she would have undertaken was to Pug's collar or her own bonnet strings.

'You know, what I said before?'

The voice was so low that in my distraction I believed I'd not heard and asked her to repeat her words. She started, hesitated, then stalled, and my thoughts flew anxiously from Sir Thomas Bertram's morally insentient wife to Melanie Hope's resolutely fatal despair, while my laggardly brain caught up with the sense of the words.

'Yes,' I said quickly. 'I'm sorry, I do know.' And nothing in the world was more moving to me at that moment than that one human heart can open to another. 'Or rather, I should say I don't know. But I remember what you said.'

'So,' she appeared to continue but halted as abruptly. And then there was a quite new kind of silence which I tried not to interrupt even with my thoughts.

The silence slipped around us, between us, over us, covering us, and the room, and everything in it, with the invisible lustre of possibility. But the possibility was not mine. I could only sit within it and wait.

'It was like this,' said Elizabeth Cruikshank, at last.

PART II

Who is the third who walks always beside you?

1

Age and disease and death may destroy our physical being but it is other people who get inside us and damage our hearts and minds. My work has occasioned ample example of this but it was Elizabeth Cruikshank who really made me understand it.

Understand. The act of standing under. A word I had used perhaps every day and yet never really analysed.

That night I dreamed I was in a forest, and the trees, tall as pylons, formed a high screen above my head. I was walking a narrow path, through the thickly knitted trees, so thick that I have an impression of holding up my hands as if to protect my eyes and face, when a barn owl flew out of the fretted darkness and savagely bit me.

It is the borrowed truths we cling to most tenaciously, and as Gus was always intimating, our profession tends to adhere to rules which have little to do with natural human exchanges. That long winter afternoon, which grew into evening, while I sat with Elizabeth Cruikshank and she told me her story, I abandoned all the accepted methods of working.

From time to time, she would get up from the blue chair and drift about my room, apparently inspecting the objects I had on my desk: the lump of volcanic lava from the holiday in Sicily I took before I went to medical school, where I had all the predictable student thoughts of daringly staying on and living a life of honest labour; the ugly silver inkstand, which had belonged to my mother's father, the judge, and which I never used but had the residue of an ink my grandfather, quite unselfconsciously, would have called 'nigger brown' encrusted on the bottom of the glass inner well; and the small round bell which was my only tangible link with Jonny.

The bell had been on a pair of red slippers embellished with smiling clowns' faces, and when our mother finally brought herself to gather his things together, I stole one night, when I couldn't sleep, into the spare room, where Jonny's socks and pants and shorts and T-shirts had been set aside to be donated to some charity. I guess that, thrifty as she was, my mother couldn't bear the prospect of the sight of her dead son's clothes on her surviving child. I don't recall what I felt about seeing Jonny's things all piled up there to give away, but the idea now is painful. I don't remember either, though I know I must have done it, tearing the bell from one of the slippers.

I see Jonny still, sliding on the polished parquet floor of our hall, which used to stretch before my eyes in palatial dimensions and reason tells me I would now find cramped. He's in the dressing gown, one of the few garments which escaped redistribution to become mine, unless, perhaps, it was passed on before he died: a camel dressing gown, with a blue-and-red twisted cord around the collar and a plaited blue-and-red tasselled cord for the waist, and he's wearing the slippers of which only one, the left, has on it a bell. My mother must have known I kept the bell under my pillow, because she would have seen it when the sheets were changed. She never mentioned it. But she would never have guessed that I sometimes rang it for Jonny in the night.

Elizabeth Cruikshank was speaking to me and I saw she had picked up the bell, which was cupped in her hand, as if it were as fragile as the blown egg I have also on my desk.

'It was his voice I heard first.'

I wondered if she might ring the bell and, if she did, whose spirit would be summoned – Jonny's, or another's presence. But she replaced my relic, unrung, as meticulously as if it were the eggshell. I dare say she had ascribed its precise value to me – as I said, she had the knack of seeing through to the back of one's mind.

'Where did you hear it?'

Voices count. The first contact a foetus makes with the world is the parental voice. In the slight pause before she answered I had a recollection of Jonny calling to me from the bathroom: 'Davey, come on, Davey, quick, hurry *up*, the water's getting cold!'

'In the bath. I was in the bath!'

As she said this she smiled and I had a shock, because, suddenly, the moon danced and I saw her naked, not at all like Wanda Williams, with whom I had dutifully and dolefully gone to bed. I don't mean I felt desire for my patient; I didn't, or not in that way.

'I see.' I was smiling too, partly because of the coincidence of the bathrooms. 'So, go on then, tell me.'

In those days, I had one of those electric coffee-filtering devices with a hotplate – the sort which made a bitter-tasting liquor if you left it too long, a monster of a machine. It catered to my one true addiction. I am frequently advised by concerned acquaintances that for reasons of health and longevity I should eschew coffee. Longevity has even fewer attractions for me today, but even if it had, I could never care enough for it to forgo coffee. I reckon we drank tankerloads of coffee that evening, Elizabeth Cruikshank and I.

At one point, I sent out for sandwiches. Maguire poked her head round the door, expecting me to have finished for the day and ready with some quip, but sharp enough to suppress it when she observed the two of us in serious conversation; though not before I'd said, 'Any chance you could run down to the canteen and get Mrs Cruikshank and me a round or two of sandwiches? Cheese and pickle and ham, in my case, I don't know what she might want?'

And Maguire, efficiently interpreting the brief signal for the same order from my patient, was off and back again with a reassuringly piled plate of sandwiches, plus some of the ropy fruit, a wizened orange and an over-red Snow White apple, which the canteen palmed off on us.

It is said that when we touch pitch we are defiled. But when we touch, or are touched by, another's story, that also affects our being, and more radically. I can still recall the almost visceral sensation with which I intuited something large and cold roll away inside my patient, as she embarked on the tale that, for so many years, I was to learn, she had had shored up inside her.

As she had already told me, as a young librarian she had rented a run-down flat, up in the roof of one of the big, white, stucco-fronted houses in Camden Square. The flat was sparsely furnished by a stingy landlord, and among its several deficiencies was an erratic immersion heater which regularly broke down. While she was prepared to put up with a good deal, she shared another of my mild obsessions: a fondness for baths.

People shower more nowadays, but I still prefer the comfort of a warm bath. It was my patient's love of baths which brought about her meeting with Thomas Carrington.

A sculptor, Cecil Bainbridge, rented the flat below, and one morning, when the landlord had promised, and failed for the third time, to call for an inspection of the faulty heater, my patient decided, for her unusually, to take independent action. Bainbridge's air of absent-minded shabbiness had softened her customary defences. They'd exchanged a few pleasantries, so with no one else to turn to, she knocked on his door to enquire about a plumber.

'You're welcome to borrow my bathroom while I'm away,'

he offered. And, gratefully, she accepted a spare key and the use of his hot water in return for some minor plant-watering duties.

Some days later, as she lay in the bath, enjoying a sense of daring at the temporary tenure of a strange environment, she heard a voice. Someone who wasn't Cecil Bainbridge was speaking in the next room where, secure against intrusion, she had left all her clothes.

The unexpected voice startled her. But she was surprisingly unafraid. There was something in the timbre which reassured her. Or didn't, at least, alarm her.

Helping herself to Bainbridge's bathrobe, she listened at the door. The voice appeared to be conducting a conversation, but there was no answering participant in this dialogue. Maybe whoever it was was on the phone and in the room where without a second thought she had left all her clothes.

She called out, 'Who is that?'

'Who's this?'

'Who are you?'

'I might ask the same question.'

The bathroom door was pulled back and a tall, beaky-nosed man stood there, his glasses steaming up in the warm air.

'I'm a friend of Bainbridge's' and 'I'm a friend of Cecil's,' they simultaneously explained.

'I should hope so,' the man continued, 'seeing that you're practically naked as nature intended in his bathroom.'

She explained, still less embarrassed than she might have been, about the plumber and the landlord.

'Plumbers and landlords are not natural bedfellows.'

'Is "naked as nature intended" a quotation?'

'A film. It used to be on at a seedy cinema in Piccadilly where they showed non-stop porn. Or what passed then for porn. It wouldn't now. As a boy, I was beside myself to see it.'

'And did you?'

'Sadly, no.'

'Is there someone else here?'

'No. Why?'

'I heard you talking to someone.'

'Only to myself. Don't you talk to yourself?' He had taken off his glasses and was looking at her with bright brown eyes. 'Surely you must. I'm Thomas Carrington, by the way.'

'I'm Elizabeth Bonelli. In a way I do.'

'What way? Are you Italian? You have an old-master look.' He looked at her consideringly. 'Giorgione, maybe. Nice.'

'Half.'

'Half talk to yourself or half Italian?'

'Both, I suppose. I do talk to myself, but not out loud. At least, I don't think so.'

'I find I have to say things aloud so I can listen, because I'm the only person who understands me well. Where are your clothes, Elizabeth Bonelli?' He spoke her name with an easy and enchanting familiarity.

The thought of her clothes lying exposed in the next room embarrassed her for the first time and she began to flush. 'I'm surprised you didn't notice them.' She wished she could remember what knickers she'd been wearing.

'I was preoccupied,' Thomas said. 'Talking to myself and then having to think up some answer to me. It gets wearing. Do you find that?' He still had his glasses off and he looked at her again, his head on one side.

'I should get dressed,' she said, ignoring his other question.

But she didn't get dressed. Or not for a while.

2

She seemed anxious to assure me that it wasn't sex which detained them. It's a funny thing, but in my job you don't take much interest in sex. Or rather, the interest you take is of a pretty disinterested kind. Like any other topic it can lose its appeal if it becomes a staple of your trade. I am not speaking about my personal experience, you understand.

Extensive sexual expertise is not something I can boast of. Bar was probably my most rewarding partner. It doesn't always follow that character is consistent in the bedroom. I've known mousy-looking women who were tigers once they had their clothes off, and vice versa. But Bar in bed was a reflection of Bar out of it: uncloying, considerate, appreciative, kind. Olivia had none of these graces, indeed the very opposites by turn, which, I'm sorry to own, may be what attracted me to her. It is a peculiarity of the human male that the poison which can destroy us has this pernicious allure. The shrewd Elizabethans were aware of this: it's not for nothing that their slang for orgasm was 'to die.'

In any case, it was with no diminished interest, rather the reverse, that I heard my patient, wrapped in the borrowed bathrobe, had done no more than talk to this stranger, for, she calculated, over three hours. Only when he said, 'You should get dressed, you'll get cold like that,' did she think about doing so, while he left the flat, promising to be back soon.

She didn't even go upstairs to her own place to change into something more presentable than the dull skirt and sweater she'd been wearing, or to put on the make-up she was conscious of lacking after the bath. She was too worried that he might return and, finding her gone, give up on her.

'It sounds stupid but I prayed.'

'You weren't in the habit?'

'I prayed to something, I don't know who or what.'

Whomever her prayer was addressed to, it was answered. Thomas returned with shopping bags filled with food.

'Did you cook?'

'He did. I couldn't have done a thing.'

'What did he cook?'

In fact, it was shortly after this that Maguire was dispatched for sandwiches, the description of that first shared meal activating a sudden vicarious appetite in my patient's single audience. I could picture her hungry – not merely for the omelette that had miraculously been prepared for her, but hungrier still for the affection she had been denied – leaning, on Bainbridge's kitchen table, towards the myopic stranger, upon whose somewhat thick lenses the light spun, in dancing dazzling points, in the tall London house, in the flat where neither belonged.

It was this air of not-quite-belonging which had so characterised her for me and it came to me that it must have filled her with extraordinary delight, but a delight of the kind that is freighted with tension, seemingly to have commanded, with so little effort, this intense focus. To be paid such unusual attention was a cordial to her famished heart, which might well have given wings to almost unbearable hope.

But it is a hallmark of the damaged that when it comes to their own desire instinctively, ruinously, they tend to court its opposite. So at the point when it dawned on her how much it mattered that he should stay, she suddenly asked, 'Shouldn't you be going? Haven't you things to do?'

And Thomas, looking at his watch, said, 'Oh hell! Damn and blast, I should.'

Even so, he didn't go at once but lingered further over the table, still talking.

'He talked better than anyone I had ever known. Not that what he said then was anything I could easily reproduce, but I don't know . . .'

'I expect you do.'

'It was as if . . .' Again she stalled.

'It cancelled the loneliness?'

She appeared to consider this before saying, 'It was as if I were meeting someone whom I had known intimately and from whom I had been separated for a very long time.'

'And he felt the same?' It crossed my mind that this was what I would feel were I to meet Jonny.

She made the wounded-bird gesture with her hands.

'How could I tell? I'd never talked so comfortably to anyone before. He seemed to like me, and to want to go on talking. But how could I know he wasn't like that with everyone? He seemed so easy, so fluent, I couldn't imagine that had much to do with my being there.'

Of course she couldn't. Your average egotist is armoured against disappointments for, to the egotist, he or she is the un-disputed centre of the whole world. That my patient had been given sight of something rarer and more compelling than this I understood. We all long for someone with whom we are able to share our peculiar burdens of being alive.

3

Besides his voice, it was his hands she remembered most, though she had not been conscious of taking them in at the time. Capable hands, she told me, with square fingers and clean nails. I don't know if at that point I glanced at my own, or if I only tried to picture what they were like. Clean and neatly clipped, I would have hoped. My mother used to say that it is the small details that betray character.

Of what they talked, on that first meeting, I am left with an impression rather than detail. I doubt she could have given me with any great exactitude more than the broad brush strokes which – between bites of sandwich, eaten ferociously – she made that winter afternoon. In any case, it is not the substance of a conversation but the way the heart irradiates it that infuses it with meaning.

Thomas, she learned, was an art historian whose work took him abroad and only occasionally back to England. He had an Oxford base in someone else's house. Bainbridge, from a long habit of personal trust – and the generosity she herself had enjoyed – had bestowed on his friend a house key and the invitation to stay whenever he found himself in need of a London bed. She gained half an impression that maybe there were other beds available, should Thomas have wanted to take advantage of them, but he preferred Bainbridge's because the hospitality came, by and large, with no strings.

Finding himself the previous evening unexpectedly late in London after a lecture, Thomas had tried on the phone and failed to get Bainbridge (notoriously unpredictable in his movements) and had therefore taken up the standing invitation. He had stayed the night and was out buying a paper when, unaware of any other presence, my patient had arrived to take her daily bath. That much she discovered in Bainbridge's kitchen, over the Formica table.

What her part was in their conversation again I can only guess. Compared to Thomas's, her life appeared to her barrenly uneventful. She told me she mostly listened while talk flowed from the confiding stranger.

In all exchanges there must be one who listens and one who speaks, but there can be no revelation without someone to whom it is revealed. I am in a position to make this judgement, since it is as listener I have spent most of my working life, as I did that afternoon and evening when I sat with Elizabeth Cruikshank. But even as I listened, trying to catch and make sense of the thread of her meaning, I was spinning invisible threads of my own.

Later that afternoon, after yet more engrossing conversation, Thomas left the flat, having taken her number, with sincere-sounding promises to call her the following week, when he expected to return to London to take up more of Bainbridge's hospitality and replicate this happy meeting. There was no hint, she insisted, of any romantic involvement.

'There was the reference to *Naked as Nature Intended*,' I couldn't resist pointing out, but she dismissed this with the vehemence which the sandwiches seemed to have inspired.

'That was only a joke.'

Privately, I thought otherwise. Gus once suggested that in the first encounter between two people the seeds of what will grow between them are sown. He was speaking of his patients, but I have come to believe that this is the case with all our important associations. The first time I met Olivia I got caught in her blouse, and I met Bar sitting beside her at a conference where I borrowed her pen, which I never returned. And Gus, well, Gus introduced me to Caravaggio.

My patient and this man had met while she was naked under a borrowed bathrobe, and from her account, the two of them had sat talking together with unusual intimacy for over three hours. That some sexual alchemy, however unrealised, had been constellated seemed likely. She admitted that she returned to her own flat in a mood of tense excitement and spent the rest of the day searching the shops for a frock worthy to meet Thomas in again.

'Did you find one?'

'Yes. It was much too expensive.'

'What was it like?' Living with Olivia had developed in me some sort of eye.

'It went to the Oxfam shop long ago.'

It took over three weeks, during which her hot water was finally fixed by the recalcitrant landlord, before she plucked up courage to approach Bainbridge, whose key she had annoyingly – for it would have provided an excuse to make contact – returned, and for whom she had already waited many evenings on the stairs for possible news of his friend. But when she rang his doorbell there was no answer.

Days later, when, after digging into her dwindling courage, she tried his door again, it was answered by an unfamiliar man with the news that the restless sculptor had departed to Australia for six months (she remembered having seen, on the hall table, post addressed to him with a Sydney postmark). Evidently their acquaintance had left too little impression on her neighbour for him to think of informing her of his sudden decision to leave.

This smaller dereliction amplified the glaringly larger one, the continued non-reappearance of Thomas, on whose word she had tremulously but hopefully relied. The shock of her incorrect estimate of her value to him must have sharpened the larger shock of disappointment.

Gus believes that somewhere we all know everything, and that what is generally called intuition is merely a stronger than usual capacity to disinter information and bring it to light. But, like the delicate artefacts recovered from long-sealed tombs, these buried truths are liable to crumble and perish under the harsh beam of scrutiny. It takes a strong immunity from doubt to sustain any belief, and it would have taken a steadier sense of self-worth than my patient's to trust to the truth of an impression born out of one lightning reckoning of her inexperienced heart.

She slid, slowly at first, for Thomas's seeming interest in her had burned into her consciousness, then, as days became weeks, more rapidly into the crippling assumption that the parting promise of soon-to-be-renewed contact was no more than a polite tactic for getting away; and that the intense pleasure she had taken to be mutual had been merely the reflection of her own naïve desire.

As she sat by a silent phone, for more bleak evenings than she cared to recall – her contacts were few and her friends sparse – she castigated herself for her presumption, for her ignorant susceptibility, for her ludicrous vanity in daring to hope that this man, of all men, could want her, of all the ridiculous cast-away souls in all the ridiculous world.

But the chastising self-remonstrations, the lessons she rehearsed to herself sternly at night – when she slept fitfully – or in the day – when her attention over her library duties wildly wandered – proved pointless, and she was to learn why the commonly advised remedy of 'pulling oneself together' is one which is recommended only by those who have been spared the doomed attempts to apply it.

The fact is, the only lasting safety from sorrow would lie in some kind of drastic surgery of the human faculty of affection. My patient's heart having been so swiftly and suddenly suborned, her affections were thoroughly compromised. She was taking the first hard steps in learning that the way of things as you go on is not the way when you try to go back, and there exist invisible turnstiles which, having let us pass easily through them, yield to none of our most strenuous efforts at return.

4

She made two last brave attempts at not losing touch with Thomas. One was to write to Cecil Bainbridge. She gathered, from his tenant, that his mail was being redirected to an English address and she wrote saying how sorry she was not to have had a chance to see him before his departure and boldly asking after his 'friend' whom she had met while enjoying the 'kind loan of the bathroom.' She waited some further weeks, in various states of agitation, for a reply that never arrived. Bainbridge was either too indifferent or too preoccupied.

The other, less practical but bolder in scope, was to enrol as a student at the North London Polytechnic.

Thomas had mentioned, in the context of her living nearby, that he had once delivered a lecture there for the art history course. 'I thought he might do another one day,' she told me.

The stay at the poly was brief. The impulse which led her to take the course was founded in something too liable to express itself in a perpetual anxious monitoring of any passing male figure who remotely resembled Thomas to leave much energy available for disciplined study, to which she was anyway unused. And the vigilant watching spawned a further anxiety: her sense of what Thomas looked like had become insecure. All she could have sworn to was a pair of spectacles on a beaky nose, and those capable hands; hands which had never touched her but were associated in her mind with a deftly turned and supremely delicious omelette eaten at Bainbridge's red Formica table.

It was then that she met Neil.

I imagine I gave an involuntary sigh, because here, at last, was an answer to the question that had hung in my mind over that egregious husband. After so devastating a disappointment it would make sense to turn to a Neil.

To her astonishment, Neil, after their first night together, continued his attentions. He invited her to a long-running musical and then to a film about racing cars. In bed he was passably attentive, though it was clear to me, if not from anything said directly, that there was in her no answering spark. She did let slip that one anxiety she had was that she might accidentally call Neil by Thomas's name. That there had been no actual lovemaking with Thomas was, I understood, immaterial. The most passionate sexual encounters originate in the mind.

From this I concluded that she had little expectation of being found physically attractive, and as I knew from Olivia's example, the assumption of sexual attractiveness is half the battle. My patient was no film starlet, as my mother might have said, but there was a delicacy about her of a kind that stirs the heart more than the cruder sexual responses. I doubted from what I had gleaned that Neil was a man to value this. To him, I guessed, she would have been no more than a reasonably personable girl willing to go to bed with him.

After a mere few weeks, she gave notice to her landlord and, with a determination to distance herself from a scene of what she saw as the grossest humiliation, moved from Camden to be with Neil. By now, thoroughly sick at heart, she longed to be free of the ritual of vainly searching the post for news. She left no forwarding address, since she wanted to ensure that the rapacious landlord would not pursue her; she had informed all the necessary billing authorities, and her few acquaintances had been told of the move.

The association drifted into an unspoken engagement. In those days, it was unusual for young men and women to cohabit, and in moving in with Neil she had acted with a disregard for social form. Which didn't, I pointed out, prevent her following convention in marrying him.

She flushed hard at this and her expression took on the faint mulishness that I was beginning, affectionately, to recognise.

'He wanted me to,' she briefly explained.

It was explanation enough. After the disappointment over Thomas, for someone with so little sense of her own worth to be wanted at all would have been an irresistible balm. And Neil, she began to insist again, was not a bad man.

'He was solid, he was responsible, he was fair-minded, he was –'

'He sounds dull,' I interposed. I felt we'd had enough of this. 'It's not wrong, you know, to find someone dull.'

'He was dull,' she gratefully accepted, taking another bite at a sandwich. I had long since surrendered any claim on the pile.

'You know,' I said, sensing I had made ground, 'we'll do better if you don't feel you have to make the best of all this. Things become clearer if not made the best of. It'll be simpler in the end.'

'It was awful.'

'Yes,' I agreed, 'it must have been.' It's naïve to pretend that life for many people isn't pretty wretched much of the time.

'Awful.'

'What was it that was so awful?'

'He got on my nerves,' she attempted. The mismatch of their sensibilities had already conveyed itself. Like the grate of a rough cloth on sensitive fingers, Neil would have set up in her a perpetual sense of being on edge. 'Poor Neil. He couldn't help it.'

She was right about 'poor Neil.' We never make anyone happy who does not make us happy. And yet this elementary emotional equation is rarely recognised. The reasons for choice of partner are obscure and what passes for love is generally a decidedly mixed bag: lust, anxiety, lack of self-worth, sadism, masochism, cowardice, fear, recklessness, self-glory, simple brutality, the need to control, the urge to be looked after; most dangerous of all, the desire to save. There are other, happier, ingredients: kindness, compassion, honour, friendship, sympathy, the wish to help, the attendant wish to be good, though these finer impulses can often wreak more havoc than the more blackguardly ones. Seldom, very seldom, do two people unite through sheer reciprocal joy in the other's being.

'So you married him?' I persisted, conscious that this would needle.

'We were married, yes.'

'With bridesmaids and orange blossom and so on?' I continued uncharitably.

'With bridesmaids.' She made it sound like confirmation of a diagnosis of cancer. 'They were Neil's sister's daughters and they wore lilac dresses and had lilac in their hair.'

'Real lilac?' My curiosity was genuine.

'Artificial. Neil's mother chose their clothes.'

'And your own wedding dress . . .?'

She made a face. 'White satin.'

I let it go, though it struck me that her face, with its worn marble planes, might suit white satin.

She added that her mother had enjoyed the occasion since it presented the chance for a new outfit and that her father had startled her by crying when he gave her away.

Although she had spoken pretty freely, without prompting, at this point one of our old silences arose. I found myself dwelling on the previous evening, and the sense of loneliness I'd been conscious of with Olivia out again.

My patient's account of her marriage was engendering some parallel assessment of my own. I couldn't envisage a life without Olivia and yet what did I really know about her after all these years? Our initial meeting had set up that pattern of entanglement and disentanglement which had left us both little wiser about the other's private needs or desires. Olivia knew the details of my past but had no feeling, or none I was aware of, for its persistent implications. I could hardly have avoided telling her about Jonny – but the telling amounted to no more than the bare bones of the situation; any idea that this was a loss which had left me lame would have filled her with scorn, or maybe alarm. And yet I knew, in a sense, she was my attempted solution to Jonny. She'd filled a gap, or hadn't so much filled as distracted me from it, diverted me with a version of desire which had kept me from the pull of that other black hole. I wasn't in love with her, I doubted that I had ever been in love with her, though no doubt I had told myself that that was what it was at the time, and there were times now when I wasn't sure that I even liked her. But, though I was ashamed of this, I needed her and the need held me.

And what about Olivia? What was her 'need' of me? I was aware so often of letting her down. The understanding I brought so readily to my work failed me in my private life, and failure tends to bring indifference or, at best, a defensive incuriosity in its train. Was I to her what the uninspiring Neil Cruikshank had been to his wife? A disappointment? An object of guilt? A substitute for some dark horse whose existence I was ignorant of?

'My mother-in-law was called Primrose,' Elizabeth Cruikshank tossed abruptly into the silence, tersely adding, 'She called me "Liz."'

On the map of human choice, there are highways and by-ways, crossroads and narrow tracks, and cul-de-sacs. And along these routes are to be found abodes of graciousness, citadels and hovels, palaces and boltholes. And there are the houses of shame into which we creep because we feel we are worth no better. In time, my patient and her husband moved to Gerrards Cross, to a bungalow built in the grounds of Neil's family home.

The house, built in the fifties, with the profits of the family's civil engineering business, was red-brick and militarily regular in its proportions, which were reflected in the layout of the garden. The rooms were correspondingly large, decorated in a range of colours that were the inspiration of a local interior designer whose friendship with Primrose Cruikshank expressed itself in the choice of the pale yellow which she took as the house's aesthetic 'theme.' The suites of furniture were matching, as were those in the bathrooms, and the Cruikshanks were in the vanguard of fashion in importing bidets and Swedish showers.

The grounds were extensive enough to support the planning and construction of the dwelling to which, shortly after their wedding, the young Cruikshanks were imported.

Primrose Cruikshank was active in the large garden, the local church, and bridge parties, and had a crisp perm, which resembled the coat of her Pekinese dog.

'She was called Connie. It became my job to walk her. The dog, not the mother-in-law.'

'"Connie," as in Lady Chatterley?'

'Yes. I got into trouble with Primrose for suggesting that.' She delivered one of her rusty laughs.

'She didn't like you?'

'She loathed me. And she knew what I would loathe. It was "Liz" at first sight. I wasn't what she had in mind for Neil at all.'

This raised my estimation of Neil until she added, 'Neil made me feel I was the one in the wrong.'

'So he wasn't loyal?'

'He wasn't *dis*loyal. But he was never really on my side, you know?'

'I think so,' I fudged.

'He tried to be fair.'

'Oh dear. Fairness isn't good enough, is it?'

'I didn't know that then. I just felt on my own.'

Poor young woman. Her flight from her dangerously kindled passion had led her to this isolated pass. 'Were there no allies?'

'I got on all right with Duncan, my father-in-law, but he was away at his office most of the time and it was Primrose who wore the trousers. Neil was their only boy and she doted on him. To be fair –' She smiled. 'To be fair,' she repeated, to establish she recognised the irony of this, 'she guessed I didn't love her son.'

'Was he loveable?'

'Isn't everyone somewhere? I thought that was what we were supposed to think.'

'Let's not bother with "supposed."'

'You're supposed to love your patients, though, aren't you?'

'That's a kind of "Have you stopped beating your wife?" question.'

She considered this and then floored me by coming out with a more direct one. 'Why do you do this? Is it love or damage?'

'Possibly both,' I said shortly, though, with the exception of Gus, my colleagues would say that in admitting this I had already said too much.

It was a question I had never put so directly to myself, though, naturally, it was an implied question of my own analysis. But the things you believe you see objectively are not necessarily the things you subjectively comprehend. I was aware that I found relief in deciphering others' pain, but there was a sense in which I had chosen to remain in the dark over the mainspring of that impulse, and the bluntness of her question set off a subtle shudder which was reverberating through me as I followed the drift of her story.

The meddlesome Primrose pursued the policy of oppression which my patient accepted as her due. She took a position at the local library until the birth of their first child, Max, kept up some part-time library sessions until the arrival of Amanda, and then gradually succumbed to the round of coffee mornings, church bazaars, and garden parties which formed the accepted pattern of middle-class married life in the Gerrards Cross community.

It sounded to be a dispiriting but not unusual scene, variants on such routine social displacements being the common theme of much of so-called civilised life. It might have formed reason enough for an independent spirit to wish to make some radical move, which might even have been expressed in the most radical of all moves: the departure from not merely an aspect of life but from life itself. But, on the whole, dullness baffles enterprise and it generally takes a stiffer jolt than the threat of another church bazaar to break out of the status quo.

'And Max and Amanda?' I enquired. I hoped her children, at least, might have brought her some joy.

'I wasn't allowed to bring them up as I wanted. I loved them, of course I did. But not in the way I longed to. Primrose thought I was over-indulgent and Neil always backed her up. The children were packed off to boarding school as soon as it was feasible.'

'That must have been difficult for you.'

The little dismissive shrug hurt me, from which I deduced it hid pain.

'They're fine. Max has just started as a chemical engineer and Amanda's training to be a dentist.'

'Do they know you're here?'

'Yes.'

'And they visit you?' Maguire's report suggested they hadn't.

'I prefer they don't.'

'But they would miss you, had you gone for good?'

I half expected her to deny this, but instead she said, 'It's hard to be with people who don't like you.'

'You feel your children don't like you?'

'They don't *dis*like me,' she corrected. 'It's just that they don't "like" me. It's not their fault. They don't know who I am.'

'Well, it's a wise child that knows its own parent,' I agreed, and maybe because I felt I had been a little pompous, or maybe because of the reference to children, which Olivia and I had never had, and noticing that time was getting on, I excused myself in order to ring home.

I wasn't surprised to get no answer and I left a message to say that I'd be back late. I was careful how I phrased the words, conscious they were being overheard, which didn't prevent my patient asking when I returned to my chair, 'Shouldn't you be going? Haven't you things to do?'

The very words she told me she had used to the absconding Thomas.

'No,' I said, 'I shouldn't be going anywhere.' As I spoke I heard a new note of resolution in my voice. 'And I've nothing I'd rather do than listen to you right now. That is, if you don't mind?'

5

In the autumn after the young Cruikshanks were packed off to boarding schools, which, from my patient's description, sounded to be of depressing mediocrity, an Italian cousin of her father's died.

'How did your parents react to your marriage, by the way?'

'They were thrilled, particularly my mother. She thought I'd done very well for myself with Gerrards Cross.'

It's alarming how often children marry to fulfil the parents' fantasies for themselves.

A legal complication, relating to Italian inheritance tax, made it expedient for one of the family to go to Rome. My patient, who had never before taken advantage of her Italian blood – any impulse having been crushed by an unhappy holiday in Rimini curtailed, at the mother's insistence, after three days – volunteered to go in place of her father, whose health was beginning to trouble him and who was gratifyingly thankful for her offer.

'That was brave of you.'

It was then, I think, that she must have mentioned her birthday and her sense of somehow starting a new term. 'I felt the children had finally gone. I needed, I don't know, something – I'd been such an ineffectual mother.'

'It's hard to be effectual on your own.'

Being unused to travel, and with a sense of nervous anticipation, she arrived early at Heathrow and, having checked in and acquired her seat, was hesitating over whether to go through to the departure lounge or to fritter time in the airport shops.

It was the hands she saw first. The owner of the hands was crouched, with his back to her, at the end of the check-in line, adjusting the strap round his suitcase. By the time he stood up and turned round, her knocking heart had recognised him.

'Good Lord,' Thomas said, pushing his glasses up his nose in a gesture which she realised had never left her mind. 'What are you doing here?'

'I'm on my way to Rome.'

It was fifteen years, eight months, and three days since she had last seen him.

'Good God, so am I. What flight?'

It was the same flight.

'Stay where you are,' Thomas said. 'No, don't stay where you are. Come over here while I check in. Don't dare to disappear!'

At the counter, he magisterially changed her seat so they could sit together. 'I was scared sick,' she told me, 'that my longing to sit with him was so transparent it would frighten him away.'

Dazed, trying not to count her luck, praying that Neil or Primrose would not suddenly materialise, like malign figures in a fairy tale, and whisk her back to Gerrards Cross, she moved through to the departure lounge, where he steered her towards a café and ordered double rations of toast and coffee.

'I have to drink lashings of coffee,' Thomas explained, 'or I shall fall asleep for a hundred years and a thorn hedge will grow round me and then only a kiss from a beautiful woman will wake me. I've been up all night looking for my passport. It's always in my travel bag and then suddenly it wasn't. Lucky I checked before I left. Does that happen to you? Do you like coffee? I forget. Have some more.'

'I don't think you could have known whether I like coffee or not. I've never lost my passport, but I don't travel much.'

'I always thought of you as a sensible girl,' Thomas said. It wasn't clear if he was referring to the travel, the coffee, or the passport. 'Didn't we drink coffee at Bainbridge's that day?'

'I remember you made me an omelette.'

Her heart, which had always rested quietly under her breastbone, was burning through her chest.

'I was going to make you a cheese soufflé the next time.'

'I'd have liked that.'

'I would have liked it too,' Thomas said. 'I'd better pay the bill. Look, it says on the screen we're boarding. They're bound to be lying, but people bag all the overhead locker room if you don't get in first.'

On the plane, he organised her luggage – 'Specs? Oh, that's too unfair, don't tell me you don't need them yet. Why are you going to Rome, as if you need a reason?'

She explained about the mission for her father.

'Of course, you're half Italian, aren't you? I've forgotten your name.'

She began to say 'Eliz –' but he interrupted.

'Don't be absurd, naturally I know you're "Elizabeth." The other one.'

'It was Bonelli, but it's Cruikshank now.'

'So there's a Mr Cruikshank? Who is he?'

'Someone I met soon after we met.'

'Tell me all about him.' She'd forgotten his trick of putting his head on one side. 'Do you know, the Indians believed that the eyes of twin souls are an identical width apart?' He had taken his glasses off and was looking at her with his bright brown eyes.

'The American Indians?' was all she could manage.

'The Eastern ones. It was a Vedic belief. The eyes are the entrance to the soul so only kindred spirits can gain access.'

They spent the flight absorbed in the kind of conversation she had not dared to risk rehearsing since the brief but splendid afternoon they had spent, her in her neighbour's dressing gown. It was as if a river which had gone underground had as abruptly reissued with a silent roar. The flow was rolling on, apparently uninterrupted, from their first encounter, though neither broached the subject of the unexplained loss of contact. As they ate their airline meal – 'Isn't it like hospital food? We need more wine!' – the mystery must have hovered between them, enlivening, with its possibilities, the predictable lunch and the unspectacular wine.

When, early in the afternoon, they arrived at Rome and there was some hitch with the baggage, she stood among the impatient bodies of the other passengers – worrying volubly over their bags – praying that hers, and his, had been stolen, or left behind at Heathrow, or gone to Helsinki or, better still, to Hell, anything to postpone the closing-off of this unlooked-for loophole in time. But his shabby case, with the buckled strap, arrived on the conveyor belt, which rolled relentlessly past them like a parody of time, and soon after her own, less venerable, and altogether ordinary, travel bag arrived, and he carried both to the station, as all the luggage trolleys had been commandeered.

They took the train to Trastevere and then there was the matter of the taxi.

'We'll go to your hotel first and then I'll know where to find you,' Thomas said. 'What time shall I come?'

'When?'

'When? Tonight. Or this afternoon. I have to see someone immediately but, no, look, take a taxi, would you, and come to mine? Come as soon as you can after five and we'll be in time to walk on the Palatine and catch the view.' He wrote the name and number of his hotel on the label of her suitcase.

Having bathed and, in high agitation, changed her clothes several times – nothing that she'd brought to wear being anywhere up to the mark – she took a taxi to his hotel, where she stood outside to recover herself before walking into the lobby, where it took a further five minutes of forcing her courage to ask the receptionist to ring to say she was there.

When Thomas came towards her across the marble floor, it was as if a lift were crashing down inside her, leaving her lips so stiff and bloodless that it was hard to mouth the polite formula she eventually found to greet him with.

'This is nicer than my hotel.'

'Change then and come here.'

It was a close evening, and they walked past the hideous Victor Emmanuel monument and climbed Michelangelo's noble steps to the Capitoline Hill, where the copy of the statue of the stoic Emperor Marcus Aurelius sat, in fine bronze sandals, astride his fine bronze horse. And then Thomas steered her round by the Tarpeian rock, and down the stony Via della Consolazione, named to console those whose fate was to be thrown from the eponymous rock.

'I hope they died quickly,' she said. 'It looks a little tame to be sure of an instant death.'

At the top of the Palatine Hill they surveyed the ancient Forum: the austere, ruined arches of the mighty basilica of Constantine and Maximilius, before which St Paul might have preached; the semicircular remnants of the Temple of the Vestal Virgins, Rome's most nubile debutantes; the elaborately decorated arches, of Septimius Severus at one entrance to the site and, at the other, of Titus, on which, he told her, the sack of the Temple in Jerusalem is celebrated in the triumphal sporting of the Jewish menorah.

Beyond all this, he pointed out a dazzling vista of light and shadow, tall *campaniles*, greening cupolas, imperious *palazzi*, dominated by St Peter's supremely self-confident dome. 'How do you feel?'

'Lucky to be here.'

'Lucky me to be the one to show it to you first.'

Descending through terraces of oleander and pale blue plumbago, and old stone basins gently overflowing water, he led her back out of the Forum and through little squares and cobbled streets and arches till they landed up in the Campo de' Fiori, where the only flowers now to be found are on the stalls of the daily market held there.

A gang of cleaners were engaged in dispatching petals, leaves, rotting figs, wasp-infested grapes, crushed walnut shells, sweet papers and sluicing the square of its patina of fish scales, but there was still a solitary flower seller, whose stall was pitched at the feet of the statue of the luckless Bruno, put to death by the Inquisition, Thomas explained, hustled, his tongue in a gag, under cover of darkness, and burned on the site of his statue at a hastily erected stake, for refusing to deny his refutation of Catholic dogma.

From the lone flower seller they bought yellow roses and laid them at the base of the dark-cowled effigy, in memory of the burned man; and close by was a congenial-looking *osteria*, where they ate lamb cooked with artichokes, and strawberries steeped in white wine.

Walking back, the sky turned indigo and crackled and then growled. 'Jove's throwing things,' Thomas said. 'I expect he's committed a marital indiscretion and Juno's in a rage.'

The rain came, first in outsize drops, then, suddenly, drenchingly, and they ran along shining, perilous cobbles to his hotel, where in the vestibule he touched her shoulder and said, with equal lightness, 'You'll stay, won't you? It's better.'

In the stuffy hotel bathroom she ran water into the wash-basin, dipped her hands and splashed her face, took off all her clothes, very fast, dropping them on to the floor, to get it over with, and when she walked into the bedroom Thomas had taken his off too, and they stood looking at each other, saying nothing, with her now so faint that she was afraid to move.

But he must have moved, for suddenly the space between them had vanished and he said, 'Look, our bodies fit. I knew they did.'

Afterwards, fused from a frantic, fervent, mutual exchange, which seemed to reach right down and through to the level of the molecular, wet, from sweat and rain, and wrung out and beached up, at last, on the hard foreign mattress in grateful, glad exhaustion, they made the promises of children, playing, as if they will play for ever, in some sequestered garden, where the shadows are lengthening and elsewhere, in a parallel universe, the adult world is preparing to summon them back inside.

'Don't let me go again.'

'I'm never going to let you go.'

'I don't ever want you to let me go.'

'That's settled, then.'

Piteous words, as I heard them in my wintry Brighton consulting room, her face, the three or so feet away from mine, as pale and as distant as the moon. Their vows, repeated now, in her flat tone, conveyed, as plainly as if she had spelled it out in poker-work, the stark fact that nothing is ever settled between two human souls, for nothing is or can be settled until we are finally done and gone.

But lovers are children; and I suppose that when you feel you have made true love, you believe you've found a back door into eternity and cannot afford the notion that it may not be open to you on your return.

6

It wasn't until the following morning that she risked raising any query over his unexplained disappearance, for even after a night of further feverishly joyous engagement she told me she was reluctant to open her eyes lest, for a second time, she find herself abandoned.

But then a foot found hers and in her ear she heard a reassuring snore.

'You didn't mind the snoring?' Olivia always poked me in the back when I'd drunk too much and snored as a consequence.

'I found it comforting. Like sleeping with a long-backed pig.'

'And was his explanation equally reassuring?'

'It was upsetting. But it clarified everything.'

On the evening he had left her, he explained as they sat in bed – knees propped congenially together, drinking coffee and eating croissants – he was due to meet a colleague, a Milanese art historian, whose visits to London were few, which was why, he took pains to say, he had not forgone the meeting for the greater pleasure of her continued company. He met the colleague and they discussed their shared area of research, but towards the evening he began to feel seedy, as if, he said, he was on the point of coming down with a nasty flu. He made his apologies to his colleague, cancelled their dinner, caught an early train back to

Oxford, walked home from the station, and retired to bed feeling pretty rough.

The following morning he said he felt so ropy he stayed in bed. His last distinct memory was feeling diabolically shaky in the bathroom, finding himself unequal to his usual shower, and wondering if he could manage to pee without keeling over.

The next thing he was conscious of was a pain in his arm as a nurse in the hospital was changing the drip.

'Septicaemia?' I hazarded.

'Nearly fatal. He was found, thank God, by a friend who was dropping off a book.'

'So he must have been out of action for a while?' Septicaemia's a bummer. More young men died of it in the First World War than were ever done in by enemy fire.

'Weeks in hospital. And after that he was as weak as a kitten and not up to much. And when he was feeling a bit more like himself and rang me . . .'

'The bird had flown?'

'We worked out he must have rung about ten days after I finally left.'

'And you left no number?'

'Who was going to ring me? I couldn't live with the anxiety of not hearing from him a second longer,' she bleakly declared.

'What fucking awful luck!' I allowed myself. On the whole, I refrained from swearing, and never with patients.

'Awful,' she echoed bleakly. 'And you see, all the time Thomas was mortally ill, instead of being with him, and being there to look after him, I was with Neil . . .'

I did see. It was an outrageous snub of fate.

'And Thomas, what did he make of this?'

'He thought what I'd thought, that I couldn't have been so interested in him after all,' she almost wailed.

'But he tried, at least? He tried to find you?' I hoped almost savagely that he had.

'He did, he was much more determined than I was. But as I told you, I had closed down that part of my life completely. He even rang Bainbridge in Australia, but of course Bainbridge didn't know where I was either, and in the end he gave up. We'd only met that once.'

'But you'd made an impression.' Since she'd embarked on her story, she was informed by quite a different spirit. I could feel for myself how their encounter might have stayed in Thomas's mind.

'Apparently.'

'So what had happened to Thomas all this while?'

'He'd married too. In fact, he married one of the doctors from the John Radcliffe, whom he met while he was ill. But he wanted children and his wife didn't. I gathered she was very dedicated to her career. He said in the end it seemed pointless being together, and they parted, though they remained friends.'

'So he was free when you met again?'

'He was free,' she agreed.

'And you found you got on as well out of bed as in?'

'Oh, it wasn't just sex!' She dismissed the suggestion with scorn. 'If he'd been paralysed I would have minded, of course, for his sake, but nothing essential would have been lost. I loved his body – but that wasn't the point. It was as if we knew each other from way back, always, I mean really knew, not just the surface pleasantries, the deep down things that no one could know because you don't know them yourself, until you meet someone who knows them for you. It was the effortless knowing and being known that was so extraordinarily –' She halted, searching.

'Comforting? Like the pig?'

'Comforting, yes, but also –' She looked around as if my room might hold the clue for the word she wanted.

'What is that egg? I mean, what bird?'

'I was told it was a thrush's. *And thrush / Through the echoing timber does so rinse and wring / The ear, it strikes like lightnings to hear him sing.*'

'Who is that?'

'Hopkins.'

'I like the lightnings.'

'Yes. Poor Hopkins.'

'Why "poor"?'

'He thought sex was wrong, or his own sort was.'

'Poor Hopkins,' she agreed.

When I left Bar, I was too cowardly to tell her what I was doing, so I did what cowards do, I wrote her a letter, the recollection of which makes me go red with shame. In it I suggested – so original was my insight! – that I was doing her a favour, and that she would be better off without me. It's a bad thing to do, that: deny the truth of someone's feelings because we find them inconvenient.

Bar sent me the egg – which we'd found in an abandoned nest in the pear tree in her garden, the weekend when I half proposed to her, and she, half jokingly, as I excused it to myself later, accepted. She sent the egg in a box, and within the swathe of protective tissue and cotton wool there was a note: *Don't teach your granny to suck these!*

'The thing was' – she was gently rocking the egg in her hand – 'it all seemed so uncomplicated.'

'Human associations generally tend to be complicated.'

'With us it wasn't. It was simple. That's what I found so hard to believe. It was the straightforwardness which was the mystery. I don't mean it was dull.'

She laughed, and again I saw the dancing moon. 'We were passionate, passionate, intensely so in Rome, but what I took from it was this sense of being utterly and unquestionably known. And utterly and unquestioningly liked for it.'

'To be both thoroughly known and thoroughly liked for it would be a tremendous allure.' I was conscious of a touch of envy.

'Have a bath,' Thomas said, when they had finished breakfast and he had concluded his explanation, 'and I'll bring you another cup of coffee and talk to you, and then we'll go and visit the most perfect secular building in the world.'

On the way, they passed Bernini's little elephant valiantly balancing an ancient Egyptian obelisk on its back.

'Why does it have acorns on its cope?' she asked.

'You know, I don't know,' Thomas said. 'Maybe because oaks are as strong as elephants.'

He led her round to the back of the Pantheon and pointed out the remnants of the marble facing and the dolphins and the scallop shells in the few extant fragments of the frieze.

There was a single remaining column. Peering up, she spotted something on a small roundel just above the capital. 'Is that a snake?'

'Clever person. Most people don't spot it.'

They walked back past the elephant and round to the entrance where a man in a dirty blue frock coat and a powdered periwig tried, unsuccessfully, to sell them tickets for a performance of *The Barber of Seville*. 'Did you know, Rossini used to compose in bed by an open window so he could lie down and look at the sky while he transcribed the music in his mind? He was so lazy that when some sheets of a score blew away, rather than trouble to get out of bed to retrieve them, he wrote a whole new section.'

Preoccupied, she wasn't really attending. 'Do you think it's an omen?'

'The snake?' He always seemed to know what she meant.

'Yes.'

'A snake in our paradise?' Better still, he never pretended not to know.

'Yes.'

'I had a snake once. A grass snake called Doris. I found her at my grandmother's, where I used to be sent in the holidays, and I kept her one summer in a tank in my room there – nobody noticed: no one ever noticed what I did, which had advantages – till I saw for myself it was cruel and freed her. I met her quite often afterwards, by the greenhouse. For the Greeks and the Romans, snakes were symbols of healing. It depends how you want to read it, Elizabeth Cruiksnake.'

('And was the Pantheon the most perfect building, did you think?' I asked.

'It might have been the floor of Heaven that morning with the discs and squares of different coloured marble shining in the rain.')

'Look,' Thomas had said, gesturing upwards.

There were few others there, as with the threat of further heavy rain the majority of sightseers were cautiously waiting to judge the likely course of the weather before venturing outside. Her eye followed the arc of his hand to the singular hole in the great domed ceiling through which the sun was posting a tremulous pole of pale light on to the yellow marble below.

'What is it?'

'The oculus. It's what gives the effect of diffused radiance.'

'And lets the rain in?'

'That's its peculiar beauty. I was here once when it was snowing.' He fluttered his fingers and she could see the slow, dizzy descent of flakes. 'The ceiling isn't as the Romans would have seen it. It was gilded, but the Vatican nicked all the gold.'

'I like it better bare.'

'I certainly like you better that way.' He squeezed her shoulder. 'Are you cold?'

'No. Just a goose walking over my grave. It's . . . I can't find the word.'

'It's the harmony. The proportions are impeccable: it can house a perfect sphere.'

She gazed up at the coffered ceiling, denuded of gold, enjoying the spareness. The Vatican was welcome to its plunder. 'It's tranquil,' she said at last, feeling the luminance seep into her bones, as if, after all, all would be well.

'Because it hasn't a wrong note. It's the geometry of grace.'

In my mind's eye, I pictured the pair of them, fugitives from the cynical world, rejoicing in the unlooked-for security of their freshly discovered alliance as they wandered together, in comfortable companionship, through ruins and old churches, palaces and secluded gardens, within the ancient lineaments of the hilled city that has looked on centuries of lovers, their passion, pain, and ardour, and seen all vanish before its consummate indifference.

'It was the most remarkable seven days of my life. I wrapped up my father's business as soon as I could – with Thomas's help it wasn't too taxing – and then we did everything together. There was nothing we didn't enjoy.'

'You were fortunate,' I suggested. 'Rome is a numinous city but it has its sinister side.'

'Yes. Thomas said you feel the presence of the ranks of the dead more than in any other city in the world.'

'That's where Keats gave up the ghost,' Thomas said, pointing to an upper room. They were walking up the Spanish Steps to collect some of her things. It was raining again and they had had to buy flimsy umbrellas and bash their way through the stouter-umbrella-bearing crowd. 'We'll go and pay our respects to his spirit and then we'll go to the cemetery to pay our respects to his mortal remains. You'll like it there: there's a pyramid.'

'A pyramid?'

'An insignificant Roman had it built as one of those self-aggrandising memorials. When Keats realised he was dying, he sent Severn to do a recce of the cemetery, and when he came back and told Keats there was a pyramid, he was as pleased as Punch.'

'Who was Severn?'

'A devoted friend. A hearth companion. He was with Keats till the bitter end.'

'What's a hearth companion?'

'Someone who sleeps beside you at the hearth and watches your back in a fight.'

There were almost as many cats as graves. Hand in hand, they walked the stone paths, through cypress and pine and bay and olive, and past two regal palms by Caius Cestius's impressive pyramid, searching for Keats's grave.

'The other thing he liked about being buried here,' Thomas said, when they had found the pine-cone-scattered grave – Keats side by side with the loyal Severn, like an old couple tucked up in a double bed – 'was the flowers. Violets were his favourites and Severn said that when he came back with the report of where his sick friend was bound, Keats was "joyed to learn that there were violets covering the graves" and said he almost seemed to feel them growing over him.'

Small piping birds, signalling that the rain had finally stopped, had begun to weave through the branches of the pines, and butterflies, like white pansies, were crookedly navigating the tilted gravestones.

'His name isn't even here,' she said, thinking of the Roman nonentity's pyramid and reading the epitaph: *Here lies One Whose Name was writ in Water.* 'It looks too ordinary for such a great poet.'

'Death is extremely ordinary. It happens to everyone, though people seem to forget this. It's why you and I mustn't waste time.'

'D'you think we will?'

'I don't know, Elizabeth.'

His eyes had the serious look she wasn't quite equal to, and to change the subject she said, 'Why was Keats in Rome?'

'Supposedly for his health, to escape the perilous British fog. But maybe he came to die. He was the sort who, unconsciously, would have known where to die. It's not a bad place to choose, Rome.'

'We should have brought violets.'

'We shall next time.'

'You've not said why Thomas was in Rome.'

'He was researching his subject, Caravaggio.' So that was the connection. Silently I blessed Gus. 'Thomas was possessed by Caravaggio. He talked to me about him all the time.'

It's a feature of love that it can invade any subject. I intimated as much, but she repudiated the implication.

'It was never boring, because Thomas so loved his work.'

'And love is never boring?'

She swept aside my feeble squib of sarcasm. 'Not if it's real, and Thomas was a true enthusiast. It was an extraordinary education. We must have visited every available Caravaggio in Rome that week.'

'A memorable courtship!'

I was conscious again of that sly undercurrent of envy beneath my slightly stuffy tone. I warmed to Thomas's passion, which, even second-hand, infused his most pedestrian observations with its ardent light. But it probed some vague and painful discomfort of my own.

I glanced at my patient in case the shade of something personal had registered and saw a gleam streak her face. For the first time in our acquaintance she was crying. An unspoken injunction had relaxed and it must have released us both, as for the first time too I addressed her by name.

'Would you like to stop, Elizabeth?'

'What's your other name, Dr McBride?'

'David. My family call me Davey.'

'I prefer David.'

'You can call me David if you like.'

'I don't want to stop, thanks, David. Unless you need to?'

'I don't need to, Elizabeth. I want you to go on.'

7

She returned to England determined to end the marriage but stopping, to stoke her resolve, at Thomas's west London home, which bore the unmistakable marks of its owner's character.

The house, with dark green paintwork, stood at the end of a mews overlooked by a tall church spire. Its plaster façade was partly obscured by tangled boles of wisteria and passion flower. The rooms were small but orderly, blessedly free of ornament – for which the fussily crowded Gerrards Cross rooms had produced a particular aversion – save for several arresting abstract paintings, some antique pots, a painted wooden saint, with what looked like a wall eye, and a strange fragment of what turned out to be the nose of a life-size seventeenth-century porphyry horse.

There were books, in double-depth bookshelves, piles of records, a chess table set with ivory and sandalwood chessmen, tattered Turkish rugs, worn leather armchairs, potted herbs, racks of wine, a collection of coffee pots with intriguing glazes, an easel with a large unfinished oil of a lime tree, and a pervading smell of coffee. The gilded old French bed of carved walnut was graciously accommodating and the mattress, after Rome, easy on hard-worked bones. It was, as she conveyed it to me, ten worlds away from Gerrards Cross.

'Do you have to go?' Thomas asked the next morning, watching her dress. 'We can send for your things, or buy you new. You look better without anyway.' In Rome he had thrown out – with cries of 'Hideous!' – most of her underwear.

Over breakfast he said, again, 'Don't go.'

They were in his pea-green dining room, eating toast and drinking coffee in wide white porcelain cups transported, in a brown paper parcel, from Rome. The shuttered windows opened to the cobbled mews and a white cat jumped from the garden fence on to the ledge outside. As she described the scene, drinking the bitter coffee from my machine, from an old CND mug I'd had as a student and Olivia had long ago relegated, I glanced to see if the evil orange tom had reappeared. But only the quince tree was palely visible through the dark. It struck me that the difference of scene resembled some hideous moral metaphor.

'I have to go,' she told him. 'I can't simply never go back.'

'Why? I mean, why not?'

'I owe Neil some sort of explanation.'

'Okay,' said Thomas. 'What's that going to look like? What is an "explanation" of love, please?'

'It's decency,' she protested.

'It isn't,' Thomas said. 'It's guilt. You imagine by talking to him you'll make it better. You won't. You'll make it worse. He won't understand. He can't understand. He doesn't love you. That sort don't. They don't know how to love.'

'But that isn't a reason for me to behave badly.'

'For God's sake,' said Thomas. 'Behaving "badly," as you put it. What's that? By Neil's lights you'll be behaving appallingly badly by leaving him for a complete stranger. Anyway, why not behave badly? What's wrong with bad behaviour? Bad behaviour, good behaviour, what's the difference? Do you think you know? Really know? And you do know, don't you, he'll feel better if you behave, as you put it, "badly"? You'll be doing him a kindness if he can say you've behaved like a trollop. Be a trollop. Abandon him. Abandon your principles. They aren't yours, anyway. They're made up. You should stop making yourself up.'

'I don't know what you mean,' she said. She wasn't quite prepared to cry.

'Look,' said Thomas, less fiercely, 'it's like this. You aren't the person you've made yourself out to yourself to be. You're another person, quite a different one, maybe not too nice at all, I don't know. I don't care. I don't love you because you're nice. What's nice, anyway? They can be "nice." Let them be. I'm not.'

'You are nice. And I can't believe you love me.'

'No,' said Thomas. 'You can't. Understandably. But I do, as it happens. It's no credit to you, actually. It's just a fit.'

'A fit?'

'Not as in mad. Or epileptic. As in match. As in hand in glove. No, not in glove. As in hand in hand.'

'It's still hard to believe.'

'I know that. It is hard. Good things are. Good things are much harder to believe than bad things. Much. Human beings are shockingly bad at believing good things. They prefer bad news. That's one of the secrets I know. It's why I don't want you going back to drink at the fountain of bad faith. The water is tainted. Foul. It'll give you a taste for the bad again. Pah!' He made a spitting gesture.

'They're not bad people, really.'

'They are not good people, Elizabeth. They are a lot of things but "good" isn't one of them. They are conventional and mean-spirited and fairly cruel. They have shut you in a dark room and you are starved of nourishment and deprived of light. It's very terrible for people like us to be without light.' His passionate face was as serious as a priest's.

'I don't know,' she said. 'I don't know, I don't know. I'm not used to this. I don't know what to do. I don't know how to manage it.'

'Listen,' said Thomas. 'There's no "used to." Nothing in life prepares us for what happens next. Nothing. Okay? It's not that you "get used to" things. That's a made-up nonsense. Things happen and you do what the occasion demands, if you can. If you have the courage. And the wit. And the will. That's all. Listen to me. If there had been a winged chariot I could have laid hands on that day we met at Bainbridge's, I would have said to you, "Excuse me, but now you have finished the omelette I have made for you – which, though cooked in Bainbridge's pathetically useless frying pan, wasn't at all bad – may I escort you to my chariot, which happens to be handily parked outside this rather crummy flat off the Camden Road, and take you away for all time?" And you would have come. Because then, at that moment, *at that precise moment*, you knew what was good for you. It's my fault. I should have gone out and found a chariot.'

'There aren't many winged chariots around in Camden.'

'Yes, well, I blame the Tories,' Thomas said. He picked up the cups and took them out into his yellow kitchen and began to rinse them noisily under the running tap.

Watching the white cat on the window ledge she said, 'I'm sorry. I don't mean to be feeble.'

An indecipherable sound issued from the kitchen.

'What?'

'YOU ARE NOT FEEBLE!' Thomas yelled suddenly. 'That's the trouble. You're FORMIDABLY STRONG!' He walked back into the dining room and picked up the coffee pot with the complicated green-and-brown glaze. For half a second it looked as if he was going to throw it at her. Then he put it back down on the table, extra carefully, and said, 'So, are you going back, then? You know, you're stronger than me.'

The cat had jumped down out of sight. She wondered if Thomas's shout had disturbed it. It hadn't really disturbed her.

At some level it pleased her, but still she said, 'I'm not. And I shan't be away long. I promise.'

'You are,' Thomas said. 'And you will, because you do things your way. That's another thing I know. You think I'm strong because I sound off and go on about things and am very direct and seem very full of myself – no, don't contradict me, I know what I am and how I seem! – but the truth is, I am much, much feebler than you. I just go on like this to keep my end up. You think what you're doing is right and that gives you strength. You see, I know I'm not right. I know there is no right. The only "right" I am is that I know what I like and what I want, and what I like and what I want is you, more than anyone else in all the world does, or could. But you won't believe that – the one thing I know and am right about you won't believe. And don't remind me later that I said so. I don't want to be reminded later that I'm right. There's no comfort in being right. I never understand why people imagine there is. And don't say I've just said I'm right about this when I've said I don't believe in right. I know I have. And don't make promises either. That's more making things up.'

Two days after her return to Gerrards Cross, while she was caught in a cross-bias of missing Thomas yet fearful at having to deliver her news, Primrose suffered a stroke.

'I can't come,' she explained to Thomas from a phone box. She had walked in the wet to find the necessary privacy. 'Not yet. It would be too unkind.'

'Yes,' said Thomas, 'but you know what? It's less unkind in the long run to be unkind right away. What's that noise? Cows?'

'Rain. It's raining. But it's not like the rain in Rome.'

'Of course it isn't. What are you wearing?'

'A raincoat.'

'And on your feet?'

'My feet?'

'Your lovely feet. They're like a saint's feet in a medieval painting. I want to know what horror you have bound your long white feet with in Gerrards Cross.'

'I'm wearing wellingtons.'

'I hate to think of those saint's feet in wellingtons. Are they green? The wellingtons, not the feet.'

'Yes, green. It's wet. What's wrong with wellingtons?'

'I knew they would be green. I can just imagine you, all respectable in your raincoat. I bet it's beige, isn't it? Don't answer. I know it is and I don't want to know. You could go barefoot. You could open the door of that phone booth – does it smell of urine? I suppose drunks don't piss in Gerrards Cross, do they? – and throw the wellingtons into the night and walk out barefoot, like the lady in "Raggle Taggle Gypsies."'

'Who are the Raggle Taggle Gypsies?'

'I'll sing it to you.'

Standing in the phone booth with the rain sluicing down round her, she heard his bass–baritone voice.

> *'She kickèd off her high-heeled shoes,*
> *All made of Spanish leather-O,*
> *And it's out in the street,*
> *In her bare, bare feet,*
> *To dance with the Raggle Taggle Gypsies-O.*

'Only in your case it's green wellingtons rather than shoes of Spanish leather-O. Kick 'em off and walk back to me. Go on, Elizabeth Cruikshank, be like the lady, dance in your bare feet to happiness, I dare you.'

'You're always wanting me to take things off.'

'You look better in nothing. They've terrible taste, in Gerrards Cross. You've caught it. Did you know that?'

'I'm sorry.'

'What for? Your taste will improve in two shakes of a lamb's tail when you come to live with me. It's okay, really. Just squashed. Speaking of which, I'd like you squashed under me right now. You squash well, d'you know that? Very well for someone so bony.'

'I can't walk out now and leave Neil to cope on his own. He's not up to it. My father-in-law's in a flap and Neil's devastated.'

'So what if he is devastated? Do him good. He could do with a bit of devastation. But he isn't really.'

'He keeps crying.'

'Oh,' said Thomas. 'Crying! I can cry, if you want. Crying's not hard. Anyway, he isn't really crying. He's faking. Like women faking orgasm. Disgusting!'

'Thomas, please . . .'

'What?'

'Don't.'

'Don't what? Cry? Okay, I shan't cry.'

'Don't be nasty.'

'Why not? I feel nasty. What's wrong with nasty? At least nasty isn't fake.'

'He needs me, Thomas.'

'"Need," hah! What is it? A sad contest. A sordid jostle for position. If it's a competition, then I need you too, if it comes to that. I'm unused to missing people and I'm not enjoying it.'

'It's not the same.'

'Why not?'

'He cares about her.'

'Ugh! "Cares"! What a word. He doesn't "care" about her. He's probably quite glad this has happened. Secretly, he probably wants her dead. That's okay. Mostly people only care about themselves. It's only love that makes you have a tittle or a jot of feeling for anyone else, and even that's pretty paltry. But it's a start. You've something real to go on, not a lot of milk junket and crocodile tears. Listen, Elizabeth. Don't be fooled by this stuff. It's bogus. Fake. I know about fake. It's my life's work. I know real and I'm real. I may be intemperate, difficult, maddening, and often foully unpleasant – as you are learning – but I'm real. And you're real too. Don't lose sight of that in your effort to be liked. It won't work, anyway. They'll never like you.'

'Thomas.'

'What?'

'I'm sorry. Really.'

'Elizabeth, I'm sorry too. Really.'

When she visited ten days later, using as an excuse the reappearance of an old friend from her library days in London, he took up the cudgels again. They had returned from the National Gallery, where he had taken her to see the Caravaggio *Supper* painting. He had a knack, she had noticed on the plane, of carrying on a conversation as if there had been no interruption.

'You don't even like your mother-in-law. "Primrose," what a misnomer! She should be called "Russian Vine."'

'What's that?'

'Surely you know what Russian Vine is? Gerrards Cross must be coming down with it.'

'Primrose never lets me touch the garden. I leave all that to her.'

'Russian Vine's the horticultural sin against the Holy Ghost. It's an evil creeper, which pretends to innocence but gets into everything, goes everywhere, takes everything over. It's rampant and predatory and vile and foully and criminally invasive. Like Hitler with Poland. Morally, we should shoot anyone who grows Russian Vine.'

'It's more that she doesn't like me.'

'How could she? She's a Russian Vine. Russian Vines don't know about liking, they only know about smothering. May I point out that I do like you? Immensely.'

'I like you immensely too,' she said, miserably. 'But I can't leave with her like this. Not yet.'

'Why not yet? Do you imagine there's going to be a better time? Believe me, there are no better times for doing difficult things than the very moment you perceive how difficult they are. That's another thing I know which I know you'll pay no attention to.'

'I'm sorry, I can't. I can't behave so badly.'

'Does not behaving "badly" mean reverting to Gerrards Cross knickers?'

'Thomas, I can't be seen putting on nice knickers to visit Janet.'

'These are not just not "nice," these are terrible knickers. They make you look like a gym mistress.'

'I'm afraid I just grabbed what was in the drawer.'

'Okay, I'll just have to take them off.'

A fortnight later, allegedly visiting the same friend for a trumped-up trip to the theatre, she tried to mollify. 'We're getting a live-in help. When I've got her properly organised I'll break it to Neil.'

'Nothing could ever be "properly organised" in Gerrards Cross. It's a contradiction in terms. Who is this library friend, anyway? What on earth is that you're wearing?'

'What?'

'The thing on your back?'

'You mean my coat? Don't you like it?'

'Elizabeth, it makes you look like a dead sheep.'

'Well, it's sheep skin.'

'For God's sake, take it off.'

'I was going to – what are you doing?'

'I'm throwing it away.'

'Why?'

'Into the dustbin with it. There.'

'Thomas, at least let me give it away to someone. That's very wasteful.'

'You can take it out tomorrow if you like. Tonight it stays there. I don't want it in my house. I suspect Neil bought it you for Christmas, or your birthday – don't tell me, I don't want to know. He only bought it for you because he hoped it would make you look unattractive. Unhappily for him, that's impossible. When is your birthday, incidentally? I think I should be told. I shall buy you something decent for that, but I'll buy it tomorrow to replace the dead sheep. Meantime, we aren't going anywhere where you'll need it, the bedroom's perfectly warm.'

Over supper of kedgeree he enquired again about the friend she was supposed to be staying with.

'Janet? I met her years ago in Camden. But I've given your number as hers, just in case they need to ring me. They won't, but just in case.'

'Darling person, do I adopt a permanent falsetto to answer the phone in case that bloody old bitch rings to check up on you? My other friends will be the tiniest bit surprised.'

'Thomas, please. It won't be long.'

'Elizabeth, please, it will be. Also, what kind of man believes that his wife, after all this time, has suddenly taken to visiting a friend he has never heard of? I would knock you down rather than stomach such garbage. He doesn't believe you. D'you know that? It's another nonsense. I should have locked you in and forbidden you to leave here when we came back from Rome. You don't know what's good for you. No, correction. You do know what's good for you and you don't like it. You don't like what's good for you, that's the trouble. You don't trust it. You won't come now.'

'I will. Of course I will.' She was crying. 'Thomas, don't be like that, I'm trying.'

'You are trying. Extremely trying. I've never met anyone so trying. And I'm not being "like" anything except myself. I see things you don't see. It was there from the beginning. You didn't wait for me. You went and married him. You didn't wait. I should have seen. I should have stopped you when we came back from Rome. I knew I should. I could have stopped you. I could have done. At least I've disposed of that terrible coat. Thank God the dustmen come first thing tomorrow. Good riddance! Ah no, too bad! I'm not letting you out of bed now.'

8

I have wondered sometimes if compassion isn't the most dangerous enemy of promise because it so readily wears the mask of virtue. *Com passion*: with passion. But it wasn't any aspect of passion, I concluded, hearing Elizabeth Cruikshank's story, which kept her from going to Thomas. It was something more insidious, which the golden blast of the stolen days in Rome had dislodged but failed finally to banish.

It reverberated in the dulled tone in which she reported the resumed monotony of life at Gerrards Cross, which had taken on for me, as well as her impatient lover, the desolating atmosphere of a polite suburb of Hell.

'Why did you really stay on in Gerrards Cross?' I asked.

'I don't know.'

'Didn't you believe Thomas?' I wasn't sure that I would have done.

'I did believe him. But . . .' She paused and stared again at her coffee, while I felt some discomfort again over the clumsy mug and the lack of a gracious Italian cup. 'I did believe him,' she repeated, 'but it was more . . . I can't explain.'

'Was it that you couldn't believe your luck?'

'Yes.' She sounded grateful. 'That was it. I couldn't believe my luck.'

I've thought more about luck since I had this conversation

with Elizabeth Cruikshank. Luck is the heart's genius, but it is sustained by belief. And the head, so often at odds with the heart, mistrusts belief and has secret, and often violent, purposes of its own. What I was hearing in my patient's account was something I recognised in myself: the faltering spirit that cunningly allies itself with decency.

'You imagined you weren't worth it?'

'I wasn't worth it.'

I let this pass. 'And how did Thomas take your disbelief?'

'I don't know. I knew he minded. Though, now you ask, I don't believe I believed either that he really minded. It's a hard thing to explain.'

'I think I understand. But he stayed?'

'Yes.' Her voice was a dry whisper. 'For a while.'

After initial vociferous protests, she said, Thomas lapsed into a semi-permanent ironic note over what he referred to as 'bearing the Gerrards Cross.' The postponement of the life they had conceived together in Rome continued. Primrose's long arm of control was merely extended from her wheelchair, and my patient developed the subterfuge necessary to visit the mews.

It's hard to be sure how far you can know another person when you perceive them only through the prism of another's perceptions. And yet, for all his differences from myself, I felt I had begun to understand Thomas. I liked him. I liked him, it occurs to me now, in much the same way that I had begun to like Caravaggio; that is, coming from an initial reserve.

Among the elements I admired in him was the guerrilla war he fought against Gerrards Cross. Round about this time, it seemed, Primrose seconded the Church as ally.

'Was she religious?' I didn't really need an answer to this.

'Not remotely! But she fancied the vicar.'

'Ah yes. Clergy tend to attract transferences the way psychiatrists and analysts do, but they aren't as a rule so prepared for them.'

'I shouldn't think he was, poor man.'

'What was it about him?'

'Oh, he was young and good-looking and sympathetic.'

'And naïve?'

'She used her condition to get him to come round and talk to her. She was a powerful presence in the church community. He couldn't very well say no.'

I have often thought there should be a book written on the need to say no. 'And what did she want with the vicar, your mother-in-law?'

'Thomas said she was enlisting him on the side of "right."'

'Right,' Thomas declared one evening, 'is a terribly wrong concept.'

They were eating supper in bed, cheese on toast with chutney. Thomas, I had been noticing, was a master of the bedroom snack.

'But there is such a thing as "right,"' she suggested.

'I don't know. Or rather, we don't know. I dare say there is, but I doubt that any human being would recognise it. Think of all the terrible things that people do in the name of "right." It's almost always bullying and invasive.'

'Where does the idea that right is right come from?'

'God knows. Or rather, God doesn't know, I shouldn't imagine. God, if there is one, would be most unlikely to be fussy about right or wrong.'

'Primrose thinks God is "right."'

'What would a Russian Vine know about God, please? An RV would just smother God with its own insidious presence. Smother Mother, ugh!'

'She's become very thick with the vicar.'

'Poor sod,' said Thomas. 'She'll be trying to enrol him in the Russian Vine Church of Moral Righteousness. I should lend him my secateurs.'

'He might need them. She's got a crush on him.'

'What's his name? I'll buy him a pair and send them to him anonymously.'

'Why is sex so rarely right?' she asked a bit later, trying to brush toast crumbs out of the bed.

'Because it's extremely rare for the right people to have it together.'

'How do you know who's "right," though?'

'You do know,' he said. 'You know when it happens. You're right, I'm right. We don't need to be righter than that. Sex with the wrong person can be fun, and often is, or it can be frankly terrible, but never right.'

'I don't know what right we are talking about now.'

'Neither do I,' Thomas said. 'Shut up for a moment. If you've got rid of those crumbs, I want to see how right we can be again.'

Later still, disengaging herself, she said, 'I don't do this any more with Neil.'

'I don't want to know what you do with Neil.'

'But I don't. I want you to know.'

'I've said, I don't want to know.'

'Thomas –'

'No, please, Elizabeth. Listen to me. What you do with Neil in that hell-hole is your affair.'

'I wouldn't because it would be wrong.'

'I've said already, I know nothing about right or wrong.'

'You do, though. You said, earlier, about right not being right. It wouldn't be right of me. It would be wrong.'

'I've said I don't want to know. And I don't know, and don't want to know, because I don't believe anyone who talks about it – not even you – knows about right and wrong. Or, indeed, right *or* wrong.'

'But I don't want to –'

'Elizabeth, stop, please.'

'But I don't want to do any wrong to you,' she insisted.

'Okay,' Thomas said.

In the short silence she heard a car door bang and a woman's voice call out, 'You've forgotten your keys, you'll forget your stupid head next.'

'You ask me about right and wrong. I'll tell you. I think it's wrong that you are there and not here. I think it's wrong because it's dangerous. I think it's wrong because it's a kind of perverseness in you. I think your reasons for being there are frankly lousy and suspect. But I love you, so I'm putting up with it. Which might be right, I don't know. And it might be wrong, I don't know that either, but if it is, I don't care. What I do know is this, and this *is* right because it is what is right for me, so hear me, please, okay? I don't, repeat don't, wish to have my imagination sullied by the thought of your having sexual intercourse – or *not* having sexual intercourse, it's no odds to me – with your husband. It's not a subject I wish to entertain at any time, at any price, in any neck of the woods, but especially not – *especially not* – here with you in my own bed. Right or wrong, I don't wish to know. Okay?'

'Thomas –'

'No, Elizabeth!' He had jumped out of the bed and stood facing her, naked and furious, his myopic eyes darkly bright with rage.

Looking at him quite coolly, she appraised his long, spare body as an artist might. You're like a painting yourself, she thought.

'I've told you. You're stronger than me. I have only myself. You believe you have right on your side.'

'Who says? I never did.'

'I do. I do. I can feel it. I feel it here.' He smacked the palm of his hand against his naked chest, which made a surprisingly loud noise. 'You believe in pissy things like good manners and adultery.'

'I believe in not hurting people.'

'And do you think you will prevent people being hurt by staying on in Gerrards Cross? Do you? Do you? Listen, here's who you'll hurt. Let me tell you: *one*, me, i.e., Thomas Carrington, okay, let's not count him because he loves us, and we don't count ourselves, so let's try *two*, Elizabeth Cruikshank, née Bonelli, well, we don't count her either, do we?, because see *one*, Thomas Carrington loves her, et cetera, et cetera – so let's move on to *three*, Neil Cruikshank, we'll do better with him because he doesn't love us so he counts more than *one* and *two* put together, but look, if you stay he'll love you, if anything, even less, because my hunch is he's really longing for you to leave him so he can be a real martyr, but, look, finally, *four*, hurrah! at last we've hit the jackpot, Primrose Cruikshank, aka the Russian Vine, who is going to get hurt worst of all because she's dying, my darling, just dying for you to run off and fulfil all her direst prophecies about you so she can say "I told you so" to her ickle son and fall into the unfortunate vicar's arms and – and – don't you see, DON'T YOU SEE – ?'

'Thomas, Thomas darling, don't, don't, Thomas . . .'

He was crying and she held him tight in her arms and they were both crying and then it all seemed all right again.

It was partly this row that persuaded her to go to Paris with him a few weeks later.

'I wish we could go back to Rome,' she had said after they had made it up in bed with the cheese-on-toast crumbs.

'Why is it, no matter how you brush them out, crumbs stay in a bed for ever and a day? We can do nearly as good as Rome. We can go to Paris, if you can extract yourself from the RV's toils.'

Thomas, it appeared, wished to visit the Louvre to examine a Caravaggio. They stayed in one of the small Left Bank hotels, short on light and smelling of tobacco and that faint aroma of something exotic, which might be no more than vanilla, but anyway a smell which once seemed unique to France.

The hotel was near the Musée de Cluny, which they visited to look at the medieval artefacts and tapestries, and also, beneath the museum, the robuster Roman baths. She told me she preferred the remains of the latter to the pale tapestry ladies and courtly flowers and ivory-backed looking glasses and intricately jewelled caskets. 'Maybe just because they were Roman and by then I was prejudiced in favour of all things Roman but I liked that the baths seemed so practical.'

'I've always admired the Romans' plumbing,' I agreed.

'Thomas was keen on their drains.'

I was mildly chuffed by this evidence of a shared taste between myself and the uncompromising Thomas. 'And Paris, you enjoyed it?'

I could hardly imagine she hadn't. To be with her ebullient lover in Paris struck me as offering another peak of joyous possibility. Bar and I went to Paris once and it has remained in my memory as three of the happiest days in my life. We had to drag the mattress on to the floor to sleep, because the hotel bed was so ropy and dipped so much that we rolled into each other. We made quite a bit of the dip, I seem to recall, before we repaired to the floor.

But it seemed that I'd misjudged this Paris visit, because her face clouded.

'No.'

'No?'

'The Roman baths were the best part.'

'Oh?'

During their visit to the Louvre Thomas had announced that he would be moving at the beginning of the year to Milan. My own heart practically juddered to a stop at hearing of this new turn of events.

'We were looking at *The Death of the Virgin* when he told me.'

'What did he say?'

'You know,' she said, 'it's not the big things that demolish you. It's the way, for example, people push their glasses up their nose.'

'I'm sorry.'

'I can tell you what he said exactly. He said, about the picture, "That's my idea of a difficult repentance." Then he said, "I'm going to go and live in Milan for a while. They've offered me a job there."'

'What did you say?'

I expected her not to respond, but she said, apparently calmly, 'Not what I felt. I must have asked some stupid question about his house – I loved that little house – because I remember what he said in reply. "I'll keep that in case you ever come to live with me, but while I am waiting I might as well take up this offer. It's a good one." It was a good one. A chair at Milan University.'

'Thomas was older than you?' I'd not enquired about his age.

'He was forty-five. How old are you?'

'Forty-five.' My laugh was embarrassed. In my imagination Thomas had seemed younger; more youthful in spirit, anyway, than my middle-aged self. The coincidence flustered me. To hide the awkwardness I asked a more than usually direct question. 'What did you feel you wanted to say to him?'

'Oh,' she said wearily, 'I don't know. Now you pin me down, what did I really want to say?'

She got up and walked over to my desk, put out a finger, and touched Jonny's bell, as if she were going to refer the question there. But, instead, she walked back and stood grasping the back of the blue brocade chair with her blue-veined hands.

'I wanted to say' – her voice lifted – 'I wanted to say: Don't go, stay, please stay with me. I am not myself any longer because now I am yourself, or you are myself, I no longer know, or some other strange new self that exists between us. I don't know what I shall do if you take that away from me. I am terrified, scared to death, scared witless at what you are saying. Show me that you understand. Show me you understand that I am standing here, looking at the blood-red dress of the mother of Christ, and the blood-red hanging over her deathbed, and my heart is bleeding away inside me, blood-red blood inside. Take away this terror that I am losing you, you must take it away because only you can, only you in all the world have ever been able to help me. If you won't understand what I don't understand myself, because I can't myself understand why I don't come to you, you might as well strap my hands and gag my tongue and bind my eyes and take me out by night and burn me at the stake, in dire darkness, in blind and filthy darkness, as you told me – when you loved me first, before you told me you loved me first – they did to the astronomer Bruno in Rome.'

'But I didn't say it.'

'You should have done.' I didn't intend to be cruel.

She seemed to acknowledge this, because she walked round and sat down carefully in the chair again and said, 'I know I should but I didn't know how.'

We sat, unwilling to meet each other's gaze, which was when I said, 'D'you fancy a drink? I've got a bottle of Scotch in my drawer,' and she said, 'Thanks, I'd love one. I wasn't Bruno, you see. At his trial he said, "Perhaps you, my judges, pronounce this sentence against me with greater fear than I receive it." By the way, what time is it?' and I got out the bottle of Famous Grouse, which I kept for my own private emergencies, and poured a couple of tumblers full, and we sat and drank together in companionable gloom while I mentally dispatched the General Medical Ethics Council to perdition. I reckoned it was a legitimate prescription: we both badly needed something to lift our spirits. I didn't bother to consult my watch: we were past such considerations by this time.

And I suppose because I couldn't take any more emotion just then, and felt we could both do with a break, I said, 'Tell me about the painting.'

'Which painting?'

'The one you were looking at when he told you.'

'*The Death of the Virgin*? For the rest of my life I shall remember it.'

When I was last in Paris I visited the Louvre to see this painting and I could hear Elizabeth Cruikshank's emotionless voice describing it to me all those years before.

'It's a scene which is usually called "The Dormition," the so-called transit of the Virgin from this life to the next. Except that Caravaggio has dared to paint it as if it is the end and there will be no life to come.

'She's young, his Mary. White-faced and exhausted, worn out with sorrow, and laid out, dead, with big, veined peasant's hands, and her feet, all ungainly, sticking out of her shift, with no attempt at elegant piety.

'John, the beloved disciple, is standing at her head and all the other disciples are shuffling up to pay their respects, and you can tell from their posture that they're crushed with the profoundest grief. He took the story from *The Golden Legend*, a medieval book, popular then, of the lives of the saints, and the legend was that, at Mary's death, the Apostles were all miraculously transported to her bedside, though the real miracle in this scene is Caravaggio's execution of it.

'Mary Magdalene, who's washed the dead body, is sitting beside the bed, and he's painted her folded over almost in two with the weight of her despair. It's the second death she's had to bear, you see, and you can tell it's defeated her. I remember looking at her and thinking: Yes, I know how you feel.'

'How did you feel?'

She pondered. 'It was a kind of second death for me, too.'

'Because you felt you were losing him again?'

'Because I felt I was losing him again. You know, they hated Caravaggio, for that painting. He used his whore as his model for the Virgin. She wasn't what they had in mind at all.'

'What did they have in mind?'

'Oh, you know, sweetness and light. Transfiguration. Certainly not some clapped-out prostitute. The picture of death wasn't what they wanted either.'

'I suppose death never is.'

'No.'

'What did "they" want for that, would you say?'

She considered again. 'Hope. Hope that this isn't the end. It's not allowed to be, is it? I mean, people, even people who aren't religious, don't like to think that it is.'

'I suppose not.' I contemplated the plate empty of sandwiches and the browning apple core she'd gnawed to next to nothing and felt a snatch of her wolfish hunger. 'What did Thomas mean by repentance?'

'"A difficult repentance" was what he called it. I'm not sure. Maybe . . . no, now you ask, I don't really know. In Caravaggio's day they thought she was a prostitute, Mary Magdalene; it was her he was referring to. But I doubt he meant that sort of repentance. He didn't go in for that kind of thinking.'

'Nor did Caravaggio, from the sound of it.' The painter's was clearly a nature which needed to rattle swords at piety and convention. 'I imagine that's why he didn't let them have what they wanted for their image of death.' It crossed my mind to ask if she shared the painter's unsentimental view of the afterlife.

'For me that's its virtue.'

I didn't need to ask the question. 'And did he go? Did Thomas go to Milan?'

Her voice sounded kind, as if reluctant to speak words she knew might hurt me. 'Oh yes, he went. People do go in the end. They get tired of waiting.'

9

According to Gus, the philosopher Diogenes walked the streets of ancient Athens at night with a lantern searching for one honest person. He might have searched just as vainly for a trusting one.

It is hard to account for the common human resistance to happiness, unless it is that we would rather be crippled by what we lack than risk the pain that is one potential consequence of placing our secret selves in others' hands. The desire to be loved is as basic a need as the desire for food or drink. But to take delight in being loved requires nerve. For where life is most ardently awakened it can be most excruciatingly extinguished and the fear of that possibility can tragically become the wet blanket which smothers the sacred flame.

That they were congruent spirits, these lovers, I didn't doubt. There exist irresistible affinities in nature, and the human psyche is only a part of that vast pool of possibility. So it is not improbable that there are souls who, through some undetermined radar, recognise a natural rapport without recourse to the usual blundering empirical means. I have no explanation for this phenomenon. Freud's most famed British disciple, the psychoanalyst Ernest Jones, met his first wife a brief three times before he proposed to her; and when she died, and he married again, he married his second wife three weeks after their first meeting. Both marriages were counted unusually happy.

My patient's account inspired confidence: confidence in the authenticity of this example of these incalculable confluences of affection. A confidence which, in her, had plainly faltered. She had told me that the mystery was the straightforwardness between her and her lover, but perhaps it was the very straightforwardness which made for the complication. Unlike our animal cousins, humankind seems pitifully ill-constructed for simplicity.

Or love. Confidence, *con fides*, with faith. It takes faith to love. But perhaps it takes greater faith to be loved: beloved, the meaning of my own name.

'David means "beloved" in Hebrew, I expect you know that.'

Her voice had echoed my unspoken thought. The sense of eeriness was underlined when she suddenly pronounced: *'And the king was much moved, and went up to the chamber over the gate, and wept: and as he went, thus he said, O my son Absalom, my son, my son Absalom! would God I had died for thee, O Absalom, my son, my son!'*

A memory from schooldays surfaced. 'King David's lament?' I wasn't called after that David, but I was much moved myself at the words she had quoted and, like my namesake, felt unusually close to tears.

'Thomas recited it to me once. I learned it by heart.'

'I was useless at scripture, I'm afraid, but I like what I remember of David. He struck me as reassuringly fallible.'

'He committed adultery.'

'Is that why Thomas recited it?'

'No. It was when he took me to see Caravaggio's *David*. Do you know it? You might like it, I think.'

'Why would I like it, Elizabeth?'

At that moment there was a rattling of the door, we both started, and Lennie stuck his head round it.

'Jeez, sorry, Doc. I thought the light was left on by accident.'

'It's all right, Lennie.' Instinctively, I glanced at my patient, who had risen from her chair and was taking refuge by my desk, where she had picked up Jonny's bell again. I noticed that at no point did she show any interest in handling the lump of lava or the inkstand.

'Don't bother about the room this evening, Lennie. I'm working late.'

'I can come back. No trouble.' Lennie's face was endearingly, and irritatingly, eager.

'No, it's fine. I'm not sure when I'll be through.'

'It's no trouble, Doc,' Lennie repeated. I could tell he longed to be given trouble.

'I know, Lennie. It's good of you. But leave it for tonight. Maybe in the morning . . . ?'

Lennie's efficient receptors had homed in on something unusual and he was looming in the doorway, still hoping to get a better view, so I stood pointedly in his line of sight and gave him a firmly cheerful 'Goodnight, then!' and shut the door rather close to his face.

'I'm sorry about that,' I said to Elizabeth Cruikshank. 'Please, do go on.'

'I'm being a trouble to you.'

'No, you're not. It was he who was being the trouble.'

'He's fond of you.' I took this as requiring no response as she continued: 'The *David* is almost Caravaggio's last work. He was outlawed from Rome on a murder charge and it's thought he painted this to butter up Cardinal Borghese, who was one of his most influential patrons and a cousin of the Pope's and could therefore help engineer a pardon for him. David is holding Goliath's head at arm's length by the hair, and the face, Goliath's face, looks monstrously sad. Both their faces do.'

'All sadness has something in common.'

'Yes.'

I remembered the burned-out look in the eyes of a Vietnam veteran I'd treated once. He'd won a Purple Heart at nineteen and when he returned from the war, a national hero, no one would employ him.

'It's through such pain that we learn to know ourselves.'

But the cost is steep and the knowledge not for the fainthearted.

'Caravaggio painted Goliath's head in his own likeness. His face had been badly wounded in the fight that led to the murder charge, and it's as if he's given the mutilation to Goliath. Thomas said that he had read somewhere that an artist is someone who knows he is failing in living and feeds his remorse by creating something fair, and that summed up for him both the painter and this painting.'

'And David is the fair?'

'Poor David. You can see in his eyes he's already anticipating another death.'

'He would have understood death from the moment he'd killed.' My veteran still dreamed about napalm victims. 'I've seen that look in the eyes of soldiers.'

Her own grey eyes looked into mine and she said again, 'Poor David.'

'Poor human beings,' I acceded, somewhat awkwardly. The ambiguity made me uncomfortable and perhaps for this reason I resorted to Gus. 'There's no cure for being alive.'

'Maybe your friend likes Caravaggio because he understands that.'

'I'm sure that's true.' It had crossed my mind that Gus would like Thomas too.

'He was likeable.' It wasn't clear if she was referring to the artist or if she had once again read my mind.

The two of them kept in touch, mostly by letter. In those days there was no email or mobile phone to enlist in the transport of love. Thomas wrote to her at the little house which he urged, even without his presence, she use as a refuge. *I insist you get away from the Russian Vine and the hideous ornaments*, he wrote. *I shall think of you, without ornament, naked as nature intended in our bed.*

He returned for holidays, when the closeness of their bond reasserted itself and harmony seemed to be repaired if not entirely restored.

And Thomas, anyway, was now absorbed in a project which might well have distracted him from any imperfections in his personal life.

Caravaggio, she explained – as I sat in my chair, with her sometimes sitting opposite, sometimes pacing about or standing, her back pressed against a wall, gesticulating with her thin hands, which, as the evening went on, seemed to acquire their own hectic life – died in dire circumstances. His, I was gathering, was always an intemperate disposition, one which diced – almost as a necessary imperative – exuberantly with danger, and I wondered, as I listened, what compulsion it is that some – women almost as often as men – have to mount an assault on life in order, perhaps, to feel more acutely for the blows it returns. For much of his life this need to provoke and deal out violence put the artist regularly in prison, and for the latter part of it he was on the run from the murder charge in Rome. But he was desperate, too, to be freed from the overshadowing threat he had almost deliberately placed himself under and return to the city that had seen the execution of his finest work and where, while his character was most reviled, his talent was most revered.

By this point in his career, at not quite forty, Caravaggio was widely celebrated as a genius and, on the strength of this reputation, was in high hope of a pardon for his alleged crime. In anticipation of what had been as good as promised, he travelled up the coast, from a safe retreat in Naples, on a felucca, on to which he'd loaded paintings intended as a further palliative offering for Cardinal Borghese, the most influential of his Roman patrons.

The felucca put in at Palo, a small port with a fortress, hard by the mouth of the Tiber, where for an unexplained reason he was once again imprisoned, possibly because the commander of the fortress believed he was still a wanted man with a price on his head, or possibly because he was taken in error for some less distinguished malefactor. By the time Caravaggio had bought his way out of prison, the boat, with its matchless cargo, had set sail again, now in the opposite direction from Rome, back down the coast towards Porto Ercole.

In an effort to recover the precious paintings, Caravaggio set after the boat, determinedly travelling nearly a hundred gruelling kilometres alone, in high summer, through long stretches of undrained mosquito swamp, where he contracted a fever, only to find on reaching Porto Ercole that the boat had already left, bound again for Naples with the irreplaceable cargo of his work still aboard.

Perhaps the second loss was the last blow to the seemingly indefatigable painter's morale. With repeated friction, even the toughest tether will fray. Frustration and despair over the missing work dragged his spirit down, which, coupled with the effects of a raging fever, finally proved fatal. Caravaggio died, unaware he'd at long last been pardoned, far from his beloved Rome, unattended by anyone known to him, in the isolated Porto Ercole's inhospitable and poorly appointed infirmary.

'God,' I said, when she finished this sorry account. 'Another piece of foul luck.'

'Yes.'

'I could do with another drink. How about you?'

I all but clinked her glass. We seemed to have become allies not merely in her misfortune but companions in others'.

'I can see why Thomas liked Caravaggio, the man, not simply the work.'

'Yes.'

'He was real.'

Caravaggio had killed so he understood remorse. Perhaps he killed in order to understand it.

'Yes.'

'He had courage.'

He had fashioned the image of grave young David to be his own nemesis.

'Yes.'

'And spirit.'

The artist's spirit, for which a larger reality must always be a more considerable matter than his own puny existence.

'Thomas loved those qualities in him.'

The story she told of Caravaggio's lonely trek in pursuit of his lost paintings struck strangely at my own heart. The painter who appeared to know the subject of death most intimately had risked his own death for his work, the work which itself presents death in its most terminal and unredeemed light. And death bested him, as it must in the end, though in this case the defeat of such a determined will, at such a point, seemed to me a matter for more than common regret. I felt I wanted to reach out and clutch him to me, embrace this maddening, driven, troubled, troublesome person – shake some of the nonsense out of him, and try to shake some sense into him – question him, discover who he was, and why he was. And it hurt me, with an almost visceral pain, that he was gone, and while he could speak to me still, through his, by her account, almost unbearably marvellous paintings, there was no means whereby the reverse could be the case. Or would ever be the case, because of death's incorrigible asymmetry.

It was not known how many paintings were included in the original boatload. Only three turned up when the boat's cargo was finally retraced to Naples. A *St John*, possibly Caravaggio's last work, was recovered by Cardinal Borghese, after a dispute with other claimants, and hangs still in the Galleria Borghese. The other two, another *St John* and a *Magdalene*, disappeared, so far as I understood from her account, for all time.

But Thomas, she explained, had found a reference in a letter which suggested that when the Cardinal's emissary went to Naples to assert his claim to the recovered hoard, there was another painting that had been stored there, possibly the disputed *Road to Emmaus*.

'The same subject as ours in the National Gallery?'

'Yes. And there's another, later, *Supper* in Milan. But there are occasional references in various sources to a work known as *The Road to Emmaus*. It's been generally assumed that this was merely a misnomer for the two *Supper* paintings on the same subject. But in a letter from the Marchesa di Caravaggio, the village from which he was named, who took Caravaggio in and put him up in Chiaia, near Naples, before his last journey, there's mention of "figures on a road" in a painting still in her possession: one he didn't have shipped to Rome.'

'And it wasn't known about before?'

'There was speculation but, as I say, it was assumed the title was misquoted. What name a painting gets ascribed isn't, as we tend to assume, set in stone. The painter, in fact, only rather rarely names it. More often the name is acquired by usage. Anyway, Thomas thought he might have a clue to the possible whereabouts of this other Caravaggio.'

'He must have been over the moon!' I felt quite elated myself.

'He was. It absorbed him entirely.'

I caught something in her tone. 'You minded that?'

'I misread it.'

'What did you misread?'

'I suppose I thought he was tired of me, instead of just tired of waiting for me. I'd been sort of expecting it, d'you see?'

10

Of course I saw. I, who had a problem even believing that I am remembered by my patients, let alone my friends or my wife, felt a swift and acute sympathy. To a diffident soul, even Thomas's trenchant affection might, at a distance, have grown to seem fantastic and implausible.

A pity beyond all telling is hid in the heart of love, and if what I recount now is coloured by my own emotion, it is because I was no longer a bystander in these lovers' story but had become involved. I make no apology for this, insisting only that what follows is as it lingers in my mind when so much that might have more seeming relevance to me has long left it.

Thomas had found the letter from the hospitable Marchesa, in whose house Caravaggio had in fact been born (his father, I learned, was his steward), in a batch of bills, mostly relating to the painter Giorgione, which he bought from a dealer in Milan. Recalling their first conversation, and Thomas's reference to Giorgione, I raised my eyebrows.

'It was because of Giorgione that Thomas bought them, if that's what you're wondering. There was an ink sketch of a woman's face in the margin of one of the invoices and he . . .'

'Did he think it looked like you?'

'I think so, yes.'

The letter spoke of a painting, making no mention of the artist but referring to it as *Il Signore Andando ad Emmaus*. Attached behind this letter, so it had perhaps not been scrutinised before, was another letter, which suggested the first letter was a means of establishing the painting's provenance to a potential buyer. This second letter was from a Mantuan agent, Gentile Ottavio, addressed to a French collector, in Aix-en-Provence, and described the painting as having been originally sold for 110 scudi, a high price in those days for a contemporary painting. So, whoever the artist was, clearly it was counted valuable.

By a lucky stroke, Thomas's doctoral thesis had explored the history of the Aix collection, in which he had traced a number of the Aix paintings back to another collection which had later been dispersed, through a family's fortune failing, in sales in and around Rome. But even with his prior knowledge the detective work took up time, and he had a programme of academic studies to organise and oversee, so he delegated part of the work to his research assistant.

The assistant was attractive, eager, and decidedly taken with the new *professore*.

'And you were jealous?'

'Not to begin with.'

'But later?'

'I became jealous.'

'Why? I mean why specially?'

'He kept mentioning her.'

'That's generally a sign of innocence. He would be more likely to suppress her name if she was important to him.'

'You aren't rational when you're jealous.'

'Of course not. I'm sorry. Please go on.'

That summer, nine months after they had met en route to Rome, Thomas rang her by arrangement at the little mews house.

'How is the passion flower?'

'It's fine, I think.'

'You have to watch passion flowers. They're like me, they look full of buck and gusto but underneath they're tender. Do you know why it's called passion flower?'

'I don't think I do.'

'Look at it. Go on, go and look now.'

'I'm talking to you now. I'll look later.'

'And the Albertine? How's my Albertine? They have the best of scents, but they're terrifically thorny and prima donna-ish to make up for it. Be careful of your dear hands.'

'The Albertine's fine too. I've sprayed it and tied it up and I wear gloves.'

'Good. And the lilies, how are my lilies? Angelic?'

'They're well too and smelling heavenly. You'll be able to see for yourself soon.'

Pause. 'I'm not coming back this summer, Elizabeth.'

'Why not?'

'Claudia has found what she thinks may be a lead to the *Road* painting.'

'So?'

'So I'm going to pursue it. It's the only time I have.'

'It's the only time you have with me too.'

'You can come here.'

'I can't, you know I can't.'

'Why not?'

'It's the children's holidays.'

'Okay. Then you have to choose. Holidays with children or me.'

'What will I say?'

'I don't know, Elizabeth. I would say, Max, Amanda, I am going to spend the summer with Thomas. Because I love him. I love you too, and if, finally, I find the will to go and live with him, I will love you that bit better, and more honestly, and in the end that will be better for everybody. Because living a pretend life is the very devil. But that is only what I would say.'

'Would you really say that?'

'I don't know, Elizabeth. I believe so. Remember, I don't have children.' He didn't, as he had in the past, add that he hoped to have children with her some day but merely asked after the Russian Vine. 'No, don't tell me. Unless you've slipped a dose of weedkiller into her gin and tonic I don't want to know.'

When they had finished talking, she made herself coffee in the pot with the complicated glaze and went outside to the garden, with one of the white porcelain cups they'd bought in Rome, and studied the greenish-white petals of the passion flower, its corona of fine purple filaments, and the five yellow stamens and three dark pistils at its dark heart.

One of the things Gus had instilled in me was the danger of seeming to pounce. Not that I am by nature a 'pouncer,' but he put into words what I hope tact would anyway make instinctive. So I didn't rush out with what was uppermost in my mind, which was 'What did you feel about having – or not having – Thomas's children?'

The subject of children was not my strong suit. If I was unsure-footed about them with my patients, it was because I was unsure-footed about them with myself. The whole issue of children produced in me one of those mental blurs which I knew to be an index of undigested pain, and Elizabeth Cruikshank's attitude towards her own children betrayed some similar confusion.

The slight girlish demeanour concealed, as I was learning, a strength of passion which, according to the usual natural laws, should have also found its object in children – and I wondered if it was maybe the very intensity of the desire which had held its expression back. Or if the children conceived so near that early loss of Thomas had fallen under its shadow. Yet, surely, she must have longed for her lover's child.

'Did it worry you that he didn't mention wanting children?' I refrained from observing that it was the first I'd heard of it.

She looked out into the deepening night and I glanced at my watch, almost by accident, noted it was pushing nine, and only faintly wondered if Olivia would be home and questioning what was keeping me.

'I think that was one of the things I couldn't believe.'

'Couldn't or didn't?'

'Are they different?'

'I would say so. Think about it.'

He met her at Milan airport and seemed as thrilled as ever to see her.

'You came!'

'I came.'

'Why, as a matter of interest?'

'Thomas, how can you ask why?'

In the wide white bed, made up with linen sheets, in the white bedroom of his white Milanese apartment, in the high modern block she said, 'It's so unlike the mews.'

'It isn't. Both are as nice as pie.'

'Thomas, why is it called a passion flower?'

'Didn't you look? It's got a crown of thorns.'

'The other "passion," then. Not our kind.'

'Is it? All passion leads to suffering, I think. Passion is suffering, most of the time. Why, really, did you come?'

'I wanted to see you.'

'That's not a proper answer. I shall fine you. Right, that's a hundred scudi. A steep fine.'

'What am I being fined for?'

'For wriggling evasion. On your honour, Elizabeth Cruik-shank, née Bonelli, what made you come here after all?'

'I wouldn't have seen you all summer otherwise.'

'Yes, and . . . ?'

'I thought you were annoyed with me.'

'Dead right, I was. And . . . ?'

'I thought you might . . .'

'What?'

'Take some sort of revenge.'

'Oh, Elizabeth.' He sat up in bed and his face reminded her of that other time, before he went to Milan, when he had shouted at her and cried. 'You thought I might sleep with Claudia.' It wasn't a question.

'Yes.'

'Oh, Elizabeth,' he repeated.

'I'm sorry.'

'You should be.'

'It happens.'

'Yes, it happens. But if that were going to happen I'd tell you. I'd say, "I'm getting tired of this and I'm worried I might just accept Claudia's often-intimated invitations for me to peel off her tight black dress and undo her all-too-visible black lace bra and take down her matching lace knickers – and don't ask how I know what her knickers are like, you don't need personal evidence to be sure that an Italian woman of Claudia's type is fussy about that sort of thing – and fuck her, as she would like." That's what I'd say. She looks like a pig, by the way, to me at least she does, poor creature, not that that makes any difference. You know what I say is true.'

'Yes.' She felt sick as a dog.

'Elizabeth, I don't fuck about. You should know this.'

'Yes. I'm sorry.'

'I don't fuck around either because I don't fuck about. You seem not to grasp that.'

'I do. It's just that –'

'It's just that – no, hear me, please! I'm speaking! – it's "just that" you don't believe me. You have no faith in me, or my words. You imagine that I say what will please you, and myself, and then go and do quite other things. You don't believe that I mean what I say. Do you? Do you? You believe that while I say that I love you, and need you, and want you, I am secretly plotting to fuck my assistant. Don't you? Don't cry, answer me. Well, DON'T YOU?'

'I'm sorry.'

'You know what? You aren't going to like this, but I'm going to say it anyway.'

'Don't say it.'

'Okay, I won't.' He turned away and she noticed again how vulnerable naked shoulder blades look. 'You're my hearth companion,' he had said to her, by the castellated gateway in the old walls, as they were leaving the dead Keats behind in the cemetery in Rome. Maybe a hearth companion had to watch the other's back even against the companion's own self.

'I'm sorry. Say it.'

'Okay, I will. What people imagine is generally what's in their own minds, not what is in other people's. You imagine I am planning to fuck Claudia because that's what you might do. I'm sorry to have to say this. Actually, why am I saying that? I'm not sorry. You see, lying is catching.'

'Thomas, I wouldn't.'

'Not Claudia, no. Not fucking, maybe, because that's not your style. But unfaithful, yes. You don't believe I'm faithful because you're not.'

She was crying too badly now to say anything.

'Oh, I don't know,' said Thomas. He rolled on to his back and flung an arm over his eyes and lay there speechless for several minutes. Then he said, 'I'm knackered. You must be too. Let's get some sleep.'

His long body in the wide white bed didn't touch hers once all that night while she lay, listening to the hysterical moan of the Milanese traffic, with sore dry eyes.

In the early morning, she looked at his sleeping form, at the mercy of the cruel dawn light, with one square-fingered hand flung not across her breast but across his own dark-haired one, as if to protect it. The sheet, lying in folds where he had drawn it round him, had to her the look of a shroud.

The following morning he took her to see Caravaggio's other *Emmaus Supper*.

Since she spoke of this to me, I have visited the great Pinacoteca di Brera, in Milan, and seen the painting too. It is as like the London *Supper* as chalk to cheese.

Caravaggio painted it in 1606, around the time he was indicted for the murder charge. The dimensions of the two paintings appear identical and the composition is much the same: the two startled disciples, the pivotal figure of Christ; the only difference being that, rather than one, there are two awkwardly uncomprehending servants placed at his other side. But the mood is vastly different. Where the London *Supper* is intense in colour, the foodstuffs on the inn table luxuriant and plentiful, the perspective steep, the light almost insolent in its raking brightness, in the later painting the autumnal vividness has attenuated to wintry blue and browns, the paint thinly applied as if to let in light. The light glows at the picture's centre, sombrely incandescent, the perspective is enfolding, the meal only the bare essentials, the atmosphere grave.

On the left of the picture is an eloquent emptiness and

Christ is no longer the renovated young renovator of the earlier work. Here he is bearded, world-weary, fragile, fatigued. Observing him, I felt that he had returned with reluctance from the restful shades of death to our brash world of necessary light.

'How different it is,' she suggested. As different as the two of them were that day from the day she had stood beside him in London and looked at the companion painting. Her heart burned with the recollection of it.

Thomas said nothing but simply stood studying it. He had a particular posture when he was absorbed. Slightly stooped about the shoulders, like a heron. She watched him, gangling and heron-like, pushing his glasses up his nose and squinting sideways at the painting. Then he said, 'They are, very different, but don't start saying you like one more than the other. I can't stand favourites.'

'I wouldn't dream of it,' she said stiffly.

He walked off and ahead of her, and she had to hurry to catch up. 'So where shall we lunch?'

'Wherever you like.'

'Thomas, how do I know? I don't know Milan. You live here.'

'I don't live anywhere,' said Thomas. 'You should know that.'

'What are you talking about?'

They were outside now and crossing the noisy road; still striding ahead of her he yelled over his shoulder, 'I DON'T LIVE ANYWHERE! I DON'T CARE WHERE I LIVE!'

'Don't shout.'

'Why shouldn't I shout?'

'I don't want other people hearing us.'

'Why not? They won't understand what I'm saying. Even if they do, they're Italian, shouting for them is normal.'

'It isn't for me.'

'Oh, you . . . !' he said, and swept into a dingy-looking

restaurant, where voluble greetings indicated he was a valued regular.

'You see,' he said, over a bottle of wine and a heaped plate of pasta and a recovered temper, 'it's this. Most people make themselves up. They wrap themselves up with a lot of tinsel and flummery: precepts and morals and habits and fibs and shams and other pathetic dishonesties. Artists don't do that. Or rather, if they do, they make sure to unwrap themselves when they work. The greater the artist, the less wrapped up they come. When I say "artist" I mean writers, poets, composers, and so on. Caravaggio was a shit of the first order. He was a drunk, a gambler, a cheat, a liar, a thief, a fornicator, and a murderer – a thorough-going dyed-in-the-wool bastard. Except for this: when he was painting, he didn't wrap anything up. I don't believe he wrapped much of his life up either. Whoever had to deal with him had to like it or lump it.'

'Was he really gay?'

'Who cares? He was the type who would try all sorts, mostly to get away from himself. He was a fugitive through and through. You can't get away from yourself so easily, but I doubt he had much clue about personal love.'

'And the impersonal kind?'

'Well, that's the thing. He must have done. You couldn't paint those pictures otherwise. You couldn't, could you?'

'I don't know.'

'Yes, you do. What do you feel when you look at them? Go on, what do you? What did you feel when you looked at that one today?'

She said, hesitatingly, 'My heart hurt. But that was about us.'

'No, it wasn't. Or rather, it was. Because we're in it too. You, me, Caravaggio. His heart burned, you can tell it did. That's what burned you. It burned through him till he had to paint that painting, and it probably burned right down his arm and into his hand.

Hah!' Thomas wrung his own hand in the air and the waiter, mistaking it for some urgent request, hurried across the crowded restaurant to replenish the breadbasket. 'He painted that *Supper* while dangerously sick and very likely already on the run, in mortal fear of his life. But he had to do it. You can tell. *It* made him paint it. What is so interesting is that this is the tranquil one. It's the other one that's febrile. That figures too.'

'Why?'

'Because a real artist knows the other side of himself better than the side he's in at the time. You don't paint as you are; you paint as you're not. But you only know what you're not through knowing what you are.'

She considered this, taking what was left of his bread and mopping up the tomato sauce. 'And the other *Supper*? Our one in London?'

'Same thing,' said Thomas. 'Same story, same hand, same heart. Different mood and perspective, that's all.'

'Like with us?'

'Exactly,' Thomas said. 'You've got sauce on your cheek. No, not there. Here. Look, I'll lick it off for you.'

11

The next day they flew from Milan to Rome, which could hardly help reviving memories of their first flight there together.

'You know,' she said, 'I was beside myself in case I wouldn't be able to sit with you on the plane.'

'Don't be silly, of course I was going to arrange it.'

'We mustn't forget to take violets to Keats,' she suddenly remembered.

He was about to respond when a stewardess came round and served them bottled water, with a flourish, as if she were offering champagne.

'We need himself to turn this into wine,' Thomas remarked.

'D'you think he did?'

'He did if they believed so.'

'But belief can't alter the physical substance of the world.'

'It can alter people's perception of it. Belief does alter people, marvellously, if only they'll believe it.'

'Thomas, what did you see in me all those years ago when we met at Bainbridge's? I don't get it.'

'What a phrase. Please don't disfigure your pretty mouth with such phrases.'

'All right, I won't. But what?'

He looked past her to the window, through which the sky was casually parading a cerulean blue. 'Look out there. Tiepolo would have been in his seventh heaven. Do you know what the seventh heaven was? Never mind, I'll tell you another time. I'll tell you what I saw at Bainbridge's.' He paused to sip his water from the plastic beaker. 'Ugh! Do you think they just fill those bottles from the tap and sell them for a fortune? I bet they do!

'I saw you had a very pretty shape, even beneath Bainbridge's hideous dressing gown. I saw you had an even lovelier smile, a Leonardo smile, not like that blowsy, running-to-fat, self-satisfied Mona Lisa creature, but like the Virgin's mother, St Anne, un-selfconscious and serene. I saw that here was someone who didn't make herself up. That's what I saw most clearly. In your own way, you're an artist, because you have an artist's ability not to pretend. Very few people' – the square-fingered hands made emphatic gestures – 'very, very few have the capacity to withstand the temptation to become someone altogether unlike themselves. You have it. You have, or had, it naturally.'

'You mean I haven't any more?'

The candid gaze was unblinking. 'You've been living under horrible conditions. It's almost impossible not to pick up the atmosphere in which you live. It's why I've been on at you to leave Gerrards Cross. You imagine it's for my sake. It's not. Or, rather, it is, because your sake is my sake. An atmosphere like that vitiates the spirit. It creates confusion. It confounds the good. It makes you doubt me, for example. You know, don't you, that Neil is having an affair?'

'How do you know?' She felt a stab of excitement.

'Because of what you've said. You've picked up duplicity and suspicion from that poisonous atmosphere.'

'But I'm duplicitous too.' For the moment she didn't want to contemplate what he had said about Neil.

'I'm sorry I don't help.'

'Thomas, you do help. You help me more than anyone has ever helped me in my life. I'm sorry I'm a trouble to you.'

'It's no trouble, Elizabeth. I'm sorry for your sake it's so hard.'

'And Rome?' I asked. I wanted it to be as significant for them as before.

'I only stayed a night.'

'Why?' My tone was as passionate as Thomas could have wished.

'Primrose called me home.'

'How? Why?'

'I rang from the hotel. I had to, for the children. I left a number and she rang back.'

'And?'

'She said I should come home, that something serious had happened. I'd told them I was taking someone's place at short notice on an art history course – of course I'd emphasised the last-minuteness of it, as if it were a cheap deal, so it was hard to argue for staying on. Especially when faced with the children.'

'What had happened to the children?'

'I pressed her, but all she would say was that it was serious and that I should come home. I thought Max must have got into trouble at school. They were always – quite barmily, it seemed to me – expelling boys for smoking. I knew he smoked. I caught him once at the bottom of the garden and he said, "Mum, you won't tell Granny, will you?"'

Good for Max! It sounded as if he'd known his mother better than she'd implied. 'And was it that? Had he been expelled?'

'No, he hadn't.'

'So what was it?' Suddenly, I was overtaken by a colossal anxiety which crashed over me like a tidal wave.

'Would you mind if I lie down?'

'Of course not, but . . .'

I had nowhere for her to lie. My analyst's couch was at my private rooms. You don't ask psychiatric patients on the NHS to lie down.

'I'll lie on the floor. I often do when my back hurts.'

'Of course. Is it hurting now?'

'Yes.'

'I'm sorry.'

'What time is it? It must be late. Do you want to go?'

'It doesn't matter what the time is, and I don't want to go.'

Thomas watched her repack, lying on the bed. He lay with one hand behind his head, watching.

'Don't look like that,' she pleaded at last.

'How am I looking?'

'Indifferent.'

'I'm not indifferent, Elizabeth. I'm as unindifferent as it's possible to be. I'm tired, if you want to know. Bone-tired. And I know when I'm defeated. I told you, you're stronger than me. People who think they're right always are.'

'I'll come straight back as soon as I've sorted out whatever it is.'

'How do you propose to "sort out" blackmail?'

'There's obviously something wrong.'

'Yes,' said Thomas. 'You're right. There is. Blackmail is wrong. Blackmail is very wrong and should never be succumbed to.'

'I thought you didn't believe in right or wrong.' But she wished she hadn't said this and went over and knelt beside him on the bed. 'Are you all right?'

'I'm tired, I told you. I didn't sleep much last night.'

'I'm sorry. I thought I was the sleepless one.'

'Don't be absurd. How could I sleep with you lying there in a state? What do you think I'm made of?'

'I'll come back,' she said again, kissing him on the forehead.

'Where will you come to? I might not be here.' They had planned to hire a car and drive to the monastery whose collection Thomas had arranged to visit.

'I'll ring the hotel. You can leave me a message.'

'Elizabeth. Be brave. Face her out. Cut the Russian Vine down to size. It's what she's trying to do to you. Don't be cut down. Stay here. Stay here with me. I don't want to cut you down. I want you. And you don't want to go.'

She had never wanted to do anything less in her life, she told me, but early the next morning she left him, still in bed, and took a taxi to the airport. She didn't lie on the floor to say this. She walked across to my desk and stood with her back to me and explained that Primrose had brought her from Rome to inform her that Neil was divorcing her. He, they – almost certainly Primrose, because, as she said, 'Neil wouldn't be so crude' – had set a private detective on her who had followed her to Milan. He had photographed her going into Thomas's apartment and coming out with him the following morning. He had also followed them to the Brera, 'repository of Napoleon's finest looting,' Thomas had called it.

I don't know quite why that struck me as the last word in gross invasiveness, since even a private detective has his job to do. The Gerrards Cross contingent, prior to receipt of these instances of vulgar proof – which, I gathered, were merely the final nails in a coffin which had been eagerly constructed – had already taken counsel's opinion. The fact that Elizabeth had abandoned her children during their holiday, in order to conduct this adulterous liaison, was, Primrose averred, with singular satisfaction, likely to ensure that custody of the children would remain with Neil. In any case, she was sure 'Liz' would understand, it would be too great a disruption, at this stage in their lives, to remove the children from their family home.

'It was your home too!'

'I didn't want it.'

'The bitch!' A bloody old bitch, Thomas had called her.

'I suppose she was only defending her own.'

'It wasn't the correct legal position, either, I imagine, about the children?'

'I don't know. I didn't bother to fight it. I felt she was right about not disrupting them and they were away at boarding school much of the time. They liked their grandparents' home.'

'I see.' The tidal wave had withdrawn, leaving an outwash of depression. Where was Thomas's fighting spirit? 'And what did Thomas say? He must have been relieved about the divorce.'

'Where did these come from?' She had turned round with Bar's egg and Jonny's bell cupped in the palm of each hand. They gave an impression of devotional offerings in some long-vanished rite.

'The bell belonged to my brother.'

'Older or younger?'

'Older. He died when I was five.'

'I'm sorry.'

'He died stopping the traffic to see me to safety.'

As I was saying this, with an extraordinary sense of ordinariness, I perceived that this indeed is what Jonny had been doing. It wasn't, was it, that he hadn't seen the lorry, as I had always supposed? Or had told myself I supposed? As the familiar scene reassembled in memory, a blind was sliding quietly up and revealing that my brother had seen the lorry, and that I had not been, as I had always imagined, on the pavement at all. It was I who had stepped heedlessly out into the road, and the lorry was looming terrifyingly towards me – and now I saw, as if it were happening there and then before my shocked eyes, that it was Jonny who had been on the pavement and had sprung between me and the approaching vehicle, holding up his hand in a vain attempt to halt its fatal progress.

Again she said, as if she feared I'd not heard, 'I'm sorry.'

'It's all right,' I said. 'It was a long time ago.' Forty years, three months, and twelve days. A long time to have carried around a lie.

'Thomas died,' she said. 'That seems a long time ago too, though it's only just over seven years. If you don't mind, I might lie down now.'

12

I must have known Thomas was dead – though I had not known I had known. I read once a remark of Harold Pinter's: *Apart from the known and unknown what is there?* At first I thought it a smart observation, until it occurred to me that all serious matter exists somewhere between the known and unknown. I knew and didn't know that Thomas was dead. But then, I had known and not known about Jonny.

She lay on her back on the floor, in the pool of light made by the Hermes lamp, with her hand behind her head – as she had told me Thomas had lain, the last time she saw him, watching her pack to return to England – and told me how he had died. And if you'd produced a couple of pins I would have lain on the floor beside her.

Thomas's belief was that a minor painter, Paolo Geraci, a follower of Caravaggio but in no way his equal, had got his hands on an original and had used it as a base for his own *Road to Emmaus*. Thomas had verified that a painting with this title was in the collection of a monastery, north of Rome, and his plan was to examine it and, if need be, persuade the monastery to allow it to be investigated further. There were problems with this, since, in stripping down to any earlier work, the upper layers of a painting must necessarily be removed, so that any later work, albeit of potentially lesser value, will be destroyed permanently in the process. It is, thus, inevitably, a risky business, but as she said, if there was any chance an original Caravaggio was to be uncovered, then Thomas was the man to convince the most cautious.

They had planned to make this investigative trip together and she had hoped he might reschedule the appointment with the monastery for her return from Gerrards Cross. Hearing her say so, I felt the futility of this. It suggested, painfully, to me that at the end she had lost touch with the mind of her lover.

He set out, dogged and alone, for his appointment with the monastery's curator, driving up into the mountains, and he never reached his destination. An alert driver noticed the hired car, askew and dangerously close to a vertiginous hairpin bend. Stopping to investigate, he found an unconscious heap over the wheel.

Thomas survived a cardiac arrest for two days in intensive care, while back in Gerrards Cross she was frantically trying to trace his whereabouts. When she finally tracked him down, it was through Claudia in Milan.

'She met me at the airport when I made it back to Rome. I didn't want to see her, but she seemed to want it, and, you know . . .'

'I know about not wanting to upset people because we are upset ourselves.'

'She made my upset seem very small beer. She must have doubted that Thomas and I were at all close.'

'And was she like a pig, at all?'

'You know, there was something faintly porcine. I felt mean thinking so, when I met her, because she was a nice enough girl and also exceedingly glamorous. But Thomas had this devastating eye. He could see the essence of people.'

'It's a great gift.'

'I'm afraid it makes you lonely.'

'It would make you lonely. Great gifts do.'

I'd no need to ask if she'd got to Thomas before he died: my bones had already informed me.

'When I finally got to the hospital in Rome, I spoke to the consultant whose care Thomas was under for that brief spell. A kind man. He took trouble to give me his time without making me feel he was doing so. He was most upset that they'd failed to save him.'

'I'm sure.'

'He confirmed it was probably the septicaemia which had compromised the healthy functioning of Thomas's heart. If he'd been found sooner, they'd have had more chance. You know, when I was lying with my head on his chest I could hear an arrhythmia.'

('It's like a bird,' she had said once, 'your heart, trying to get free from a snare.'

'You're the bird,' he had replied, drawing her down to him to dismiss her concern.)

'The doctor was kind, but he couldn't answer all my questions and you know' – the words had come fluently but here she stumbled and, hardly a pace behind, inwardly, I stumbled too – 'distress places a burden on the heart. I'd upset him. He was uncharacteristically passive that evening. I thought it was disappointment in me, but I feel now he was already unwell.'

'We all tend to project our own concerns.'

'I don't believe Thomas did. Or less than most. He was unusually clear-eyed.'

She confided she had had a fantasy that he might be buried in the Protestant cemetery, where they had gone together, on that first fine reunion, to honour Keats's remains.

'I take it he's not buried near Keats?'

'No. But I did go there and I took violets.'

'He would have liked that,' I felt able to say. 'Where is he buried?'

'In Kensal Rise. He'd have hated *that*, but I had no say in it. I've never even been there. His wife organised it all.'

'And did you meet her too?'

She crooked her head towards the blue brocade chair. 'Yes, through that.'

'What?'

'What's in my bag. Thomas's notebook. He'd written my name over his address, to say where, if the book was lost, it should be returned. Very decently, his wife did so. Or, rather, she wrote to me care of the mews – I still had the key – and asked if we could meet.'

'And did you?'

'We met there.'

'And was it difficult?'

'It was awkward, certainly. For some reason, I ended up recounting what Thomas had told me the first time I stayed, after we returned from Rome: a mews is so called because the first was built on the site where the royal hawks had been mewed.'

And quite distinctly I saw a bird's hovering image over the spire which, she had told me, lifted her heart every time she approached her lover's home. 'What did she make of that?'

'Oh, she took it in her stride. I felt she grasped the awkwardness.'

'What was she like?'

'A doctor. Practical. Steady. Unimaginative, which would have been difficult for Thomas, but I didn't dislike her.'

It made sense. Particularly after his drastic illness, a highly strung soul like Thomas might have been drawn to someone who offered a sense of security – before he learned that security, finally, is always an inward matter.

'And the notebook?'

'Oh, David.' She sat up on the floor and put her head in her hands.

Years later, when I visited the Louvre to find *The Death of the Virgin*, and saw for myself the figure of the grieving Magdalene, I recalled Elizabeth Cruikshank's doubled-over form, sitting on the hospital floor of my consulting room with an empty plate and glass beside her. A difficult repentance.

But when I spoke of this to Gus Galen, he told me that what we translate as 'repentance' means more accurately, in the original Greek, a turnaround, or change of mind. *Metanoia*. I would rather say a change of heart.

'It's so like him,' she said, looking up. 'His ideas, his sketches – of faces, flowers, seed pods, trees, buildings; quotations he'd liked, words – he'd a passion for unusual vocabulary – accounts of places he'd visited, people he'd met on trains, dreams, cloud formations, recipes (lots of those), fragments of poems, and things he'd written about me.'

'Nice things?' The banal question hid the degree to which I was moved.

'Better than "nice."'

I didn't ask her to amplify, but she got up and went to the brown bag and took out a green leather notebook. 'I've always loved the smell of this.'

She turned the pages till she came to what she was looking for and read:

'*Elizabeth here last eve and the world restored for me. I keep thinking she will discover how insufferable I am. How little really I have to give her except my plain difficult self. Is one self enough? Well, it's all I have to give her and she may have it if she wants it . . .*

'*Elizabeth rang and I wanted to fly down and scoop her up and run with her, head down against all takers, like a rugby player with her the ball. But I must do what I'm worst at and be patient. People have their own inner clocks. I'm a fast-ticking one, she's slower.*'

'He was right about the clocks,' I said. I'd noticed that what goes awry between people is often a matter of mismatched timing.

'He was right about most things. This is what he wrote the morning I left, the last thing he wrote, in fact: *E off this a.m. from Rome, summoned by the Gerrards X. I was too knocked up even to see her off at the airport. God knows what she'll be met with. A crooked deception, no doubt. It's funny how you imagine loving someone is enough to make them believe you love them. Love needs belief, not to exist but to work. Without belief love is hobbled and lame.*

'He was right about that too,' she concluded.

'About belief: is it yours, then, that if you hadn't left he wouldn't have died?' There was no point in mincing words.

'Of course it is. What do you think?'

I waited, wondering if this was a rhetorical question. 'What do I think . . . ?'

'Do you think he would be alive if I hadn't gone trotting back to Gerrards Cross like a tame poodle?'

'I don't know, Elizabeth.'

'I know you don't "know." But what do you think?' I said nothing and she said, 'Thomas would have told me.'

'Okay,' I said. 'I'll tell you what I think. I think your Roman consultant was right. Septicaemia can jeopardise the functioning of the heart. It could have led to a ventricular fibrillation, which can lead to cardiac arrest, and to death. It is also true that emotional distress can be a trigger of this kind of fatal arrhythmia in someone whose heart is already under strain. So it is possible that had you not left him as you did he would not have suffered the attack. It is also the case that had you been with him you might have succeeded in getting him treatment faster, and the sooner a cardiac arrest is attended to, the likelier it is that the patient will be saved. However, it is also not only possible but likely that this fatal episode would have occurred anyway, that it had nothing to do with your leaving but was purely a consequence of an impairment which had never been diagnosed. It should have been, if, as you say, an arrhythmia was detectable, which suggests to me that Thomas was careless of his own safety and that he would have died in the car with you beside him, or later at the hospital, even had you succeeded in getting him there sooner than was the case. To my best knowledge, that is what I think.'

'Thank you,' she said gravely. 'That is exactly what I wanted to hear.'

'It's what you knew already.'

'It's what I knew already,' she granted. 'But I needed to hear it. I could never have put it so clearly to myself. It is good of you. You can't have enjoyed saying that.'

'I'm sorry you weren't with him, Elizabeth. Very, very sorry.' I doubt I had ever been sorrier for anything in my life, except Jonny.

'Yes. So am I. Thank you for listening to me. And for telling me the truth.'

'Thank you for telling me what you have told me. And for telling me to tell you the truth. It was brave of you.'

'It was brave of you to tell me.'

'Why did you wait seven years?'

'Before I tried to top myself?' She was smiling, to reassure me.

'Well, yes. If it's not an intrusive question.'

'It was the rain,' she said simply. 'The rain this October was so like the rain that October in Rome, when we were together first. And I kept thinking of Keats's epitaph in the cemetery and Thomas saying that we mustn't waste time.'

'I'm sorry,' I said again. There didn't seem to be much else to say. Except, 'Thomas's Caravaggio *Road* painting? Did anything ever turn up?'

'I never bothered any more about it. It wasn't my first concern and he was gone and, well . . .'

'I understand.'

'It didn't seem worth pursuing. Nothing did.'

'Of course.'

'Nothing,' she said again, 'has seemed worth much since.'

'I'm sorry,' I said again.

'I know you are.'

I thought of something else. 'Was Thomas right about Neil? Did he have a mistress?'

At this she laughed quite gustily. 'He'd had her stowed away for years! Long before Thomas and I met on our way to Rome. He told me, Neil did, before the divorce.'

'Who was she?'

'A harmless woman who worked in his office, called Norma, with a matronly bosom and those spindly legs top-heavy women often have. He asked me not to let on to Primrose that he'd told me. It made us quite conspiratorial. Poor Neil, he had a guilty conscience about it – not about having a mistress, I noticed he was unapologetic about that, but about using my adultery in the divorce. In the end he didn't, in spite of Primrose. He behaved quite decently, overall.'

'So the Russian Vine was cut down to size. Thomas would have been pleased.'

'Well, you know, they had things in common, Thomas and Primrose. They were both uncompromising. She was all right in her way.'

But loyalty to Thomas made me protest. 'She sounds to me quite wrong. Thomas's was an altogether different order of being.'

'Yes, you're right.'

'Good,' I said, 'I'm glad we've sorted one thing out this evening to our satisfaction.'

13

We drank another whisky, and then, I think, another, and she continued to sit on my floor, from where she read me scraps from Thomas's notebook. One letter he'd copied into his book, written by Joseph Severn at Keats's death, seemed almost unbearably poignant.

Rome, 27 February 1821

My dear Brown,

He is gone – he died with the most perfect ease – he seemed to go to sleep. On the 23rd, about 4, the approaches of death came on. 'Severn – I – lift me up – I am dying – I shall die easy – don't be frightened – be firm, and thank God it has come!' I lifted him up in my arms. The phlegm seemed boiling in his throat, and increased until 11, when he gradually sunk into death – so quiet – that I still thought he slept. I cannot say now – I am broken down from four nights' watching, and no sleep since, and my poor Keats gone. Three days since, the body was opened; the lungs were completely gone. The Doctors could not conceive by what means he had lived these two months. I followed his poor body to the grave on Monday, with many English. They take such care of me here –

that I must, else, have gone into a fever. I am better now –
but still quite disabled.

The Police have been. The furniture, the walls, the
floor, every thing must be destroyed by order of the law.
But this is well looked to by Dr C.

The letters I put into the coffin with my own hand.

I must leave off.

J.S.

This goes by the first post. Some of my kind friends would
have written else. I will try to write you every thing next
post; or the Doctor will. They had a mask – and hand and
foot done – I cannot go on –

There was a recipe for quince jelly, which I wrote down. I still
have it somewhere; but I have never made it.

She also read me Thomas's speculations about the *Road* painting: *There may well be as many lost masterpieces hidden away as found
ones,* he wrote. *Waiting for someone to recognise and restore them.*

I hadn't wanted to consult my watch in case it prompted her
to leave, but it was gone ten by the time we parted and then it
was she who'd made the first move.

'I should go. You must be tired.'

'You must be. Would you like a sleeping pill?'

'Not after all that whisky, Doctor!'

'By the way, what maniac prescribed you Soneryl?'

'I stole them from Primrose.'

'Oh, Elizabeth!'

'I know. D'you know, that was almost the worst thing, when
I came round and realised that I'd survived. I thought how ter-
ribly angry Thomas would have been, especially at my using
Primrose's sleeping pills.'

'Rightly so. How did you get them?'

'I filched them from her drawer when I came back from Rome, the second time. After Thomas had died.'

I calculated. 'You mean the third time?'

'Oh yes, it must have been the third.'

'So you kept them all this while?'

'They were my exit visa.'

'Well, you've used it up,' I said briskly. 'No more Soneryl. Too bad!'

'Yes, too bad.' She got up from the floor and stretched and walked across to the desk. 'Who gave you this?' She had picked up the egg again and was balancing it on her open palm.

'A friend.'

'It's a heavenly blue.'

'I think so.'

'Thomas would have matched it to some painter's palette.'

'Thomas isn't here,' I said. 'You are.' I had no idea why I came out with that. It sounded brutal.

'I'm sorry your brother died,' she said. 'But if he saved you, I'm glad.'

PART III

But when I look ahead up the white road
There is always another one walking beside you

1

And I was glad that Elizabeth Cruikshank and I had already exchanged these words, because when I opened the door of my room Bar Buirski was waiting outside.

I touched Elizabeth on the shoulder. 'Will you be all right to –?'

But she was ahead of me. 'I know my way back by now.'

'Goodnight, then.' The world we had returned to seemed a shadowy place and I admit that I didn't want her to go. I would have had her for a hearth companion any day.

I caught a glance at my unexpected visitor before she answered 'Goodnight' and went quickly down the badly lit corridor. I watched till she rounded the corner before asking, 'What's up?' Bar would never come to the hospital, certainly not so late, without a pretty sound reason.

'I thought you might know where Dan is.'

'No.'

'He said you were playing squash tonight.'

'Hell, was I? I'm sorry. I must have forgotten. I had this emergency and –'

'My meeting was cancelled so I walked over to the court, but he wasn't there – or in the bar. And he's not been home. I wondered if he was maybe with you here?'

'No.'

'Oh,' Bar said. 'Well, I wanted a walk and I was passing, so thought I'd call by and see.' She continued to stand there.

After a minute too long I said, 'Look, I'm pretty nearly dead on my feet. Let's go for a drink and then I'll drive you home. He's probably gone round to the Powells' or something.'

I got my things from the room and we went and found my car, which I'd left sloppily parked that morning. Someone had left a note on the windscreen: *Kindly show consideration for other drivers*. Probably Mackie. The idea of having to clear this up made me feel extremely weary. I drove, humming to avert conversation, to a decentish bar which I knew from experience wouldn't be too rowdy or smell too foully of cigarette smoke, where I ordered a couple of whiskies, which, considering what I'd drunk already, I shouldn't have done. Though in fact I might have drunk nothing but the purest spring water all evening for all the drunkenness I felt.

After I'd downed a gulp of whisky I said, 'D'you remember that weekend we spent in Paris?'

'When was that?' Bar asked, and I was about to remind her, a little chagrined, when she laughed and said, 'Of course I remember, don't be silly. It was one of the nicest weekends of my life. You took me to the Louvre. I'd never been.'

'So I did. What did we see?'

'Oh, everything. Too much to remember. I thought you would despise me for knowing so little about art.'

'But I knew next to nothing about art.' If we had happened on *The Death of the Virgin* I would have walked past it.

'I thought you did. I thought you were terribly intellectual and cultivated, and I felt inadequate and inferior.'

'Oh, Bar!'

'I did, Davey. I always did. You always seemed so lofty.'

We fell silent. I was thinking that she must have wondered

what I was doing with Olivia if I was supposed to be so intellectual. I didn't have a clue what I was doing then. I was realising how little clue I had now.

My mind kept reverting to Thomas, whom I would now never know, who, nonetheless – here was the paradox – I now knew maybe better than anyone, save his lover, my patient, the suffering Elizabeth. Listening to her, I had come to hear his voice sounding through hers, informing it, and my ear, with its ringing insistence, its hatred of false currency, its laudable and unselfconscious directness. Thomas didn't fuck about, as he had told her. He said it like it was, or as it looked to him, and be hanged to the consequences.

'I remember you wore a red dress in Paris.'

'You bought me lilies of the valley when I was wearing it.'

'Did I?' I couldn't even picture what they looked like.

'They have an enchanting smell.'

'I'm sorry to have forgotten.'

'Women have an annoying way of remembering these things. I'm sure men wish they didn't. Davey, where d'you suppose Dan is?'

Which was when I knew she knew all the time where Dan was; and when I knew that I had known all the time too. I began to know from the moment of her enquiry, because I had had no squash date with him that evening. Even under pressure, I never forget appointments.

Bar was too old a friend to dissemble with, but I simply asked, 'Where do you think he is?'

And she said, 'What about you? Where do you imagine Livy is?'

'Well,' I said, 'perhaps home by now. I was thinking if I took you home I might ring her from your place.'

'Davey,' Bar said, 'what shall we do? Shall we just pretend

nothing's happening?' Her face looked white. I couldn't help comparing it with Elizabeth Cruikshank's face. It was a different sort of white. More chalky-looking.

'I'm not sure quite –'

I was about to prevaricate when Bar cut me off. 'You are sure. But we don't have to say anything. Not even between ourselves, if you'd rather not.'

This was so like her that I took her hand and squeezed it. 'What do you want to do?' I felt surprisingly calm at the idea that my wife was committing adultery with one of my closest friends. I must have known. It had a kind of ludicrous predictability to it.

'Go back to Paris, maybe? But we can't go back, can we?'

I didn't feel this was a question that needed answering right then, and in the end she drank a second whisky and I, overruling the tempter inside me, moved on to orange juice, and then I drove her home. The lights were on in the Buirskis' flat and I waited in the car to see if she would come down again, in case Dan wasn't there – or in case he was and she wanted me to come up too. But after a while the lights were extinguished and I assumed I wasn't needed, so I drove on home.

It was nearly midnight by the time I reached the flat and there were signs that Olivia was back, her shoes kicked off by the sofa in the sitting room. High-heeled slingbacks, two-toned navy and white. My mind conjured Thomas again, singing 'The Raggle Taggle Gypsies' down the telephone, while his lover stood listening, torn between her perceived duty and her unperceived heart, her narrow feet in the green wellingtons, as the rain washed the sides of the phone booth in Gerrards Cross; the same chemical compound but so different from the rain in Rome.

Thomas was right to have urged her so vehemently to come to him. He was right because he had grasped the nature of mortality. He had a mind free enough and a heart bold enough to take on board, properly take on board, that just as there are first things so also – it is after all, if we could take it in, implicit – there are last things. That everything in human life tends towards its ending and that any meeting, however full of hope and promise, will be the first stage in a progress towards a last meeting – and that this may happen sooner than we imagine and without fair warning. I think I can say that this was something he understood generally, because he had made me aware of it; it wasn't only a premonition of his own end.

Looking at Olivia's shoes, stylish, sexually provocative, I thought Thomas was right about that other 'death,' too. Only rarely does sex feel right, because only rarely do we have it with the right person. Olivia was never the right person. I'd lied about that: to her, and to myself. I didn't blame her for wanting it with someone else. She'd a right to it. Thomas would have agreed.

Nevertheless, I didn't feel like sharing a bed with her, so I fetched a couple of the scratchy grey blankets, which I believe were once my mother's, from the linen cupboard and stretched out on the sitting-room sofa. My neck and back had fused into an aching arch, my eyes might have been pickled in brine, and a cruel wire was cutting into my temples. I felt washed up, washed out, and insufferably weary. Elizabeth Cruikshank's story, Jonny's death, the meeting with Bar, the discovery of Dan and Olivia's liaison, swirled like a maelstrom through my overcharged brain. There was nothing I wanted at that moment more than oblivion.

When I looked at my watch next, it was 5 a.m. and a huge barn owl was pecking viciously at my left foot. I snatched the foot away in terror. So acute and disturbing was the impression of this assault that I fumbled for the table light, missed it, overturned the standard lamp on the other side of the sofa, found the overhead light switch, and inspected my foot for a bloody wound. Only then did I realise that had I been standing – as, still partly asleep, I believed I had – the sole of my foot, where the bird had attacked so ferociously, would have been protected. What I had been walking on was dream ground and not the solid earth at all.

I lay down again, and for a while hovered in that non-realm between the waking and the sleeping worlds, where, for a blessed space, we are released from mortal ties and duty's daily round. And as I lay, half in, half out of sleep, the owl flew into focus and I knew it for the same great white bird that had beaten its wings helplessly against the wire, in that far-off first dream of my analysis.

The owl had flown free, but it had returned to deliver a sharp stab to my understanding.

I found I was shuddering with cold. The grey utility blankets had slipped during the night from the narrow sofa, and I wrapped myself in one now and went into the kitchen and filled the kettle, as noiselessly as possible so as not to wake Olivia. And then, because I wasn't yet ready to contemplate what I was going to say to her, I went to my study and stood on a chair and from the topmost, dustiest shelf, where all my childhood stuff had been shoved in tottering, heedless piles, pulled down the shabby little broken-backed Bible which I hadn't opened since I was a boy.

When I opened it, I read inside, in a blue-ink, childishly curved script: *This book belongs to David Edward McBride, 29 Burlington Road, Chiswick, London W4, England, Great Britain, United Kingdom, Europe, The Northern Hemisphere, The World, The Milky Way, near The Sun.* Beneath this was appended: *If this book should dare to roam, box its ears and send it home, to the above, i.e. David Edward McBride etc.*

After leafing through, and a certain amount of skim-reading, I located, right at the end of the Gospel according to Luke, the story that Caravaggio had painted. *And, behold, two of them went that same day to a village called Emmaus, which was from Jerusalem about threescore furlongs.*

It was a bare two days since I'd walked to the National Gallery from Gus's tiny flat and found the Caravaggio and looked at it – looked and seen it, or, I should say, begun to see it, for the first time. With all that I had been hearing from Elizabeth Cruikshank, and all that had passed since, it seemed at least two centuries since I'd stood there, a different man. For – I could say this to myself, though to anyone else it would have sounded trite or pompous – I was not the same person. As I pondered this, it dawned on me that here was another mystery: that in the gap of my precisely not seeing the painting but hearing Elizabeth Cruikshank's account of it, it had acquired a new dimension, and now its diffuse brilliancy radiated something which, even as I contemplated it – anticipating the taste of the freshly drawing coffee – was searching out a moribund corner of my own heart.

I was changed. Changed by my patient, and by her story, which was also her lover's story, and my own story, and by the story of that long-ago scene, which may or may not have ever occurred in what is facilely referred to as 'real life.' But Caravaggio had made it real, through his exacting hand and eye; an eye which saw uncompromisingly through the prism of his searing heart.

Two men on a road 'threescore furlongs' long. How far was a furlong? How many furlongs made a mile? What distance had they to travel, those two, when they were joined by that enigmatic third on their unexplained journey?

I looked again at the frontispiece of the scuffed little Bible in case I had recorded any of the useful information – about pints of water and pounds and gallons and chains and acres and maybe furlongs – as I seemed to recall I had in other of my school texts. But there was only the boy's endearingly old-fashioned request that should it stray, the book's ears be boxed before being sent home to Burlington Road.

Burlington Road was where we moved to after Jonny died. Our first home without him. The first time I had a bedroom which was mine alone and where he was not some kind of presence by me at night, and I had to begin to come to terms with the fact that even during the ambiguous hours of darkness, where, in our old room, he hovered still, he was there no more. In all my life I had experienced no loss greater than this. And all my life I had denied my own part in it. I had lived with this invisible gash in my side, this breach in my dyke, this crumbling portion of my sea wall. The lorry which had crushed my brother's body, as he had placed it, valiantly, to protect mine, had also crashed the sustaining boundaries of my world.

And they talked together of all these things which had happened. And it came to pass, that, while they communed together and reasoned, Jesus himself drew near, and went with them. But their eyes were holden that they should not know him. And he said unto them, What manner of communications are these that ye have one to another, as ye walk, and are sad?

What else would they be of, the communications, as the two men made their way together on the dusty road, but the affair that had left them so heavy-hearted? They were sad, because they believed they had lost the person they loved, as I had done, as Elizabeth Cruikshank had. They had lost their heart's best treasure, and as they walked, it was natural that they should talk of this grievous loss. Except that most of us don't. Most of us haven't the knack of opening our hearts to another without reserve.

2

I had bathed and shaved and there was still no sound from our bedroom, so, with reluctance, I put on the clothes I had been wearing the day before and made myself a second pot of coffee, relieved that any confrontation with Olivia could be postponed.

From the noise outside, the traffic was only just starting up, and since there was no need for me to get off to work for nearly an hour, I took another look at the tale I'd been reading.

They must have known, really, the two companions, that this stranger was the lost friend they believed dead – though they didn't know they knew – because when they got to the inn, at Emmaus, they persuaded him to come in and eat with them. And when, over supper, he broke bread and revealed himself, and then vanished again as suddenly as he had appeared, they said to each other, by way of confirming his identity, 'Did not our heart burn within us, while he talked with us by the way?'

One heart; two people. Standing in the kitchen, looking out at a green and incandescent orange sky, in which a frail crescent moon was lingering still, my own heart burned, thinking of my brother's bright incipience given for my pitifully uninspiring life.

The phone rang.

'Davey?'

My first thought was that it must be Bar. Then I recognised with alarm the voice of Cath Maguire. The use of my first name betokened something serious.

'Cath?'

'St Stephen's have been ringing.'

'Tell me.'

'It's your wolf man. I'm sorry.'

'What?' Maguire was no panicker.

'He's tried to kill a nurse. I'm sorry.'

When I got to the hospital, Maguire was at reception waiting for me, her comely face twisted in an anxious knot. 'I'm sorry, Dr McBride, I know you're fond of him, poor soul.' She'd recovered her formality, but I was as touched as I was troubled by the concern which had led her to discard it.

'What happened? Is she all right?' My poor wolf man, I doubt you meant anyone harm!

'They'll fill you in better than me, but from what I've gathered, this new nurse was afraid of him. You know how fear breeds fear?'

I did. Fear was fingering me there and then. It was I who had ordered that the wolf man's security restrictions be lifted.

'And do we know how he did this thing?'

'I gather he tried to strangle her, with a telephone cord.'

'Jesus! How the bloody hell did he get his hands on a telephone cord, for Christ's sake?' At least they couldn't lay that oversight at my door.

'God knows, Doctor, I didn't ask.'

I drove to Haywards Heath, swearing at other drivers for my own errors of judgement, and as I walked into the hospital reception – smelling, as it always did, of disinfectant – my heart was racketing wildly between my mouth and my shoes. Although my most pressing impulse was to ask to see my patient, I was aware it was important that we deal first with the injured nurse. I recognised too that, unfairly, I wanted to blame her for this catastrophe.

The nurse had been taken off to the local medical hospital, and I was relieved to hear that, physically, the worst we had to address was some bad bruising to her neck. Her mental state, I was given to understand, was altogether a graver matter. The nurses' union was already involved, as the senior registrar informed me, a low-sized man with a serious case of dandruff, judiciously professional in his speech, but, I sensed, under a veneer of sympathy, thanking his lucky stars that he was not in my place and secretly relishing the fact. People do so enjoy another's crisis.

The wolf man was under lock and key and drugged up to the skin. But his anguished gaze locked fast on to mine as I entered the security cell where he was detained.

'Peter?' I said, and it's a curious fact but, perhaps because to me he had always been 'the wolf man' and I had seldom used his given name, only then did I connect him with 'Peter and the Wolf.' It crossed my mind that perhaps it was Peter rather than the wolf man who had committed this atrocity.

'Doctor, will they hang me?'

'No, Peter. They won't hang you. Peter, why did you do it? Can you say?'

'I said I weren't safe. I said so. They can't hold that against me, can they?'

'I don't know, Peter. I don't know what happened. Could you tell me? Did she scare you?'

'Please ask them, Doctor. Ask them, will they hang me?'

'Peter, did you do this thing because that is what you wanted, to be hanged?'

But however much I questioned him further, he spoke no more words to me, either then or later, but merely looked at me, beseechingly, with his trapped-wolf's eyes.

I did what needed to be done, approved the extra security provision and attempted to begin to establish how he had contrived to get hold of a phone. It seemed likely he had secured this during his move down a floor. One of the nursing offices had had a spare, perhaps left out on an unattended desk, and our guess was that the wolf man had lifted it quietly and later removed the cord. I was surprised he had it in him to be so forward-planning – but I should have remembered that what people have in them is often a surprise.

As I drove back towards Brighton, the traffic had increased with the onset of the day, and after a couple of near scrapes with other cars, and with anger mounting inside me, I pulled over to the Dew Drop Inn, which infelicitous pun I'd marked on my journey down.

The Dew Drop's clientele was for the most part lorry drivers, exchanging comradely badinage or reading the *Sun* over a quiet smoke and enjoying the sight of pairs of substantial breasts over plates of, equally substantial, breakfasts and mugs of orange tea. I longed to be one of their number, freed from responsibility for the crazed actions of others and to be looking, peacefully unmolested, at pictures of pretty naked girls.

I ordered the 'Full English' and two rounds of the thick white toast which, well buttered, is more consoling than tranquillisers. And a pot of tea, because although the waitress swore blind it wasn't, I guessed that the coffee was instant.

'You all right, dear?'

The tea had arrived in advance of the breakfast and I nodded thanks to the middle-aged woman whose pleasantly ordinary face was signalling a nosy concern. She left the table, and the briefly checked tears returned. I put my hands over my face and relinquished control.

Of course my poor wolf man wanted to be out of it. I must have known this. How could I not, since it was my own position exactly? It was why I so often drove with my seat belt unfastened, even as I did so, coolly and clinically noting the danger I was inviting; it was why I was always secretly longing to contract some fatal illness, so I could retire from life's gruelling demands with guiltless dignity; it was why I worked too hard, and long, over other people's affairs, because it lent to existence a point and purpose. It was also why, though I had never formulated the thought, I had acceded to Olivia's request that we never have children, for I knew that children are hostages to fortune and that a part of me would resent the claim on my affection, a ballast to ground me when I preferred not to be grounded, so that I could the more easily slip away.

And in my desire to offer up my will-to-live to other lives, I had robbed the wolf man of his escape. He would never now be free of some overruling constraint, which would shackle him for the rest of his days to a life he would rather be rid of, enough to contemplate taking another's life. And that life too would now for ever be tainted by an increment of fear.

Beware, beware of those who care! I, who cared so little for myself, had by way of compensation cared too much for others and they were the losers thereby. As I'd flicked my ignorant way through the school Bible that morning, which now seemed another world away, I had paused over Cain's resounding cry at the first recorded murder: 'Am I my brother's keeper?' The ancient question was a rhetorical one, a piece of brilliant dramatic irony, for far from being his 'keeper,' Cain was his brother's killer. And hadn't I always believed I had been Jonny's keeper? It seemed that in this case also a keeper was a killer in disguise.

It was in Jonny's stronger reality, which had never left me, and of which I had become the living custodian, that I had found the model to hold out my hand to others more obviously wanting than myself, to protect them, as, fatally, he had protected me. The recognition made me literally shake now as the tears ran down unrestrained.

The breakfast arrived and I dabbed at my face with the thin paper napkin, because in my hurry that morning I had forgotten my usual handkerchief, and ate the eggs, bacon, sausages, tomatoes, and mushrooms, my white toast, buttered thick and anointed with sweet bland marmalade, as if it were I who was to be hanged and this was my last requested meal. And then, because physically to move seemed more than I could manage, and to delay my departure further, I ordered another mug of orange tea from the nosy waitress and sat longer than I could calculate in a more dead than alive trance.

When I summoned the strength to get myself up from the table to settle the bill, I went and sat in the car, by the parked lorries, and, still unready to face any further incompetence in my driving, leaned my arms on the steering wheel and laid my face on my arms and wept uninhibitedly like a child.

After a while, I stopped crying and drove my car, pretty much without conscious navigation, till I found a way up to the South Downs. I stopped the car in a lay-by and walked up a rutted track, turning up my collar against the driving cold. I'd had no opportunity to replace the lost scarf.

I walked on upwards, and when I'd gained height enough that I could no longer see the road, I stopped and turned my face to the icy wind blowing in from the sea. It had brought in its skirts a collection of gulls, white birds in a cruel white sky, harbingers of more ill weather to come. I stood under the chilly sky and the wheeling birds, with winter-bleached grass beneath my rapidly freezing feet, and howled like a wolf into the countering wind.

I howled for my wolf man, for Bar, for Olivia, for Dan, for Elizabeth Cruikshank, and for her Thomas, who suddenly, absurdly – for in life we were perfect strangers – I missed almost as sorely as I missed my lost brother.

But I also howled for myself, because for the first time even the unreality of Jonny was not there for me, no one and nothing was there, and I couldn't for the life of me see how I was going to manage alone.

3

When I got back to St Christopher's I found Hassid outside my room. It had been in my mind that Hassid was ready to be discharged and only my indulgence had allowed him to linger so long.

'Hi, Hassid, are you waiting for me?' Who else would he be waiting for? The thought of some new demand, even a trivial one – especially a trivial one – fell like a dead-weight blow.

'Doctor, I am sorry, may I speak to you, please?'

I suppressed irritation, unlocked the door, and, with a manner as warm as I could muster, indicated that Hassid should enter too. At first I didn't register what was wrong with the room. Then I saw that the plate for the sandwiches, on which Elizabeth Cruikshank had stayed her savage appetite, was still on the floor, along with an empty mug and glass. The waste bin had not been emptied, the chairs had not been aligned into their customary military precision, the whole room smelled of whisky and had the disordered air of use.

Lennie's attentions entailed a fascist-like efficiency. That he hadn't been in was obvious. But then I had asked him to leave the room till the following day.

'It's Lennie,' Hassid said, apparently extracting, with his conjuror's skill, the name from my mind. 'He's gone.'

Oh Christ! I thought. Not now, please.

'How do you know, Hassid? Maybe he just hasn't been in today. Maybe he's unwell.'

'No, Doctor. Lennie is never ill, believe me.' Hassid's expression, portraying superior insight, was ever so slightly smug. 'It is Dr Mackie. Lennie has gone. Vamoosed.' He gestured with the elegant hand. 'Believe me.'

Jesus wept! Another matter I was going to have to deal with.

'What happened, Hassid?'

Hassid's glance was wandering to the blue chair, so I indicated that he should sit down and told him to spill the beans. Thinking of beans, I noticed the coffee machine still bore the dregs of the previous evening's marathon.

'Would you like some coffee, Hassid?'

'Gosh, thanks, Doctor.'

'It's cold. That all right for you?'

There was only one clean mug, which I gave to him while I used the mug Elizabeth Cruikshank had drunk from. Hassid accepted the mug of cold stale coffee graciously. Maybe he imagined the British medical profession preferred their coffee cold. As he settled himself in the blue chair, nursing a slender ankle across his knee, it crossed my mind that maybe he was homosexual and that this was potentially a contributing factor to his breakdown. One I may have overlooked. We'd touched on girls a little, but in deference to his religion, I had treated his diffidence as a cultural rather than a physical or affectional matter.

And then into my mind erupted a rogue voice, which uttered this heresy. I don't care! it announced. I don't care any longer what Hassid's, or anyone's, sexual preferences are, or whether they matter to them or not.

But despite this voice, I cared about Lennie's whereabouts, so while I sipped the disagreeably cold and bitter coffee – which I took a perverse pleasure in drinking – in my twice-worn shirt

and underclothes and socks – matters over which I am fastidious –
I listened to Hassid's story.

'It was your car, Doctor. Lennie found Dr Mackie putting a
note on it.'

So I was right about the author of that prissy note. 'What
happened, Hassid?'

'There were fisticuffs, Doctor.'

This wonderfully old-world word brought an involuntary grin
to my tired face.

'You mean they had a fight?' My smile must have broadened.
The idea of Mackie and Lennie in a punch-up was cheering me
up no end.

'I would say that Lennie was doing most of the hitting, Doctor. Dr Mackie didn't do so much.'

Lennie, Hassid explained, with the glee of one who brings
distressing news, had argued with Mackie and in the course of
the wrangle had become so incensed that he had hit the doctor.
Mackie had rung the police while Lennie, showing, to my mind,
great good sense, had scarpered.

'And this was all over my car?'

'Yes, Doctor. Lennie didn't like that Dr Mackie was complaining
about it. He wanted to come and see you, Dr Mackie did, but
Lennie said you were with somebody. He stopped him. Dr Mackie
shouldn't have insisted, should he, while you were with someone,
even if it was late and after hours? It was Mrs Cruikshank, wasn't it?'

It's not only Jane Austen's world that's a neighbourhood of
voluntary spies. But curiosity is one index of mental health.
High time, I thought, for Hassid to be returned to the student
environment.

'Do you have any idea of where Lennie might have gone,
Hassid?'

'No, Doctor. But he gave me this, so I think he was not
thinking of coming back.'

Hassid dug in his trouser pocket and produced a rosette in the blue and white Brighton colours. 'Dr Mackie asked me to stay and watch Lennie while he rang the police. He tried to get Lennie to come inside with him, but Lennie said he wouldn't. He said he "weren't no bleeding loony."' Lennie's thick voice emerged unmistakably through Hassid's lucid accent. So Hassid had a talent for mimicry too. Well, as I'd been noting, you never knew what people had in them . . . 'Then he gave me this and said, "Great knowing you, kiddo," and ran. Dr Mackie was angry with me, but I am not a policeman and I do not think he was entitled to ask me to restrain Lennie. I am one of the "bleeding loonies," after all,' Hassid concluded politely.

For all my concern I had to laugh, and did so a little too raucously. I would have to sort it out with Mackie. After all, I was to blame for the badly parked car. What with one thing and another the gods were ensuring that Nemesis was having a field day with me: Lennie, though not one of our inmates, was a registered outpatient and technically my responsibility.

I rang Mackie's number, got no reply, rang my secretary, Trish, and left her a message, and then went to reception to see if they could throw light on Mackie's whereabouts.

'Oh, Dr McBride, one of your patients left this for you.' Maureen, our receptionist, handed me an envelope, and although the handwriting was unfamiliar, the second I saw it, I guessed who it was from.

It was an italic hand in brown ink, and when I opened the envelope I looked at the signature for confirmation. There wasn't much else to detain the eye, for all that was written on the postcard inside were three lines.

Dear David,
Thank you.
Elizabeth Cruikshank

I turned the postcard over, but it was only a faded sepia print of Brighton Pier, the kind I'd seen plentifully on sale in the hospital shop.

'When did she go?' I had left a message for Mackie and hurried, as if my life depended on it, over to Elizabeth Cruikshank's ward.

'I'm sorry, Dr McBride, I should have said.' Maguire looked anxious. 'She left this morning, after you went, ever so quietly. She packed her stuff up and just went. We couldn't stop her, could we? She asked for you and I explained you were called away and we couldn't say when you would be back. She said she had to go, and anyway, you would know she would be gone.'

Had I known? Perhaps I had. Perhaps that was what I had understood when I had experienced that terrible sense of dereliction on the Downs.

It dawned on me that in all the world this was the person I was closest to. Closer than I'd been to anyone save Jonny. I had left the gap he had made unfilled, that door in my soul ajar. But it was through it, through the door which I had never closed, that Elizabeth Cruikshank had walked back into the known world. And somehow, in that process, she had closed the way behind her and shut Jonny out.

How this had happened, what strange emotional logic this betrayed, I couldn't begin to fathom, still less comprehend. But I felt the consequences as rudely and forcefully, and, it seemed, as mortally as if someone near and dear to me had taken a twelve-bore and shot it, point-blank, into my chest. I think I may even have gasped aloud and stooped over with the pain of it, because Maguire said, 'Are you all right, Doctor? They can't blame you for this one, surely? She was voluntary.' And because of all that had happened, and because of who Maguire was, and because even if she didn't understand why I felt as I did, and could never understand, I knew she wouldn't judge me, I put my hand on her shoulder and said, 'Cath, would you just give me a hug?' I needed to know that someone was there. And good old Maguire hugged me as hard and as close as if I were a long-lost sweetheart come home.

'I always said you were wasted on women!' I didn't bother to conceal the fact that for the third time that day there were tears in my eyes. 'Get away, you great flirt,' Maguire said, and I smacked her behind and we both blushed, from which I deduced that she wasn't as lesbian as she made out.

I found Mackie, finally, taking a late lunch in the canteen. He was forking fish fingers into his mouth, and the sadist in me noted a blotch of ketchup on the white collar of his neat blue-striped shirt. My sensitive nose was conscious that my own shirt stank rancorously of sweat.

'Colin,' I said, aware, in contrast to Mackie, that I presented a pretty crumpled sight and purposely the more genial. 'I've been looking for you. I owe you an apology for my car.' And, God forgive me, I believe I beamed.

Mackie looked uncomfortable. He was the type who, aggressive himself, is at a loss to know how to deal with cordiality in others, however assumed.

'McBride! I'm afraid events have evolved, ah, unfortunately.'

'Oh dear,' I said, disingenuously. 'I hope I didn't inconvenience you too much?'

'I'm afraid you did. You saw my note?'

'I did and I would have come to apologise but –'

Mackie waved this aside. 'That cleaner of yours –' Seeing me raise my eyebrows, he adjusted: 'I should say, ours. He behaved most aggressively over my placing the note on your windscreen. I'm sorry to tell you, he attacked me. I've had to bring a charge of assault, of course.'

'Oh dear,' I said, 'I am so sorry. I feel responsible.'

'No, no, how could you –'

'But I do, Colin.' (I applied the Christian name like a poultice.) 'Technically, he's my patient. Of course we employ him too, but obviously I must take full responsibility if his medication is proving inadequate.'

'What's he on?' As I had hoped, Mackie's professional instincts began to engage.

'Modecate, a hundred mil, monthly.'

'Ought to be holding him,' Mackie said. 'You might try reducing the interval to three weeks, I suppose. How long has he been on it?'

'Pretty much since he fetched up here about three years ago. But look, he's your line of country. I'd welcome your thoughts. I shouldn't dream of trying any talking stuff on him.'

Mackie was visibly thawing, so I pushed on while I had an advantage. 'As a matter of fact, I was thinking of using him as an example of what we can't do with talk alone in the paper I'm giving in Rome. Gus Galen's asked me to give the response to Jeffries. Look, it would be a huge help to me if I could talk some of that stuff through with you.'

This was not sheer guff, for as I was speaking I was allowing myself to become aware of something, something which, unwilling to acknowledge, I had pushed out of consciousness till now: Mackie was lonely. Mackie, in his way, was as lonely as I was. I knew nothing about him, of his life away from the hospital, and I had never attempted to discover anything. I had played on his hostility as a justification for my own dislike, but in truth I had been an accessory to the bad feeling between us. I had discouraged him because he made me feel discouraged. And discouragement, like every other emotional emission, is contagious.

But so is its opposite.

'I've not spoken to the police, as such,' Mackie was now saying. 'They were too tied up last evening – would you believe?'

'It would be a kindness to me if you could see your way to dropping it,' I said. And this time my cordiality wasn't faked. 'I've had a hell of a day, to tell you the truth.' I sketched for him an outline of the St Stephen's disaster.

Mackie took his glasses off and rubbed his eyes, and I observed that they were that pale blue colour which fades under spectacles. They were bloodshot, as mine most likely were. 'I had a hell of a day yesterday too. Fact is, my mother's ill. My sister's in Canada and the burden falls on me. I probably overreacted to your car. In the event, the police didn't come out; though it's as well someone wasn't being murdered – sorry, not very tactful in the circumstances! I'm sorry about your St Stephen's man.'

'Thanks. As I needn't tell you, it rather goes with the territory.' I heard Elizabeth Cruikshank's cool voice: *Why do you do this? Is it love or damage?* But mine and Mackie's damage were of different orders and I didn't want to get into the wolf man with him, not even on our new terms. 'I'd be very glad if the police weren't involved. I don't think Lennie's basically violent. He's just got an overprotective thing about me. I'll give him a proper talking-to.'

'Yes, well,' Mackie said, unwilling to relinquish a justified grievance too readily. 'If it happens again I'll be forced to do something. He gave me a very nasty knock.'

'I'm sorry,' I said again. 'Where did he hit you?' Other than the ketchup stain, there was no obvious mark on Mackie's impeccably turned-out person.

'It was in the, ah, stomach,' Mackie said primly; from which I deduced that Lennie's blow had in fact landed rather lower down.

Poor Mackie. Poor Lennie. Poor all of us, if we but knew it, blindly crawling along our parallel lines, unmindful that all around there are others as much in need of comfort and consolation.

'Come by my room sometime and we can chew things over,' I suggested with a heartiness born of this small victory. I doubted he would. And I had no intention of discussing Lennie at the conference. But I felt relief that the enmity between us had for the moment been dissolved.

Mackie must have been feeling something similar, because he said, awkwardly, 'Surely, yes, I'll do that, thanks, ah, David,' which was the first time he had addressed me by anything other than my surname.

'*What's your other name, Dr McBride?*'

'*David. My family call me Davey.*'

'*I prefer David.*'

'*You can call me David if you like.*'

Suddenly, I was overwhelmingly, unavoidably, uncopably tired. Too tired almost to stand. I bade a comradely farewell to Mackie, returned to reception, where I rang through to Trish and told her to cancel my afternoon appointments. I offered no explanation for this and she asked for none. It was the first time I had taken more than an hour off in all the time she had worked for me. I imagine she was too astonished to voice any reaction.

Mackie's Ford was parked with anal precision by my Renault and I was dismayed to see the figure of Hassid parked there beside it.

'Hassid?'

'Doctor, I was thinking –'

Enough was enough. 'I've spoken to Dr Mackie, Hassid. He's very kindly agreed to drop any charges against Lennie, so if you can think of how we might track him down, would you put your mind to it for me? I'd be very grateful.'

I inched out of the narrow space with the added impediment of Hassid's magisterial beckoning, but I was now fully alive to the dangers the day might harbour, and for Lennie's sake, I paid special attention to my reversing. I didn't want anything to foul up the truce with Mackie.

As I was about to pull away Hassid halted me with an imperious hand.

I wound down the window. 'What is it, Hassid?'

'Please, Doctor, it is Mrs Cruikshank.'

'Yes?' I was ready to be openly annoyed.

'Sister Maguire says she has left us. But she had not returned all her books to the library, I'm afraid.'

'Never mind, Hassid,' I said, and now the tears which threatened my composure were born of sheer fatigue. 'If you let me know what they are I'll undertake to replace any that are missing.'

I continued to monitor my driving on the short journey home. Olivia would be at the shop, so an oasis of potential peace lay before me. I was planning a sandwich, a hot bath and – the prospect was celestial – bed.

'Darling,' Olivia's voice greeted me as the front door banged shut. 'Is that you?'

I found her in the living room – with Dan. My school Bible was still lying face down on the corner of the sofa where I'd left it. Dan and Olivia were sitting on the sofa, and some protective instinct made me walk across and close the little book and place it deliberately on a table by the armchair in which I sat down. I said nothing. I hadn't, when it came down to it, anything to say.

'I was passing the shop and Olivia wanted me to run her home,' Dan suggested finally. It wasn't much of an attempt at explanation, so I didn't bother to reply to it, except to raise my eyebrows and look at Olivia.

'I wasn't feeling too well,' Olivia explained.

'Oh,' I said, non-committally. I felt that someone should do better than this and it wasn't going to be me.

'Yes,' Dan said. He looked dreadfully awkward. 'So, I brought her home.'

'Yes,' I said. 'I see.'

'I wasn't feeling well,' Olivia repeated.

I wondered how much longer we were going to go on in this vein. I felt completely detached, remote, unfussed, even a little kindly towards them. It wasn't my scrape and I was mildly interested to see how they were going to get out of it. The only thing I felt strongly about at that moment was a sandwich and my bath.

I got up. 'Don't go!' Dan said, and simultaneously Olivia said, 'Darling!'

'I'm getting myself something to eat,' I explained. 'I'm starving.'

When I came out of the kitchen Dan was standing by the window jingling his keys. He was a terrible fidget and Bar often teased him about it. I wondered how Bar was and what, if anything, she and Dan had talked about the previous evening.

'Look, I'd better be off,' Dan said abruptly. 'I've patients to see . . .' He didn't ask what I was doing home in the middle of the afternoon. He would have known I must have patients to see too.

'Sure,' I said. And sat down with my sandwich.

Olivia saw Dan to the door, where they exchanged a few words, and then came back and sat on the sofa with her feet up while I went on chewing my sandwich. It wasn't bad, cream cheese with cucumber, and a lot of pepper, though it struck me that I'd had rather a lot of sandwiches lately. When I'd finished, I got up to take the plate into the kitchen and went to run a bath. I undressed in the bedroom, put on my dressing gown, and was going across to the bathroom when Olivia called out, 'Darling.'

I thought of ignoring this, because I really did want that bath very badly, but habit is a hard taskmaster, so I called back a reluctant 'Yes?'

'Darling, will you come and talk to me?'

'I've just run a bath.'

'Would you like me to soap your back?'

This time I ignored the taskmaster. 'No,' I said. 'I wouldn't, thanks,' and I went into the bathroom and locked the door. I think it may have been the first time it had been locked except by visitors.

I lay for a long time in the bath, topping it up with draughts of hot water as soon as the temperature dropped below the level of just less than scalding and stuffing my toes alternately into the hot and cold tap, as I have done since I was a child.

I didn't try to think what I was going to say to Olivia, or how she was going to approach me. I didn't have to try not to think. My mental processes had been reduced to a state which appeared to have lost touch with any personal emotion. It was as if I had been filled from top to toe with mud, and the mud was slowly solidifying inside me. It was a dull sort of feeling but not uncomfortable. Possibly those who have been lobotomised feel somewhat the same.

When I surrendered my bathroom retreat, my first hopeful thought was that Olivia had gone out. The sitting room and kitchen were empty, but when I went to the bedroom, to my annoyance I found her undressed in bed.

'Actually,' I said, 'I was hoping to get some sleep. I didn't sleep too much last night.'

'I'll snuggle down with you,' Olivia said.

Over my dead body, I said inwardly. 'I'll take a nap on the sofa, then.'

'Darling,' said Olivia, 'I do love you.'

If, rather than what she had been doing with Dan, she had

sat up all night debating with him how to rile me most, she could hardly have achieved a wilder success. But I was too tired and too detached even to attempt to indicate as much, so I just said, 'Oh?' as unenthusiastically as I knew how.

'Darling Davey,' Olivia said.

'What is it, Olivia? What would you like to say to me?' Resigned, I watched the chimerical prospect of sleep slide away.

'Darling, I do love you,' Olivia said again.

I stood there, slightly damp in my dressing gown, not even especially annoyed this time. I kept thinking of Elizabeth Cruikshank and her Thomas shouting at her, shouting because he loved her, and crying, and then dying without her; and how hard it is to find love, and how harder still to be loved, or believe you are loved; and how often and how easily, and cheaply and wantonly, the word 'love' is abused. And – and this, as I stood there, struck me as almost the most pitiful fact of all – how much more conditioned we sorry beings are to respond to the sham, the pinchbeck which parades as love but isn't love at all.

Olivia didn't love me. She was, I suddenly understood, afraid. I wasn't sure of what, unless it was the humiliation of being found out over Dan, but that she was afraid I knew for sure. And hard behind that recognition came a debilitating ennui; for I felt myself about to be bound fast by those invisible cords of compassion which constrain us more tightly than love.

'Olivia,' I said, 'I am so tired I can hardly stay upright. I want more than anything just now to go to sleep. If you have anything to say to me, please would you say it? Whatever it is, I won't mind. I don't mind anything right now except how extraordinarily tired I am and how much I would like to sleep for a few hours, preferably on my own, undisturbed.'

'I'm pregnant,' Olivia said, with what seemed at the time startling simplicity, though afterwards, when I thought about it, I wondered what other words she could have used.

4

It turned out that I didn't get much sleep that night either, but I never cared so much as I did that afternoon when I stood by the bed and had my world pulled down around my exhausted head for the third time in a day. After a while, you go over some sort of ridge with sleep and then you feel you will never sleep again.

My first impulse when Olivia broke this news to me was to laugh. I think, in fact, I did laugh, and then I sat down on the bed next to her, naked in our bed, mostly because the news had knocked out what stuffing there was left in me. Hadn't I twice already that day remarked to myself that you never knew what others had in them till it was revealed?

'Darling,' Olivia said, 'I don't know what to do.'

This might have annoyed me again, because its helplessness was guaranteed to evoke my sympathy. But, oddly enough, I believe that Olivia, for all her skill at manipulation, wasn't alive to that element in my character. She was too unacquainted with such feelings herself.

'No,' I agreed. She was nearly forty-three. We'd stopped using any contraception a while ago. Not that we'd had many occasions not to use it.

I was wondering whether she was assuming that I knew about her and Dan when she said, 'Would you like it if we had a baby?'

'I don't know,' I said, unwilling to be drawn. And then, to get it over with, 'Do you know whose the baby is?'

To her credit, she blushed and said, 'What d'you mean?' sulkily, more like the Olivia I knew and had pretended to love.

'I mean,' I said, getting up from the bed, 'is the child likely to be mine or Dan's? It does have a bearing on my feelings about it.'

To my relief, she didn't attempt to refute the implication but asked, 'How did you know?' and continued to look sulky.

I was better able to cope with a sulky Olivia, so I simply said, 'Bar and I had a drink together last evening. She'd worked it out.'

I was intrigued to note that at this Olivia looked really alarmed. 'Bar knows?'

'Yes,' I said. 'Bar's shrewd. Are you surprised?'

'Has she told Dan?'

'Heavens, Olivia, how do I know? Bar and I aren't lovers, it's you and Dan who are.' I felt we'd better have things plainly stated.

'You were, though.'

'Were what?'

'Lovers.'

'No, Olivia, don't do that. Just don't do that, all right?' I had detected that she was about to imply that whatever it was with her and Dan was some sort of reaction to a *tendresse* between me and Bar. 'Bar and I are friends and have been for years. We were lovers for about ten minutes.' While you fucked around, I mentally added but managed not to say.

'Has she told Dan?'

'I've no idea,' I said wearily. 'Look, would you like a cup of tea?'

I watched myself bearing a tray, with teacups and milk jug and a pot of tea, to my wife, who had just confessed to conceiving a child possibly by one of my closest friends. I pictured it, even as I was carrying the tray, complete with digestive biscuits – for which Olivia, rather endearingly, suddenly expressed a wish – into the bedroom where, minute by minute, it was seeming less and less likely that I was going to get any sleep. A part of me began at this point to fuss over the time I had taken from the hospital. I had not intended to squander my snatch of freedom in this way.

'Look,' I said to Olivia, who, having delivered her bombshell, showed signs of taking up residence in the bed. 'How pregnant are you? Surely we can work it out from that?' My mind was now engaged in a calculation. I could remember the last time Olivia and I made what is laughingly called 'love': it was the night we dined with the Powells when, with the clarity of hindsight, I now perceived she had already started with Dan. The night I brought up Elizabeth Cruikshank, to avert bad feeling between the pair of them, then regretted it.

Elizabeth, where are you now? How I would prefer to be back in my room, listening to your cool voice, sharing with you the chaste intercourse of minds and hearts, than here in my bedroom with my wife trying to establish the outcome of our last unsatisfactory effort at physical intercourse.

Olivia looked uncomfortable. 'Seven, eight weeks.'

'And,' I pressed, 'when did you and Dan start up?'

'It was the day we had dinner with the Powells,' Olivia said, confirming my intuition with unexpected candour. I thought she had probably forgotten that we also had a brief encounter that same evening, but she surprised me by saying, 'The same night you and I, you know . . .'

'Fuck!' I said, with unusual pertinence, and we both laughed. One trait I liked in Olivia was that when she wasn't being manipulative she wasn't sentimental.

'And Dan?' I asked. The inner monitor coolly noted that I seemed eerily unmoved by my good friend's role in this. 'What does he feel about the child?'

Olivia's face lost its look of momentary openness and became cautious and closed again. 'I don't know.'

'But he knows?' Obviously he knew. That was why he was here at the flat when I so unexpectedly arrived. My guess was that Olivia had come here from the doctor's and summoned him. I was willing to bet that by now he was regretting that he had obeyed her call.

'Yes.'

'So? He must have had some reaction.'

'He was concerned,' Olivia said, taking refuge in the trite.

'But I mean, does he want it? Does he want to go off with you, have you have his child, if it is his child, leave Bar? What?'

Olivia just looked at me and then did something so maddening it was as well there was no blunt instrument handy to beat her over the head with. She wriggled down inside the bed and pulled the eiderdown over her face to hide.

I hadn't finished my cup of tea, but at this I got up, put it carefully down on the chest of drawers, having first found a magazine to place it on – because even though there was a saucer I am neurotic about marking polished surfaces – went across to the bed, and peeled the eiderdown back from Olivia's face. Which looked scared. Maybe she expected me to hit her, I don't know.

'Listen, Olivia,' I said. 'It's like this –' and I could not have said if I was consciously repeating Elizabeth Cruikshank's words to me. 'Yesterday afternoon and much of yesterday evening I spent listening to a woman, a patient, a suicide, I should say a failed suicide, who was describing, in words more poignant than you could grasp, how she had failed to recognise that the man who said he loved her did love her, most sincerely and dearly and genuinely, after all. And by the time she recognised this rare and precious truth, he had died, unaware that she had, at last, perceived the purity of his affection for her. Because of this miserable misunderstanding, she has spent the past years in a state of anguish. So bitter has been her self-reproach that recently she tried, really tried, not just mucking about, to kill herself, because, having passed over the chance of real love, life for her wasn't worth a straw. She is not an hysteric or an attention-seeker. She is, in my judgement, an unusual and remarkable woman, brave enough to recognise her own part in her own misfortune. Having heard her sorrowful tale, I met Bar, who had come to my room looking for Dan, and hoping that she might, by speaking to me, find that the stories he has been fobbing her off with were true. And perhaps because this woman patient of mine had spent the past seven hours telling me the unvarnished truth about herself, something in me allowed Bar also to be able to tell the truth and, maybe for the first time, tell herself the truth, about Dan, and about you and Dan. I am, as you have pointed out, needlessly bitchily, very fond of Bar. She was good to me when you were not and I'm afraid I used her badly. She has never shown a flicker of resentment over that, for which, because I don't deserve such leniency, I offer God, if there is a God, the humblest thanks. Yesterday evening, when she indicated to me what she had for a time suspected, and which, as soon as she disclosed it, we both knew to be the case, I minded, not for myself, odd as that may seem to you, but for Bar, that not content with taking your own husband from her long ago, a man foolish enough to return to you when you clicked your fingers, you felt entitled to take, for reasons which I know nothing of, but I very much doubt are excusable, her husband now as well. All right so far?'

Olivia was looking at me like a frightened weasel, so I continued unabashed.

'Last night, after these two ordeals, both of which were distressing to me, I arrived home, not knowing where you were, that is to say whether, to be frank, you were in our bed alone or in some other bed in some other venue with Dan. I made an as-

sumption, possibly a false one, that you were back in our bedroom – please don't bother to enlighten me, I no longer give a
tinker's cuss for the truth of the matter – but having no wish to
share our bed with my friend's lover, who is also my wife, I spent
a chilly, cramped, and unrestful night on the sofa. This morning,
feeling far from my best, I was summoned to St Stephen's, where
a patient, who has been under my care for years, and for whom
I have developed a sympathy, and whom, as a consequence, I had
attempted to help by releasing him from his previous security
restrictions, had tried to murder a nurse. As a result of this piece
of misjudgement on my part, this man, whose welfare was and
is my responsibility, will spend the rest of his unnatural life in conditions which, when I come to contemplate them, will make
me shudder in my shoes. I have not yet contemplated them because I have not had the strength of mind to force myself to do
so. But I shall have to soon, because soon there will be an inquiry during which I shall be questioned, long and hard, and
probably not very sympathetically, on my motives and reasons
for making this change in a treatment plan which has functioned
perfectly adequately for many years.

'I do not know how I shall begin to answer these questions
because my own motives are still obscure to me. I rather suspect
I may discover they had something to do with some notion I
had of being kind. But also I have a feeling that when I scrutinise
more closely this kindness I am claiming as my motive, it will
prove, at root, to be a kindness not to my patient at all but to
myself. In other words, it was myself I was imagining I was releasing from those security provisions and not my benighted patient. I shall pass over the possible reasons for this confusion in
me since that is not your business or concern.

'When I returned to St Kit's, more than a little undone by
this experience, I found that another patient, also under my
care, had, while I was listening to the story of my would-be sui-

cide, assaulted a colleague, also for reasons connected with me, in this case an attempt, sadly another misplaced one, to do me a kindness, kindness, you may note, if you care to, proving to be a dubious remedy.

'Happily, the nurse whom my patient attacked is not dead. She is bruised and badly scared, but her life remains intact. Happily, too, my colleague has agreed to accept my apologies for my other patient's errant behaviour and not to press charges against him. Happily, though here I am less sanguine, the suicidal patient appears to have recovered sufficiently to discharge herself from hospital. I hope and pray, though, as I say, I cannot be sure of this, that this means that all is well with her. However, all of this, the sum of it, what it means in general, and what, more specifically, it means to and for me, is weighing somewhat heavily on me just now. I understate the position. To be blunt, it has left me impatient with lies and convolutions and falsehoods and evasions of all kinds. To put it more colloquially, it's left me sick and tired of anything which resembles fucking about. You should know that at present fucking about is something I can't take. You can fuck around in your physical person, that I cannot help or change. But you may not fuck about with me in any other sphere.

'Let me tell you what I think. I think that Dan does not want this child, even though the chances are it is his. You and I have been having sex for a number of years, not very often, it's true, but nonetheless when the act has taken place, however inadequately, it has been without our using contraception. So far as I am aware, this has not previously led to any conceptions, unless there are other things you have kept from me?'

Olivia dumbly shook her head.

'Good. So it is on the cards that this is Dan's child and not mine. I also suspect that you want this child if it is Dan's but not if it is mine. After all, we have been there before and I cannot see what in the world would now have made you change your mind. I think that you are worried over whether or not to abort this child because your decision rests not on my reaction, or on me, but on Dan and on his reaction. And I think that in spite of all this you nevertheless wish me to help you sort out this muddle, both in your own mind and also, quite possibly, practically and with Dan.

'So let me now tell you what I propose.'

I paused deliberately and was pleased to note that Olivia looked even whiter than Bar had looked last evening. I had never even remotely spoken to her in this manner before and I hoped, most sincerely, that she was terrified.

'I propose going to spend the night elsewhere. I am not, please note, walking out on you. I could for two pins walk out on you. I could, it may interest you to hear, without difficulty and without disquiet to myself, walk right away from all this and find a slow boat to take me to China. There is very little here to keep me and I am no longer sure I wish to do, or can do, what I have spent my adult life doing, as it now appears to me, ineffectually, possibly even dangerously. However, for the moment, what I want most — if not a night's sleep, which I suspect will not now come easily to me — is at least the chance of some peace and quiet. In which I can think whatever thoughts I may need or elect to think without further interference. I cannot do that lying in bed beside my wife, who may or may not be carrying my child, but who is in any case carrying within her a piece of new life which, for reasons I have no need to adumbrate, may soon be extinguished. To be candid, the thought of that right now is what might induce me to abandon my plans for China and save time and money by simply slitting my wrists. I mean this, by the way: it is not idle chat or fancy rhetoric. So, to avoid that possibility, I am going to collect a few things and take myself off to some local hotel. And tomorrow morning I shall go, as usual, to work. And what I ask of you now is that you say nothing, not one word, not a single word, but allow me to leave this flat quietly and speedily and if, and only if, you do this one thing, then I promise you tomorrow evening I shall return. I shall neither take a boat to China nor will I slit my wrists, however appealing those prospects may seem to me by then, and together we shall rationally discuss the best way of dealing with what you have told me and how we should proceed.'

I had never before addressed even a tenth as many consecutive words to Olivia. Indeed, other than giving an academic paper I doubt I had ever spoken uninterrupted so long to anyone in all my life. I felt as I believe Elizabeth Cruikshank must have felt when she spoke aloud to me the words she had wanted the courage to say when Thomas told her he was moving to Milan.

Olivia said nothing but continued to look at me and then ducked back under the eiderdown, perhaps, I don't know, to stop her mouth.

I was as good as my word. I took a clean shirt, socks and underwear and handkerchief from my father's chest of drawers and packed them into my briefcase. I did not clear away the tea tray, though I felt a strong inclination to clear away my half-drunk cup of tea before I departed. I had a conviction it would be there still on my return. The idea of this irked me, but I let it ride. Before I left, however, I went to the sitting room to look for my fountain pen and something to write in. And perhaps as a result of the frustrated impulse over the teacup, seeing it on the table, I also gathered up the shabby little school Bible.

5

Although my prediction that I would sleep little that night proved accurate, once I had accomplished the task I had set myself I must have dozed off, because I woke with the sensation that a benign presence was tapping me lightly on the shoulder with two hands. I rolled over and registered the hotel curtain gently brushing against my back in the breeze which was blowing through the opened window.

I sat up and switched on Your Friendly Teasmaid and, lying on the bed, drank the blistering hot, utterly tasteless liquid it produced while listening to *The Lark Ascending* on the bedside radio-alarm. Then I shaved and bathed and went down for a pre-breakfast walk.

It was early still, few people were about, but I could see from the light gilding the line of the horizon that the day was about to come up fine. As the sun mounted higher, it made spangles on the sea's surface. I skimmed a few stones over the placid waves and threw a stick to an eager young red cocker spaniel, out with his mistress, a grey-haired woman with formidable legs that looked as if they had been put on upside down. It occurred to me that if I didn't live in a flat I could have a dog. A dog seemed suddenly a heavenly companion.

Back at the Regency Grand, I went to town on breakfast, a different affair from the Dew Drop's but no less ambitious:

grapefruit juice, stewed prunes, porridge, kippers, brown toast (the white, I surmised, being unlikely to be up to Dew Drop standard), and two large pots of ground coffee. 'Two, sir?' The waiter's face was as incurious as the Dew Drop woman's had been otherwise. 'As large as you've got,' I confirmed. I did not, as I sometimes did, feel the need to apologise.

I arrived at work with my face sandpapered by the sea wind. I was early, but I had plenty to catch up on.

The first thing which met me was a room so clean you could have eaten breakfast off the carpet, and my pleasure was doubled when there was a rap at the door and a thick voice said, 'You in, Doc?'

'Lennie!' It was respect for his pride, and not mine, which kept me from hugging him.

'Hey there, Doc! How you doing?'

'Good,' I said. 'And you?'

'Your room was in some state.'

'I know, Lennie. I missed you.'

'Yeah, well, me and Dr Mack had a ding-dong. But that Hassid, he come found me and told me Dr M was ready to let bygones be bygones. Hassid said I could come back and no hassle, right?'

'Right, Lennie. Though you must promise not to hit Dr Mackie, or anyone else, again. It's me who gets it in the neck.'

'Yeah, Doc. Hassid said. He's a bright one, that.'

'He is too.'

'Reckon he'll be moving on soon.'

'Probably.'

Lennie looked out of the window at the quince. Remembering how he had called by when Elizabeth Cruikshank was there, I thought how she had said Lennie was fond of me.

'You know what, Doc. If that kid hadn't come after me, I wouldn't have come back. An' if you hadn't taken the kid in . . . see what I mean?'

'I think so.'

'It's like my Granma says. Everything's connected. You, me, Hassid an' –'

'And Dr Mackie,' I put in swiftly, keen to take advantage of Lennie's grandma's spiritual drift.

'Yeah, right, Dr Mack too. Though I didn't half give him one in –'

'Yes, Lennie, I know,' I said. I felt it best not to dissipate his grandma's good influence by laughing.

I was due to see Hassid for a session that morning and, as an apology for his reception the day before, I greeted him with some decent coffee. He accepted the hot fresh brew as enthusiastically as he had the cold and sat in his customary position, nursing his foot across his knee.

'Well done,' I said with emphasis. 'Very well done indeed about Lennie.'

'I thought about it, Doctor, and then I thought I knew where to find him.' Hassid's voice exuded consciousness of well-merited praise.

'Where was he?'

'Under the second pier, you know? He told me once that this was his spiritual home.'

'Well, well done for finding him. He's lucky to have you as a friend.'

'And I am lucky to have him, Doctor,' said Hassid, with the faintest note of reproof.

'Exactly,' I agreed, perfectly content to be put in my place by an admonishing Hassid. 'By the way, something I wanted to ask. Have I got this right? Electrons have no material reality but are called into existence by us when we measure them?'

'Yes, that is right.'

'So in a sense they depend on us for their existence.'

Hassid looked uneasy. 'Maybe, but –'

'But they don't figure, do they, in our reality until we set about looking for them?'

'I suppose not, yes.'

'And yet you would say they exist, wouldn't you?'

'Certainly they exist, Doctor.'

'Thank you, Hassid. That's helped me.'

'Doctor, I am glad to be of assistance to you.'

'Hassid, do you think you might be ready to go back to university next term?'

'I think I would like to, Doctor. Once I have been home to see my family in Karachi.'

'Good.'

'Oh, Doctor, Mrs Cruikshank's book, you know –'

'Yes, I said I would replace it.'

'Sister Maguire says there is no need. She says the book is not important. She says that Mrs Cruikshank is welcome to it.'

'Yes,' I said. 'I think we can probably spare Mrs Cruikshank one of our books. I need to sort my own out. I've a load of paperbacks I'll never read again. I'll bring them in. Maybe you would like to catalogue them for the library before you go?'

'I would be glad to, Doctor.'

'Thank you, Hassid.' I felt that a subtle shift had occurred and that Hassid had taken on the role of my informal assistant. 'Would you like more coffee?'

'No thank you, Doctor. In fact, I do not really like coffee so much.'

'Oh.'

'But Lennie gave me some of his spirit to drink under the pier.' Hassid gave me the benefit of his perfect smile.

'Be careful, Hassid. I don't know what it was but –'

'I had only a little. A drop. Whisky. It is good stuff, no?'

'Yes,' I said. 'It is good stuff. As long as you don't overdo it. Though I expect you will. Most of us do, once we start.'

I worked through to the end of the day, deliberately avoiding any thought of Olivia and our meeting. I had no idea what I would say, or what was going to transpire. I wanted to call Bar, but Trish had mentioned that Dan wasn't in today, so I felt maybe they were embroiled in their own conversation and she wasn't ready to talk.

As I was leaving my room, the phone rang. It rang twice, stopped, and then rang again. I was in half a mind to leave it but something in the pattern of hesitancy made me pick it up. There was a silence at first at the other end and then I blessed my intuition.

'David?'

'Elizabeth.'

'I'm glad I've got you.'

'I'm glad too. I was just leaving, as a matter of fact.'

'I wondered if you might be.'

'Did you hope I would have gone so that you could have rung without having to speak to me?' A silence. 'Elizabeth?'

'It's all right. I was just thinking how well you know me.'

'I'm glad you didn't miss me,' I said.

'I'm glad too, now I've got you.'

'Well then,' I said, and waited.

'I would have come to see you before I left but –'

'It's all right,' I said. 'I know. I was called away. Oddly enough, it was the same person I had to see when I missed that session with you whenever it was.' To my surprise, I realised that it was less than a week ago.

'I minded that.'

'Yes?'

'But if I hadn't, maybe I wouldn't have said what I said.'

'Maybe,' I said. 'But I think there were things I needed to say first.'

'Yes?'

'I think I needed to say I minded too.'

'That's how things work, isn't it?'

'I think it probably is.' I decided not to introduce Lennie's grandma's take on things, but offered a mental nod of approval in her direction. 'We catch things from each other.'

'Yes,' she conceded. 'Good and bad.'

There was a pause again, but this time it was my turn to respond. 'So you're all right?'

'As all right as I'll ever be. There's always going to be a bit of me that's not quite right.'

'Well, for what it's worth, I would say that's pretty all right. It's all right by me, anyway. But then there's always going to be that bit of me that's not quite right too.'

'Thank you. That's nice of you.'

'What?'

'To say that. And to hear that someone I trust thinks I'm fairly sane.'

'I mean it. Actually, I think you're more all right that way than if you were quite right, if you see what I mean. At least from where I stand.' I was, in fact, standing. I was standing by my desk and I had Jonny's bell in my hand. Seeing her play with it two nights ago, I realised how rarely I touched it.

'Thank you,' she said again.

'Elizabeth, where are you? I mean, are you with someone, is someone looking after you?'

'I'm with Max. He's been very kind. I told him how I'd come to be unwell. He didn't seem to mind.'

'Why would he? He's your son.'

'Well, you know . . .'

'Yes,' I said. 'I do know. I know how it is not to expect anyone to understand, or be kind. In fact, I know quite a lot about how you feel.'

'Yes,' she said, 'I think you do. That's why I could speak to you. Because you knew.'

'Elizabeth, there's something I've been pondering.'

'Yes?'

'I haven't quite got the words for it but I think when you believe something, I mean really believe it, it becomes real or, rather, it calls what is real into being. It's entertaining the belief which makes it real. I'm putting this badly, because I've not found a way of expressing it for myself yet; it's something I've been thinking about, partly because of what Hassid has been telling me, or trying to, about the nature of reality.'

'I like Hassid. I'm sorry I wasn't very chatty with him.'

'I don't think he minded. Hassid's pretty robust underneath.'

'Which reminds me, I took a library book away with me. I'll send it back.'

'Yes, Hassid mentioned it.'

She laughed. 'Did he think I'd stolen it?'

'Hassid's morality is still somewhat rigid, but we're working on it.' Or Lennie was. 'Anyway, look, keep the book, if it's any use to you. A present from St Christopher's.' I meant this as a sort of joke, but there was another silence at the other end. 'Elizabeth?'

'Yes, I'm here. What were you saying about reality?'

'Oh, so far as I can understand what Hassid says, reality isn't material at all – in fact, nothing is – but let's say, or he seems to be saying, some essence of it depends upon its being perceived for it to exist. We make it exist. Or our consciousness does. Or, anyway, consciousness. Do you follow me?'

'I'm not sure.'

'I'm putting it badly. We need Hassid.'

'No, we don't. You're doing fine. Go on.'

'I don't know if I can say more except, yes, I think, very often, you, we, need a witness, or a companion, someone else to entertain the belief with, because, well, maybe because it's too hard to believe on our own. Because we don't want to face other things on our own. I wanted to tell you: I never met Thomas except through you. But I believe what you told me he said was real. I believe he loved you. I believe it not because you were trying to make me believe it but because I felt you believed it while you were telling me. You made me believe it by your telling me.' There was another silence at the other end again, so I said, 'Elizabeth? Are you there?'

And the familiar voice said, 'Yes, I'm here. Thank you. And thank you for saying it was real. You're right, it became real when I told you. It's a funny thing. I believed it, but also I didn't believe it. But it became real when I told you,' she said again.

'So, you'll be all right now, you think? Or as all right as . . .'

'I'll ever be? Maybe, just about.'

'Well, you know where I am. And this is my home number, in case you need it.' As I started to give her my number I considered and then added, 'Look, may I give you Gus Galen's number too? You can always try me at either the hospital or home, but it's possible I may be moving and Gus will always be able to put you in touch with me. You can say you're the Caravaggio person. That's how he knows you. I hope you don't mind.'

'No, I don't mind. Thank you for the numbers.'

'No,' I said. 'I want you to have them. Have you got something to write on?'

'I'll write them in Thomas's notebook so I won't lose them.'

'I'm honoured.'

'Thomas would like what you said just now.'

'I like Thomas. He's real.'

'Yes,' she said. 'I think he is. Did you have a hangover?'

'No, fortunately something happened to distract me. I should have done. Did you?'

'No. I slept like the dead.' We both laughed. 'I shan't forget our evening, David.'

'Neither shall I, Elizabeth,' I said.

PART IV

But who is that on the other side of you?

1

Gus's medical instincts hadn't deserted him. His PSA levels rose unacceptably and in the last week of March he was in hospital for a prostate operation. I visited him in the Middlesex, one of the big old central London hospitals near Gower Street.

I hadn't seen Gus since the night in early December when I was to act as a witness on Hannan's behalf and I spoke to him, in my despair, of Elizabeth Cruikshank. She must have stayed in his mind, because once we'd discussed his treatment – on which subject he was, in turn, scornfully dismissive and touchingly appreciative – and I had delivered, under instruction, the bottle of single malt in a brown paper bag – 'Stick it in the locker, dear boy, next to the incontinence pads' – she was the first topic he raised.

'How's the Caravaggio woman?'

'I don't know. Or rather, I do. She left. She left, in fact, three days after I saw you last December.'

'Really?' said Gus. 'Tell.' His face shone with curiosity.

I wanted to put my arms round his shoulders, suddenly vulnerable in their washed-out old flannel pyjamas, and tell him that he was one of the best things that had ever happened to me. But I knew he would rather hear about Elizabeth Cruikshank, so instead I said, 'It was you who were responsible, in fact. All your fault, old man,' because I guessed this would really get him going.

'How?'

'Caravaggio,' I explained. And then, because suddenly I didn't really want to get him going while he was still poorly but preferred to tell him, when he was well and ready for it, all that had occurred between me and Elizabeth Cruikshank during those long seven hours, I said, 'Look, when are they letting you loose again on the suffering world?' and Gus said, 'Next Wednesday, if their word is anything to go by,' so I said, 'Would you mind if I came and fetched you and took you back to your flat and tucked you up in bed and spoiled you a bit, and then I can tell you all about it without feeling I'm being a drain.'

Gus said, 'I'm not fussed about the tucking-up, but you're welcome to prop me up when I totter forth from this bloody graveyard.'

So that was settled. He seemed quite tickled by our arrangement and disconcerted me by asking after Olivia. To my recollection, he'd never said a word about her before.

'Ah,' I said. 'Olivia and I are parting.' Gus didn't look too bothered at this news so I continued. 'I wouldn't tell anyone else but she had a mishap which ended in an abortion, not a very easy one, as things turned out.' Poor Olivia. When I collected her from the nursing home, she looked so forlorn I nearly went back on all we'd agreed. But with a reserve which I found painful, and a dignity which left me regretful, she had insisted we stick to plan. 'She's better now. She's still at the flat and I'm staying with friends.' With Chris and Denis Powell, who had taken me in with almost no questions. It's asking too much of people that they should ask no questions at all, I suppose.

'I'm sorry to hear that,' Gus said. He looked sad.

'It wasn't my child.'

Gus brightened at this and asked, 'Anyone we know?'

'A colleague.'

'Funny,' said Gus. 'That happened to me. Wife got banged up by a research assistant of mine. Bad story. He turned out to be a scoundrel, I could have told her that. Brilliant mind. Corrupt heart. They often hang together, have you noticed? Women find it sexy.'

'I'm sorry,' I said. 'I had no idea.'

'Why would you? I never speak about it. I can't have kids, so I didn't blame her.'

'I've always imagined you as something of a Lothario.'

'I hope I've better things to do than flash my dick around,' said Gus coldly.

'Sorry,' I said. 'I don't know what possessed me to say that.'

'That's all right,' said Gus. 'I'm grateful for the vote of confidence. You saw my wife once, as a matter of fact. We were walking down Shaftesbury Avenue and you pretended not to see me.'

'Was that your wife?' I didn't bother to explain my evasion.

'That's her.'

'I thought she was beautiful.'

'Tanya? Yes, very beautiful.'

I got Gus out of the Middlesex with not a little trouble. He had me pack his things in a number of flimsy plastic bags and dropped the half-drunk bottle of expensive malt I'd smuggled in for him after insisting on carrying it out himself. It smashed, embarrassingly, on the tiled floor by the lifts on the way out. A bevy of nurses appeared, not to scold, but to fuss round and tell Gus he mustn't mind and how much they would miss him. One, a very pretty brunette, hugged him quite possessively, so I felt less apologetic for my philanderer diagnosis.

The snuff-coloured flat was freezing cold and smelled of sardines and escaping gas from the aged gas fire. There was no central heating, as Gus had a theory it was damaging to the mucous lining of the nasal passages, so I lit the fire to an alarming roar and smell of burning dust and forced open a few windows with the aid of a bent screwdriver, which I found under his bed in a green Clarks shoebox containing various rusting tools, some old cigarette cards, and a packet of perished condoms. I didn't succeed in tucking Gus into the bed but, as by now it was almost evening – he had forbidden me to lose a morning's work and I hadn't got to the hospital till late afternoon – I settled him into the peeling rhinoceros chair, poured him a large, and legitimate, glass of Scotch, and asked if he'd any requests for supper.

'Can you cook?'

'I seem to have acquired the habit lately' – in the last few months, since Olivia and I had decided to go our separate ways and when the solicitous Chris Powell would let me. I think I'd always been fearful before that if I did anything domestic it would in some way show Olivia up.

'You know what, all the time I was in that bloody graveyard I've been fantasising about scrambled eggs. Think you can rise to that?'

'Nothing easier,' I said. 'I'll nip out and get some eggs and stuff.'

I walked down Marylebone High Street and bought eggs, smoked salmon, cream, butter, bread, and milk from the supermarket and was just in time to catch the French patisserie, which was shutting up shop. A charming girl held the till for me while I havered and finally bought one of those deceptively thin dark chocolate cakes which conceal prodigious quantities of calories. I had a hunch Gus had a weakness for chocolate. Most whisky drinkers have.

When I got back, he was drowsing in the chair, so I went to the kitchen and washed up the dirty dishes and saucepans as best I could with a filthy sponge mop and then set about supper.

'Here we are. Scrambled egg on toast and smoked salmon.'

'Blimey!' said Gus, awake in a trice. 'It's almost worth having your bloody prostate out!'

He perked up still more at the sight of the cake and had

eaten two wedges with a cup of coffee, of which I found a supply in a biscuit tin sporting a picture of *The Stag at Bay*, before he
said, 'Righto then, tell me about this woman you're in love with.'

'Which woman?' For a moment I wondered if he'd misun-
derstood and meant Olivia.

'The Caravaggio one.'

'I'm not in love with her,' I protested. But I flushed.

'You are,' Gus said, licking his fingers disgustingly. 'It's not
what baboons call "in love," but that's what it is. I knew it when
you spoke about her here before.'

'What did you know?'

'That it was love you were in. I felt for you.'

'How? Why?'

'How did I know, or why did I feel? It's a thing you can't
fake. Unmissable if you know the signs. And I felt for you because it's the one thing we don't want.'

'But surely people always want love?' But as so often with
Gus, once he had said it, I knew what he meant.

'They don't. They want candyfloss and reassurance. They want
security and pats on the back and someone to tuck them up in
bed and cuddle them. Love isn't that. It's difficult. And demanding.
And a nuisance. And bloody absent much of the bloody time.'

'Did you love Tanya?'

'Don't know,' Gus said, licking his fingers some more while
I wished he wouldn't. 'Possibly. I've never loved anyone else, for
all my reputation!' I was relieved to note that he had elected to
take my Lothario comment as a compliment. 'Maybe I did. She
was certainly difficult. Bloody difficult! And a nuisance. And demanding. And certainly bloody well absent much of the time.'

'But love comes in so many different forms,' I suggested, not
very originally and more for something to say, because really I was
dying to hear more about this wife.

'No, it doesn't,' Gus said. 'That's just something made up by baboons to avoid feeling uncomfortable. Basically, love is always the same. I don't mean it's all dicks and fannies. Love isn't being up some fanny. Or arsehole.' I didn't at the time, but later, recalling this, I laughed out loud, because it conveyed something very characteristic of Gus: that even in the heat of this conversation he was trying to be even-handed about sodomy, of which I sensed he secretly disapproved. 'All that obsession with sex is a load of shite, thank you, Dr Freud!' Gus's expression suggested that if perchance Freud were concealed behind the grubby velvet curtains he'd better stay put if he hoped to escape a thrashing. 'Love is perfectly singular. It simply moulds itself to the person – obviously you don't show love to a babe in arms the way you do to your mistress. But in essence it's the same.'

'And what is it, in essence?' I asked, not expecting an answer.

'Not never having to say you're sorry, or shite like that, for a start,' Gus said. 'Got any more of that cake?'

'Have you any napkins?' The chocolatey fingers were still bothering me.

'Christ, I've no idea. If I have, I haven't a clue where they are. Love might well be what I feel for this chocolate cake. Thank you, dear boy. It's much appreciated.'

After this, I felt mean about the chocolatey fingers and, ceasing to object, as always, I ceased to mind.

'Love,' resumed Gus, when he had bolted another portion, 'is letting be. Letting the other be as they are. Like you with the napkins.' Of course my agitation had not escaped his notice. 'Wanting to help them be that, not by doing anything – you can't *do* anything for anyone anyway – but simply by wanting them to be nothing other than they are, because that's who they are so that is how you want them to be: as they are, whatever that may be. Just that. Easy-peasy, I don't think.'

'No,' I said. 'Or rather yes, it's not easy.'

'But,' said Gus, 'sometimes it is. That's the thing. Sometimes it's all you want in the world and you're prepared to fight for it. To death. Your own, if need be. You were fighting for that Caravaggio woman. And in a particular way.'

'What way?'

'Against yourself. You were prepared to take on yourself for her. That's how I knew.'

I told him then all that Elizabeth Cruikshank had told me, as much as I could remember, and some, no doubt, which I couldn't remember – because I believe now that truth is more than the accurate recall of events but something more elusive, less accountable – much as, after leaving Olivia, I had written it out for myself that long satisfying night that I spent alone in the Regency Grand. And I told him, too, of the subsequent events, as I had also tried to set them down, of my wolf man, and Lennie and Colin Mackie and Hassid, and Bar and Dan and Olivia. And also Jonny.

I explained how I had understood for the first time, that evening I spent with Elizabeth Cruikshank, my part in Jonny's death and how I had stood on the high Downs, at the moment when she might have been leaving St Christopher's, and howled to the uncomprehending gulls.

'You would. I told you, the heart registers what's what before the mind can say "Fiddlesticks!"'

'The thing is, Jonny seems to have gone. All my life he's been there – or not been there, but the not being there has been a presence, d'you see?'

'Are you saying she took him with her?'

'Not exactly.' It wasn't that. Elizabeth Cruikshank had taken nothing from me.

'You know what?' Gus said. He had polished off the cake and was running his forefinger round the plate. 'Exchange is no robbery.' He picked up the plate as if he were about to lick it and then put it down and grinned. 'I love tormenting you.

You're a doddle to torment. Know what it is about you? You're one of those odd birds who's supremely tolerant about the stuff that most people get their knickers in a tangle over. And then suddenly there's some tiny thing you can't abide that drives you nuts. I love that in you.' Gus was suddenly serious.

'Not many would,' I said.

'You know what? You're wrong about that. You're unusually loveable.'

'I've never thought so.'

'No,' said Gus. 'You wouldn't. Of course, that's partly why you're loveable. But it's also the other.'

'What other?'

'The other side of you.'

'What other side?'

'What passes for your brother,' Gus said cryptically. 'Or what did pass. Has passed, from what you say. You may or may not have been the cause of his death – who's to say that your memory of things now is any more accurate than it was before? You won't ever know.'

'I think I've been expiating his death all my life,' I said. Of course I had known this; but I had lived apart from the knowledge.

'I expect you have. But there are worse things to do in expiation – helping lost souls find themselves.'

'Or trying to be him. I'm not sure which. I'm not sure I can go on.'

'Don't, then. You're a grown man. You don't have to do anything you don't want to.'

Unconsciously catching Gus's manner of speech, I said, 'You know what? I never cry. I've barely cried since Jonny died – my mother discouraged tears. But for the past three months I've hardly been dry-eyed.' As I spoke, my unruly eyes had begun to fill again.

'That doesn't surprise me.'

'What did you mean by exchange being no robbery?'

'What I say. I expect you're right that she walked back through that hole left in your heart. Where your lost brother was; or rather where he wasn't. That's how she got into your system. She fitted. She filled the gap.'

'Like her and Thomas?'

'In its way. As I said, all love's basically the same.'

'And her?'

'Oh, these things are always mutual. Stands to reason, they have to be. You'll be in touch somehow, somewhere.'

'She did ring me.'

'She'll ring again. Or if she doesn't, you'll know where to find her. Or it will. After all, it brought you together in the first place.'

'It?'

'Whatever is behind it all. What it all adds up to, whatever that is when it's at home. Christ knows, I don't. I'm just an old fool who pisses in his pants.'

'D'you think he did?'

'Who?'

'Christ.'

'What?'

'Did he, though?'

'What, piss in his pants? Probably, when they came for him. You don't see that referred to much!'

'Did he know, d'you think, what's really behind things?'

'Oh Lord,' Gus said. 'Don't ask me. I'm just a simple Jew boy from the East End.' I was used to this brand of Gus's showing off, and because I was talked out, I waited. 'Mind you, he was one too, though not from the East End. But he knew how to tell a good story. That's why his own story's so popular.'

'He wasn't a bad physician, either, from what I can tell.'

'Same thing,' said Gus. 'Different method, that's all. Did I ever tell you the story about the great Rabbi Israel Baal Shem-Tov?'

He knew he hadn't, but I obediently made a show of shaking my head.

'Pity there's no more of that cake. Have we got any biscuits?'

'I'll look.' I went to the kitchen and made us both more coffee and found some soggy shortbread fingers in a sticky tin.

'Thank you, dear boy. I seem to need something sweet. Have one.'

'No thank you.'

'Go on. Break out a bit.'

'Gus, I don't like sweet things.'

'Extraordinary! I never quite believe that. Any road, when Rabbi Israel Shem-Tov saw misfortune looming, it was his custom to go into a particular glade of the forest to meditate. But before he began his meditation he would always light a fire and offer up a prayer and the disaster would be averted. Years passed, and his disciple Magid of Mexeritch, finding himself in a similar situation, went to the forest glade and said to the powers that be, "I do not know how to light the fire, but I can offer up the prayer," and, again, disaster was averted. Later still, Rabbi Moshe-Leib wandered into the forest, saying, "I do not know the whereabouts of the special glade or how to light the fire, but at least I can say the prayer," and once more, disaster was averted. Finally, it was the turn of Rabbi Israel of Rizhin to deal with impending doom. He sat in his study for long hours with his head in his hands. At last he said, "Listen, Lord. I cannot light the fire, or find the special glade in the forest and, forgive me, I am old and tired and failing in my wits and, to be frank, I have forgotten, if I ever knew, the words of the prayer. But I can tell the story."

'I need a pee, and I'm sorry but you're going to have to help me with this bloody zip and see I don't wet my trousers. Incidentally, how's that paper coming you're giving for me in Rome?'

2

The hotel I had booked into wasn't far from the Pantheon and, sticky after my flight, I washed and changed before walking round to the piazza, where I sat, over two cappuccinos, in one of the cafés opposite the famous rotunda, while I studied the inscription over the many-pillared portico. The temple had been built, it declaimed, by Marcus Agrippa in 27 BC.

Before going inside, I walked round to the back to see if I could spy Elizabeth Cruikshank's snake and congratulated myself on finding it, just where I'd recalled from her description, on a small plaque above the capital of the solitary column.

Thomas was right. The building was a consummate example of human invention: a great feat of engineering, the massive concrete dome apparently having been cast in one splendid piece, and yet so effortlessly encompassing the ethereal through its porthole to the sky.

I passed through the mighty studded brazen doors and wandered round the soothing interior, where I examined the tomb of the gracious Raphael and the statue of *The Madonna of the Stone*, and admired the variant marble of the floor.

Presently, to stretch my legs further after the flight, I walked up towards the Spanish Steps and caught Keats's house before it closed.

The room he died in was surprisingly small: narrow, with a

coffered ceiling of azure and gold, a marble fireplace, a desk, a chair, and a silk damask-covered barque bed, made of walnut – like Thomas's. These were not the original furnishings, all of which were destroyed after Keats died, burned under Vatican law, as was required of the effects of those who died of tuberculosis.

The courteous custodian had impressed on me that I might enjoy the use of the chairs, and taking advantage of this piece of civilised licence, I sat at the desk and looked out over the Spanish Steps, lit by the yellow afternoon sun.

Keats would have sat at this window, before he grew too weak to rise from his bed, believing his genius unrecognised, fearing his impending extinction, missing Fanny Brawne and steeling himself to miss her for all time; and desolately staring out at these same steps, wet from the February rains. I wondered if that maybe was the origin of his melancholy image of his name being 'writ in water.' He could never have guessed how that watery inscription would abide.

And when Thomas Carrington, with Elizabeth Cruikshank, had seen the same steps last, they were wet too, unless Thomas had come here again, alone, after she had obeyed that fateful summons to Gerrards Cross. From what I had gleaned, it was plausible that he might have done. I almost felt he was here now, and with me, as I sat recalling his story.

I walked downstairs and out of the house and climbed the steps, 'steep as Paradise,' his lover had told me Thomas had said of them, when they had gone to collect her things and take them to his hotel, in the palmy days of their brief time together. From the stone-balustraded platform at the top, I looked out over an ochre and green and terracotta Rome, and then descended and turned in to Babington's Tearooms, where the ambience is more English than in England, and where I was served toasted teacakes soused in butter and Darjeeling tea, in a silver-plated pot with a cat for the handle of the lid, and hot-water jug to match, and tried to keep my anxious thoughts from the paper I was to give the following day.

I woke in the night with a terrible sense of impending doom, my heart juddering violently. I wondered if I had wet myself because the sheet, and my pyjamas, seemed to be soaked right through, and while the hotel room seemed oppressively hot, so that I was having trouble breathing, my body was freezing cold.

My first frightened supposition was that this must be a heart attack. And then I recognised that it was panic I was in the grip of.

Sitting up in the bed, I breathed into my cupped hands, still pouring sweat, my berserk heart banging away, and, after what seemed an eternity but my watch told me was just over twenty minutes, the hammering abated and dwindled to an erratic flutter and then gradually returned to normal. I got up, thankfully, and made myself a cup of tea and put on a sweater and got back into bed, still shivering.

A panic attack. What was that about? I was aware that the talk had been weighing on me, but while I never enjoyed giving papers I was not unused to the experience.

The manuscript was by my bed, and as I drank the hot sweet tea, I forced myself to read it. It gave me no pleasure to do so.

It was a fastidious compilation of a couple of cases I'd treated over the past year, offering verbatim material of turning points in the treatment and a sound theoretical explanation of the underlying issues. It was well written, well argued, and fundamentally false. I'd no appetite for reading the words I'd laboured over, still less for declaiming them in public, and given my present state it seemed likely that I would be in little position to do so.

I had undertaken this wretched task for Gus's sake, because I loved him and he had wanted me to. He had asked because he had confidence in me, and I couldn't let Gus down. But nor could I face the idea of standing before an audience to read this milk-and-water stuff aloud. My recently taxed heart revolted at the prospect, and as if in confirmation of my resolve, the iron fist, which appeared to have commandeered it, volunteered a warning squeeze.

In an effort to calm my racing mind, I picked up *The Portrait of a Lady*, which I'd brought with me to read in Rome. And out of it fell the postcard I kept as a bookmark.

The meeting was packed. The choice of venue for the conference had brought larger than usual numbers eager to debate the subject of depression in this undepressing environment. I swept an appraising eye discreetly round and detected a mood of dull inattention. Jeffries had shown some slides illustrating the neural pathways in the brain to indicate the likely prophylactic effects of various new forms of drug therapy. The slides were informative but supremely unriveting.

I stepped up to the podium and surveyed my audience. The day was warm and the room hot, the air conditioning had been running noisily and Jeffries had asked for it to be turned off. Under my linen jacket my shirt was already damp.

A technical assistant, in chic army fatigues, had produced a machine able to project the postcard, and a mild hum of speculation was audible when *The Supper at Emmaus* resolved into focus on the screen.

'It's like this,' I said, and I was fully conscious of the words I was using. 'As many of you will recognise, this is a painting by Caravaggio which is to be found not here in Rome but in London's National Gallery. It is one of two paintings by Caravaggio called *The Supper at Emmaus* and it illustrates a scene in a story told in the Gospel of Luke.'

I paused to pour a glass of water from the jug on the table to prime my dry mouth.

'Two men, disciples of the recently dead Jesus, travelling to an obscure village called Emmaus, a few miles west of Jerusalem, are joined by a third party, an apparent stranger, who journeys with them to their destination, where he makes as if he means to travel on further. The other two detain him and press him to share their supper at the inn. He accepts their invitation, and when he breaks bread they recognise him for the friend they have believed dead, whereupon he vanishes out of sight.

'Please let me assure you, before I proceed, that I am not speaking from any religious position, perspective, or background. It was only when I had reason to look at the Caravaggio here that I considered the story from which this scene is drawn. I was familiar with only its bare outline before the painting sent me off to read it.'

I took another sip from the glass of water, in which angles of coloured light, from the refracted image of the painting on the screen, were mingling.

'It is relevant to our concerns here that this brief tale appears only in Luke – it is not to be found in the other Gospels – as Luke himself was very probably a physician, perhaps from Antioch. It is also relevant that the radical young Galilean he writes of, the man known as Jesus of Nazareth, was renowned among his contemporaries first and foremost as a healer with very considerable powers. In other words, both author and subject of this story were, if you like, colleagues of ours, and much of Luke's account of the life of Jesus can be read as a series of case studies of a variety of disorders which nowadays we would assume to have a psychological source.'

As I was saying this, there was a minor disturbance at the door and my peripheral vision registered a latecomer enter the hall and sit down at the far side towards the back.

'You might like to hear how I came upon this painting, for that is also relevant to my theme . . .'

I carried on, describing how Elizabeth Cruikshank had come to my attention, of my persistent failure to reach her through her cryptically broken silences until I shared my anxieties over my reticent patient with my colleague Gus Galen, and how, as a consequence of this conversation, I had returned to look at the painting to which he had introduced me. I have no idea what precise words I used; I can only say they seemed to issue unedited from my disencumbered heart.

'The history my patient finally entrusted to me is not mine to divulge. It is another story. But I came to this conference with the intention of presenting a case history, or case histories, treated not by drugs but by other, less material, methods, and I mean not to fail in that undertaking. However, the case I wish to invite you to consider is not that of the suicidal patient I have been alluding to but my own, and the part played by Caravaggio's painting, and the story it portrays, in developing my understanding.'

Here, I felt a wave of uneasiness swell in the room and for reassurance glanced at the familiar figures in the painting, the two fishermen and their recently recovered friend, and took another sip of inspiration from their dancing images in the glass of water.

'I believe that, in my dealings with this patient, nothing could have been accomplished without three factors: one, my own incompetence and attendant fear, which I was enabled to recognise through the kindness of my friend and colleague Gus Galen; two, my own desire to liberate myself from some long-term inner restriction, which I expressed in the misplaced decision over a high-security patient; three, my willingness to express my personal commitment to my patient's continued existence, which I did with uncharacteristic force.

'However, there is a further factor more critical than any of these. My patient had experienced a loss which was the catalyst of her desire to end her life. I have experienced an equivalent loss. Her loss activated feelings about my own, and while I did not speak of these directly, or not immediately, I have little doubt that they made themselves known to her and were a *vital* – I use this word advisedly – element in what unfolded between us.'

I talked on, suddenly fluent, all my distraining anxiety fallen away, and as I talked I remembered how I had always felt that the world where our real selves reside – our hopes, perplexities, anxieties, aversions, longings, fears, and loves, those elements which make up our sense of who we are – remains always invisible to others. My audience could see my speaking, gesticulating, sweating outward form, but the real David was elsewhere: they didn't know the half of me.

'This is the kind of thing which can happen, I suggest, when we dare to truly engage. Two people with open hearts, and the willingness to speak from them, create a reality more powerful and more salient than either individual. That is the essence of the meaning of that journey to Emmaus celebrated in this painting here. What transpired between myself and my patient was the emergence of a truth, born of our meeting, which only came to life through our conversation. It was not a truth I immediately recognised. Because you don't immediately recognise truth when it emerges. Very often it appears alien and strange. Sometimes downright objectionable. Nor was it a miracle, except the kind of everyday miracle which occurs when stories are told and heard in conditions of love and trust. But nothing would have been furthered had I maintained my position of professional distance and excluded my own history from my understanding of my patient's story.'

I sat down, wiped my sweating face, and polished off the tumbler of water in the ensuing silence. There was a fractured burst of applause, the chair asked for questions, and there was silence again.

Someone asked in what circumstances I would be prepared to prescribe antidepressants, and another for my views on ECT. One questioner, a young woman doctor from Poland, asked if I felt there was any relevance in the fact that the first-century Emmaus story was re-created in the seventeenth-century Caravaggio painting and was now the subject of my contemporary paper, which was a thoughtful question, and I tried to answer it coherently, though I got myself into a bit of a tangle trying to do so.

'A colleague of mine in the UK,' I said, smiling at her, partly because she was pretty, partly out of gratitude for this token of genuine interest, and partly because I was feeling almightily thankful that it was over and I would never have to put myself through such a thing again, 'would deal better with your question. She has a theory that all consciousness is connected.'

There was a further silence at this, and the chair was about to wrap things up when towards the back of the hall there was a scraping sound as someone got to his feet.

'I hesitate to add my two penn'orth after Dr McBride's moving and enlightening exposition, but with regard to the last question, and the nub of his commentary, as I understand it, there's an old Jewish tale which comes to mind about the Rabbi Israel Baal Shem-Tov.'

3

'Gus, thank you.'

I was exceedingly pleased to see him. The talk had left me shaky and, suddenly and swingeingly, depressed.

'It shut them up anyway. I liked what you said. It was good stuff. You didn't fuck about. It behoves us' – he pronounced this the old-fashioned way to rhyme with 'moves' – 'not to fuck about. Mind you, they won't have a bloody clue what you were on about. Mostly.'

'I know.'

'Not that that matters,' Gus said. 'One or two may take something in. You sow seeds and some sprout, as the man said.'

'Yes.'

'You look done in,' Gus said. 'Come on, let's get out of here. They've succeeded in getting me to lay off alcohol for the time being, but I'll buy you a beer and watch you drink it.'

We walked until we found a congenial-looking café, and sat while I drank a beer and Gus drank coffee, which truth to tell I'd have preferred. But, as he said, it didn't matter. Not much mattered. Which didn't mean that nothing mattered, either. I'd honoured Elizabeth Cruikshank's story, and Caravaggio's story and Luke's and, I hoped, my own. I wasn't up to much more.

'By the way,' Gus suddenly remarked. 'That woman rang looking for you.'

'Which woman?'

'Your Caravaggio woman, the one you were on about.'

'When?'

'Just now.'

'No, I mean when did she ring? Where?'

'Yesterday. She rang me in London. St Kit's told her you'd left, and she couldn't get any joy out of Olivia.'

'Olivia doesn't know I'm here. What did she want?'

'She wanted to speak to you. She asked if I had your number and I said you were in Rome, and then I couldn't remember where the hell you were staying.'

'I don't think I told you.'

'I forget everything these days, including what I wasn't told. Anyway, I thought I'd come myself and tell you.'

'Gus, are you fit enough to fly?'

'Nice voice. I was feeling sorry for myself and then she rang and I thought, What ho! I'll bugger off to Rome. It was a good excuse. You know what? She's a catalyst, that one. I've met those. They're the sort who slip in and you don't know what's going on but they change things. The quiet kind. Bet she's not a looker, though.'

'Her lover liked her looks.'

'Oh well, lovers.'

'He had taste. I like them too, if it comes to that,' I said a shade defensively.

'You would. Incidentally, who's the colleague you mentioned to that Polish girl? The one who said everything's connected?'

'Lennie's Granma.'

'Who?'

'Lennie's Granma. Lennie's my black schizophrenic cleaner at the hospital. Or was. His grandmother says everything's connected.'

'We'll get her to speak next time. Now then, d'you want the Caravaggio woman's number? She's here, by the way. I meant to say. She's in Rome.'

My sleep that night was dreamless, a black mole-like sleep, and in the morning I woke to the echo of Sunday bells and vivid light storming my room through the window which I'd left open, the heavy curtains undrawn.

The newly arrived swallows and martins were venturing so nearly in at the window – as I stood looking out after my bath, enjoying the sense of liberation that one's own unobserved naked-ness induces – that I felt my skin almost brushed by the currents of air, as the birds swooped by in their softly shrieking ellipses. I remembered how my notes had suggested that Elizabeth Cruik-shank resembled a swallow.

I breakfasted in a café, tucked, with an adroit Italian mix of shrewd commercialism and taste, above a church cloister near the Piazza Navona, where I lingered over several cups of coffee and continued my reading of *The Portrait of a Lady*. Then I walked across the piazza to the Francesi church, where Caravaggio's *The Calling of St Matthew* is to be found.

I located it in one of the side chapels and stood a long time engrossed, while other visitors came and went, and put coins in the machine that provided the purely mechanical illumination of the altarpieces which aids the inner kind. After that, I walked on upwards to the Piazza del Popolo, which I found thronging with people sporting red caps and white balloons, being rallied by a small darting man bawling through a megaphone.

Only in Italy would one find such a committed turnout for the Communist Party. I asked one of the bored-looking policemen standing guard over this cheerily pacific affair for the Santa Maria del Popolo and he gestured at the church with a tall bell tower, on the opposite side of the piazza, to which I fought my sweating way through the lively Communists.

Inside the cool building a service was concluding and I watched and waited while the congregation dispersed. This time it was Paul or, more properly, Saul whom I had come to see, struck blind, upended, and dashed definitively from his horse on his way to Damascus.

A church, from long tradition, offers even strangers to worship a rest from the press of the world, and as I didn't fancy fighting through the mass of Communists again, and had time on my hands, I sat in the vaulted quiet reflecting on the Caravaggios.

What they so strikingly offered was access to those moments which invade time and contain both its annihilation and renewal. That finger of Christ, pointing from one side of the room at Matthew, as he sits chatting with his cronies at a custom-house table, describes, and forces on the surprised tax collector, a shattering choice. His bemused eyes cannot evade the level gaze of his irresistible summoner, and with his left hand, the hand of the heart, he points at himself in hopeful disbelief: Is it really *me* you want? – while, instinctively, the right hand is covering the coins on the table, guarding the money he has spent a lifetime successfully raking in.

And in that split-atom second that the vicious persecutor Saul becomes the victimised apostle Paul, he is propelled upside down, body exposed like a turned hedgehog, arms flung wide against his cruel past and the prevailing inrush of obliterating brightness.

Out of his own torment, Caravaggio apprehended those staggering reckonings, where a life spins on a point of possibility, where irreconcilable worlds, which have lain, indistinguishable and slumbering, one atop the other, rear up and show their quintessential differences. And Elizabeth Cruikshank's lover had also understood the piercing inexorable truth of such moments and she had made me understand them likewise.

When we met she seemed smaller, older, the strong daylight revealing the lines on her face, so that I found myself thinking that Gus was right and that she wasn't a 'looker' after all. But once we had begun to speak, the appeal that had drawn Thomas – which is that inner condition which appearances only reflect – began once more to hover about her presence for me like a summer haze.

We had arranged to meet in the forecourt of the Borghese Gallery, and I wasn't surprised when the warm and cautious silence – which followed our initial, and inevitably reserved, greetings – was broken by a suggestion.

'I've not been here since I came with Thomas and he showed me Caravaggio's *David*. I thought maybe, if you would like to, that is, we could go and see it together?'

In those days it was possible to buy a ticket for the gallery without the tedium of prior booking, and she led me, with an air of authority, wordlessly through a sequence of gilded, statue-crowded, picture-resplendent rooms. Only when we reached the salmon-coloured marble-faced room where the Caravaggios were displayed did she indicate a gross figure of Silenus, at the room's centre, remarking that the Romans might have done better to stick to drains. She didn't add that this was Thomas's opinion, but I felt that it must have been, and it seemed entirely natural to ask, as we stood together before the painting of *David*, 'What was it Thomas said about remorse?'

'That an artist is someone who knows he is failing in living and makes something fair to feed his remorse.'

The painting, hanging on the livid marble, was like a window opening, behind the lit figure of the boy, on to a sable night.

I looked at my valiant namesake with his vulnerable young throat exposed and the blade of his drawn sword resting across the crease of his groin. David also knew those moments of choice where Yes and No collide. In the act of taking life he had moved into manhood and all that this entails – the comprehension that all our acts have consequences, which we must bear, and with which we must live consciously, if life is not to become a desperate flight from ourselves – was distilled in his dark dispassionate gaze.

'It's a subtle observation. Not assuaging it, feeding it.'

'Thomas's observations were subtle. I didn't always get them at the time.' She smiled. 'He wouldn't have approved of me saying I didn't "get them." He was terrifically fierce.'

'He minded,' I said. 'It's a fine quality, minding. I haven't minded enough.'

'You minded about me and Thomas.'

'Yes, I did, didn't I?'

'I shall always be grateful.'

'I am equally grateful to you.'

Something unfathomable stirred in her expression, and if you ask me what it was, I would have to own that, even now, I couldn't say, beyond that it seemed to issue from a far-off region of her disconcerting understanding. But it encouraged me into a further emphatic 'It is the case, I assure you.'

In some confusion, I glanced up at the youthful David's sorrowing eyes – and then, following their direction, down into the eyes of his victim; and I suddenly saw that Caravaggio has portrayed the suspended head with divided sight: the right eye was dead as a dead fish's but the left was staring at me, vital, indignant, aghast.

'I hope it won't embarrass you if I tell you there was something I'd not faced, but your story made me reconsider. I believe I was the unwitting cause of my brother's death. I couldn't acknowledge it, but also – as, meeting you here and telling you this now, I can see with strange clarity – I couldn't have helped it either.'

She waited, as if to be sure there was no more to come, and then said gravely, 'It doesn't embarrass me.'

I turned back to the boy who had killed; and gone on to become a great and powerful king.

'Would you say the lament again? I remember it only dimly, but I've very often recalled your reciting it to me in my room.'

And this is my last distinct memory of Elizabeth Cruikshank, a slight figure, standing, in the marmoreal grandeur of the Borghese Gallery, before the beauteous young man with the likeness of the mauled head of his ugly creator hanging dead in his hand, her face a little averted, the Roman sun, behind her dark hair, filtering through the blinds at the long windows, reciting, in her distinctive voice, the cry of David to his lost son, who died, at war with his estranged father, unaware how grievously he would be for ever mourned.

Would God I had died for thee, O Absalom, my son, my son!

The note of anguish hung in the air, like the after-peal of the bells which had roused me from sleep that morning, or the motes in the sun's fingers, and she looked at me and our eyes were full of tears, and the tears were the reciprocities of an understanding beyond words. I think that if I had walked towards her she might have opened her arms to me, and perhaps we should have found another, better, way of feeding our shared remorse. For a fraction of an interval, the possibility hovered between us, with the haunting words and the red-veined marble and the dusty sunlight and Caravaggio's brave self-portrait and the figure of the lone boy – and the timeless stories of death and loss and remorse, which we had shared and would always share – and I knew she was involved in the same elusive, impossible calculation. And then the moment passed.

Maybe we had been through too much to accomplish a fresh beginning; maybe we were too world-worn; maybe I felt too much in the shadow of Thomas. Her story had restored the authentic likeness beneath the clumsy overlay – but that self would always be a hesitant one: it wasn't in me to embrace her high-hearted lover's blazing disregard for certainty.

We walked outside and sat, side by side, decorously on a bench in the civilised gardens of the Villa Borghese, almost as we had sat those long hours in my consulting room, and spoke of many things, but mostly of a factual nature. I told her I had resigned my position at the hospitals but that Hassid, who had returned to university, kept in touch – intermittently, to my relief – and sounded to be doing fine and even had a girlfriend. Which reminded me.

'What was that book you stole from the hospital?'

'I thought it was a present!'

'Okay, what was the "present" we gave you?'

'It was an old guidebook of Rome. It's hopelessly out of date but I'm attached to it, because, well, you know . . .'

She asked after my cleaner and I explained that Lennie had been a headache, as I had been troubled lest he wouldn't keep up his treatment without me, but then, in a brainwave, I'd consulted Colin Mackie and Lennie had apparently transferred his loyalties and that Mackie's room was now treated with the reverence once reserved for mine. 'Probably more,' I suggested. 'Mackie is less chaotic than I am. It's an excellent lesson in how never to suppose we are irreplaceable.'

'For me you were. Are.'

'Thank you.'

'And you're not chaotic.'

'By Lennie and Mackie's standards I am,' I interposed hastily, because I was embarrassed at what she might be going to say.

She pondered more and then said, 'No, you're modest. Modesty's a fine quality. It means you let things be. It's odd how people can't do that. They seem to need to poke about and interfere. Why?'

'Probably as a distraction from themselves. I've done my share of interfering too, I'm afraid.'

I spoke, then, with distress, about my poor wolf man, and how I was still anxiously awaiting the result of the inquiry into his assault on the nurse; which led, by extension, to her reminder to revisit the fabulous Etruscan wolf in the Capitoline Museum.

'She supposedly has Romulus and Remus suckling from her, but they're later accretions. Thomas –'

'Don't tell me, Thomas deplored them . . .'

She explained how she had returned to Rome soon after our last encounter, but that she had only recently resolved to move there permanently, which was why she had rung Gus, to tell me where she was and what she had finally accomplished. As she put it, Rome was where she had been closest to her self and she had no ties to keep her elsewhere. Her son had been all for it, and had been helpful with the move, and her relationship with both children, even in this short period, had grown increasingly close. We laughed most when she told me how, before leaving England, she had steeled herself to visit Gerrards Cross, where there were matters to tie up with Neil, and that Norma had shown herself to be of strong stuff, altogether tougher than the Russian Vine, and that Primrose had appeared quite meek under the new regime.

'Maybe she misses you?'

'Bullies only rate other bullies. Anyway, as I needn't tell you, very few people in life truly miss us. It's a mistake to imagine otherwise.'

'One or two, if we're lucky, maybe.'

4

Although I did not see Elizabeth Cruikshank again I did speak
to her, because she rang me at the hotel before I left Rome. She
knew nothing of my domestic life, so I had not mentioned, when
we sat in the Borghese gardens, that my wife and I had parted,
though even without her acute intuition she would have guessed
I was married since I had left Olivia a message during our seven-
hour exchange.

She had rung, she said, to ask a 'possibly impertinent' question,
and I was pleased to hear from her again so soon.

'Fire away.'

'I wondered, was the woman who was outside your room
that night the person who gave you the egg?'

'How did you know?'

'I thought perhaps from seeing her that maybe she loved you.
The egg is the kind of present someone who loves you gives.'

'I think she did love me once. But I didn't treat her very
well.'

'It's not my business, but perhaps she would forgive you?'

Because this wasn't what I wanted to hear, I brushed this off
with a gruff 'I'm not sure I'm up to being forgiven.' But it wasn't
really that.

The whole business of Dan and Olivia had left a bad taste. I
had no idea if Dan and Bar would survive as a couple, but what-

ever I had been to Bar once, I knew her well enough to know that she was not the sort to abandon a marriage because of one lapse, however treacherous. And what I really wasn't 'up to' was becoming a further spanner in that marriage's works.

But there was this besides, which I didn't say, though maybe I didn't need to say it: I always believed she could see through to the back of my mind. Once you have experienced a certain closeness, the other kinds leave you wanting. I learned that, too, through getting to know Elizabeth Cruikshank.

From that day, in the gardens of the Villa Borghese, I have not laid waking eyes on her. Sometimes I dream about her; and when I wake I miss her. I don't know if she ever misses me. But I had no need to explain, when we spoke, why I had resigned the position through which we met, and proposed to work from that time writing, and seeing only those few patients with whom I felt an intuitive rapport.

My life since then has been uncomplicated but not unsatisfying: I have never remarried, though for some years I have had a companion, a sculptress, who prefers her own space, and sometimes company, but enjoys mine too. We get on well and I've grown fond of her children and, latterly, her children's children. She's not the sort to probe, so although I once mentioned Elizabeth Cruikshank, she has never enquired about her. And I have preferred to keep these recollections to myself, till now.

But last year, when I was feeling the time was approaching when I might wind down my practice and spend more time writing, I visited the exhibition at the National Gallery devoted to Caravaggio's last years.

He has become popular and I had failed to book ahead for an allotted date and time. I queued up for my ticket, one mild March morning, and was killing time in the shop in the Sainsbury Wing when I noticed a book, written by an Italian woman, entitled *Caravaggio's Emmaus Paintings*. I opened the book and read randomly, and across twenty intervening years I heard the cool precise voice of Elizabeth Cruikshank as her cool precise prose limpidly expanded on Caravaggio's versions of that Emmaus Supper story; describing, technically, how the paintings were executed, and when they figured in Caravaggio's own history and, finally, persuasively and elegantly, what it was in the subject matter that we might wish to absorb.

I bought the book, but I'd read none of it when I stood by the two *Supper* paintings hung, companionably side by side, at the exhibition's start.

As I stood, taking in the pair afresh, with Elizabeth Cruikshank's account of them as yet unread in my hand, I heard the words with which she described to me her first experience of love: *It was as if I were meeting someone whom I had known intimately and from whom I had been separated for a very long time.*

The two pictures could hardly be more different in mood, but the story was the same. You see the scene one way, and then you see it another, and as Thomas would have agreed, neither way is better, or more true, or right. And then it was Gus's words on love which were returning to me: *It's difficult. And demanding. And a nuisance. And bloody absent much of the bloody time.*

Love also expresses itself in absence, the paintings seemed to be suggesting: love is here, and then it is not, and then it is here again, transformed, transforming. Caravaggio was absent, Thomas was absent, Jonny was absent, Elizabeth Cruikshank was absent – but I was here, and the love I felt for each of them, as I looked at those evocations of that strange story of that strange supper with that still stranger stranger, was mingling inside me, like the light of the reflected figures in the glass of water, which I drank as I tried, hopelessly, inadequately, to make sense of all this, that time, long since, in a lecture theatre in

Rome. No analysis, however honest, could summarise what the two masterpieces portraying Luke's story conveyed. It seemed to me now a fool's enterprise.

I walked through the exhibition, in mute agitation, till I came to the portrait of my namesake with his unsought-after trophy in his clenched hand. And I looked again into his darkly comprehending eyes. 'I understand, David.'

'Excuse me?' An over-made-up American woman, equipped with catalogue, headphones, and the informative exhibition recording, mistook the comment as intended for her. I apologised, insincerely, and rapidly melted away. In any case, I had had enough: I decided I would visit the exhibition again when my emotions were in better order.

I felt that Elizabeth Cruikshank might appreciate this reminder of our last meeting, and I recounted it when I wrote to say how much I had enjoyed her book. And how especially pleased and intrigued I was by a footnote, which mentioned a painting that had come to light in a monastery, north of Rome, which, she tentatively indicated, was exciting speculation, since it was believed conceivable that it overlaid a lost Caravaggio on the Emmaus theme.

She answered after a goodish while, long enough for me to wonder if she had forgotten me. But her reply, when it finally arrived, was worth waiting for. It apologised for the delay, blaming it on her publisher's tardiness in forwarding my letter. Hers was expansive and drily amusing; but she made no mention of our time together. Except that it ended with a few words of Greek, which eluded me and with which I had to ask Gus Galen's help.

Gus, in his eighties, continues to defy cancer, and convention. From time to time, when I visit, I meet Tanya, who is still beautiful and seems impervious to the squalor in his flat. But she wasn't there the day I went with the letter, with the postmark from Rome, in my pocket. And I was glad of it.

The line Gus translated for me, which Elizabeth Cruikshank had written in her unfaltering brown script, read:

> Οὐχὶ ἡ καρδία ἡμῶν καιομένη ἦν ἐν ἡμῖν;
> *Were not our hearts burning within us?*

Beneath it she had signed her name.

ACKNOWLEDGEMENTS

I am very grateful to the organisers of the Adelaide Writers' Festival, and the incomparable Christine Farmer of Harper-Collins Australia, who enabled me to visit Australia, where the seeds of the idea for this book were sown and where I made some of the best friends a writer could hope to have. A special thank you to David Richardson, Dean of St Paul's Melbourne, who told me the story about Rabbi Israel Baal Shem-Tov and, with many more pressing claims on his time, allowed me to question him about the Emmaus story and was always generous and enlightening.

My sources for Caravaggio's life were various, but Helen Langdon's *Caravaggio: A Life* (Chatto & Windus, 1998) and Giorgio Bonsanti's *Caravaggio* (Scala, 1991) were most helpful. And my thanks to Faber and Faber Ltd for permission to quote from T. S. Eliot's *The Waste Land*, and to Stephen Page, whose help in this matter was the action of a friend.

Miss Garnet's Angel

Read on for an extract
from Salley Vickers' bestselling novel

Death is outside life but it alters it: it leaves a hole in the fabric
of things which those who are left behind try to repair. Perhaps
it is because of this we are minded to feast at funerals and it is said
that certain children are conceived on the eve of a departure, lest
the separation of the partners be permanent. When in ancient
stories heroes die, the first thing their comrades do, having made
due observances to the gods, is sit and eat. Then they travel on,
challenging, with their frail vitality, the large enigma of non-being.

When Miss Garnet's friend Harriet died, Miss Garnet decided
to spend six months abroad. For Miss Garnet, who was certainly
past child-bearing years and had lost the only person she ever ate
with, the decision to travel was a bold one. Her expeditions abroad
had been few and for the most part tinged with apprehension. As
a young woman straight from college she had volunteered, while
teaching the Hundred Years' War, to take a school party to Crécy.
On that occasion she had become flustered when, behind her back
but audibly, the boys had mocked her accent and had intimated
(none too subtly) that she had brought them to France in order to
forge a liaison with the large, sweating, white-faced coach driver.

'*Mademoiselle from Armentières,*' they had sung hilariously in the
back of the coach. '*Mademoiselle from Armentières. Hasn't had sex
for forty years!*' And as she had attempted to convey to the coach
driver the time she considered it prudent to start back for Calais,

wildly and suggestively they had chorused, '*Inky pinky parley vous!*'

The experience had left its mark on Miss Garnet's teaching as well as on her memory. Essentially a shy person, her impulses towards cordiality with her pupils, never strong in the first place, were dealt a blow. She withdrew, acquired a reputation for strictness, even severity, and in time became the kind of teacher who, if not loved, was at least respected. Even latterly, when in terms of pupils' taunts *Mademoiselle From Armentières* would be considered very small beer, no member of Miss Garnet's classes ever thought publicly to express a view about her intimate life.

Julia Garnet and Harriet Josephs had lived together for more than thirty years. Harriet had answered Julia's advertisement in the National Union of Teachers' monthly journal. 'Quiet, professional female sought to share small West London flat. No smokers. No pets.'

Harriet had been, in fact, the only person to respond to the advertisement, which had not prevented Julia from giving her what her friend later described as 'a toughish interview'. 'Honestly,' Harriet had used to say, on the few occasions when together they had entertained friends, 'it was worse than the time I tried to get into the Civil Service!'

Generally Harriet had laughed loudly at this point in a way her flat-mate had found irritating. Now Miss Garnet found she missed the laugh just as she missed Stella, Harriet's cat. The prohibition against pets had been relaxed seven years earlier when late one night after choir-practice Harriet had been followed from the station by Stella. Stella, then an anonymous black kitten with a white-starred throat, had waited all night on the stairs outside the front door of their fourth-floor flat, whereupon, on finding her, the soft-hearted Harriet had fed the kitten milk. After that, as Julia had observed, there was 'no getting rid of the animal'.

Alongside the two school teachers Stella had grown into an elderly and affectionate creature but it was Harriet to whom the cat had remained attached. Two days after they had both retired (they had arranged the events to coincide in order, Harriet had suggested, that the New Year could see them setting off on 'new feet') Julia returned from the shops to find her companion, apparently asleep, stretched out upon the sofa, her romantic novel face down on the carpet. Later, after the doctor and then the undertaker had been, Stella disappeared. Julia had placed milk outside first the flat door and then, worry making her brave the neighbours' ridicule, downstairs by the main entrance to the block. The milk she left outside was certainly drunk but after a few days she was forced to accept that it was not Stella drinking the milk but, more likely, the urban fox who had been seen rootling in the communal dustbins.

Perhaps it was not just the loss of Stella, but also her incompetence in the face of it – so soon after losing Harriet – which finally determined Miss Garnet's abrupt decision. She and Harriet had made plans – or rather Harriet had – for it must be said that, of the two, she was the more given to planning. ('Flighty' was sometimes her companion's name for Harriet's tendency to cut out advertisements from the *Observer* for trips to faraway and exotic places.) Harriet's (now permanent) flight had rendered the plans pointless; a kind of numbness had dulled Miss Garnet's usual caution and she found herself, before she was quite aware what was happening, calling in on one of the numerous local estate agents which had sprung up in her locality.

'No worries, Mrs Garnet, we'll be able to rent this, easy,' the young man with the too-short haircut and the fluorescent mobile phone had said.

'*Miss* Garnet, it's Miss,' she had explained, anxious not to accept a title to which she felt she had never managed to rise. (There had never been any question of Miss Garnet being a Ms: her great-aunt had had some association with Christabel Pankhurst and the connection, however loose, with the famous suffragette

had strengthened Miss Garnet's views on the misplaced priorities
of modern feminism.)

'*Miss*, I'm sorry,' the young man had said, trying not to laugh
at the poor old bird. He'd heard from Mrs Barry, the caretaker,
that there had been another old girl living with her who had just
died. Probably lezzies, he thought.

Miss Garnet was not a lesbian, any more than Harriet Josephs
had been, although both women had grown aware that that is
what people sometimes assumed of them.

'It is very vexing,' Harriet had said once, when a widowed friend
had opined that Jane Austen might have been gay, 'to be considered
homosexual just because one hasn't been lucky enough to marry.'

'Or foolish enough,' Julia had added. But privately she believed
Harriet was right. It would have been a piece of luck to have been
loved by a man enough to have been his wife. She had been asked
once for a kiss, at the end-of-term party at the school where she had
taught History for thirty-five years. The request had come from
a man who, late in life, had felt it was his vocation to teach and
had come, for his probationary year, to St Barnabas and St James,
where Miss Garnet had risen to the position of Head of the History
Department. But he had been asked to leave after he had been
observed hanging around the fifth-form girls' lockers after Games.
Julia, who had regretted not obliging with the kiss, wept secretly
into her handkerchief on hearing of Mr Kenton's departure. Later
she plucked up courage to write to him, with news about the
radical modern play he had been directing. Mr Maguire, Head of
English, had had to take over – and in Miss Garnet's view the play
had suffered as a consequence. Timidly, she had communicated this
thought to the departed Mr Kenton but the letter had been
returned with 'NOT KNOWN AT THIS ADDRESS' printed
on the outside. Miss Garnet had found herself rather relieved and
had silently shredded her single attempt at seduction into the
rubbish bin.

'Where you off to then?' the young estate agent had asked, after they had agreed the terms on which the flat was to be let (no smoking, and no pets – out of respect to Stella).

Perhaps it was the young man's obvious indifference which acted as a catalyst to the surprising form she found her answer taking – for she had not, in fact, yet formulated in her mind where she might go, should the flat prove acceptable for letting to Messrs Brown & Noble.

Across Miss Garnet's memory paraded the several coloured advertisements for far-flung places which, along with some magazine cuttings concerning unsuitable hair dye, she had cleared from Harriet's oak bureau and which (steeling herself a little) she had recently placed in the dustbin. One advertisement had been for a cruise around the Adriatic Sea, visiting cities of historical interest. The most famous of these now flashed savingly into her mind.

'Venice,' she announced firmly. 'I shall be taking six months in Venice.' And then, because it is rarely possible, at a stroke, to throw off the habits of a lifetime, 'I believe it is cheaper at this time of year.'

It was cold when Miss Garnet landed at Marco Polo airport. Uncertain of all that she was likely to encounter on her exotic adventure she had at least had the foresight to equip herself with good boots. The well-soled boots provided a small counter to her sense of being somewhat insubstantial when, having collected her single suitcase with the stout leather strap which had been her mother's, she followed the other arrivals outside to where a man with a clipboard shouted and gestured.

Before her spread a pearl-grey, shimmering, quite alien waste of water.

'Zattere,' Miss Garnet enunciated. She had, through an agency found in the *Guardian*'s Holiday Section, taken an *appartamento* in one of the cheaper areas of Venice. And then, more distinctly, because the man with the clipboard appeared to pay no attention, 'Zattere!'

'*Si, si, Signora, momento, momento.*' He gestured at a water-taxi and then at a well-dressed couple who had pushed ahead of Miss Garnet in the shambling queue. '*Prego?*'

'Hotel Gritti Palace?' The man, a tall American with a spade-cut beard, spoke with the authority of money. Even Miss Garnet knew that the Gritti was one of the more exclusive of Venice's many expensive hotels. She had been disappointed to learn that a Socialist playwright, one whom she admired, was in the habit of taking rooms there each spring. Years ago, as a student teacher, Miss Garnet had, rather diffidently, joined the Labour Party. Over the years she had found the policies of succeeding leaders inadequately representative of her idea of socialism. Readings of first Marx and then Lenin had led her, less diffidently, to leave the Labour Party to join the Communists instead. Despite all that had happened in Europe over the years she saw no reason now to alter her allegiance to the ideology which had sustained her for so long. Indeed, it was partly Venice's reputation for left-wing activity which had underpinned her novel notion to reside there for six months. Now the long plane flight, the extreme cold rising off the grey-green lagoon waters and the extremer fear, rising from what seemed more and more like her own foolhardiness, joined force with political prejudice.

'Excuse me,' Miss Garnet raised her voice towards the polished couple, 'but I was first.' As she spoke she lost her footing, grazing her leg against a bollard.

The woman of the couple turned to examine the person from whom these commanding words had issued. She saw a thin woman of medium height wearing a long tweed coat and a hat with a veil caught back against the crown. The hat had belonged to Harriet and although Miss Garnet, when she had seen it on Harriet, had considered it overdramatic, she had found herself reluctant to relegate it to the Oxfam box. The hat represented, she recognised, a side to Harriet which she had disregarded when her friend was alive. As a kind of impulsive late gesture to her friend's sense of the theatrical, she had placed the hat onto her head in the last minutes before leaving for the airport.

Perhaps it was the hat or perhaps it was the tone of voice but the couple responded as if Miss Garnet was a 'somebody'. Maybe, they thought, she is one of the English aristocracy who consider it bad form to dress showily. Certainly the little woman with the delicately angular features spoke with the diction of a duchess.

'Excuse us,' the man spoke in a deep New England accent, 'we would be honoured if you would share our taxi.'

Miss Garnet paused. She was unaccustomed to accepting favours, especially from tall, urbane-mannered men. But she was tired and, she had to own, rather scared. Her knee hurt where she had stupidly bashed it. And there remained the fact that they had, after all, pushed in front of her.

'Thank you,' she spoke more loudly than usual so as to distract attention from the blood she feared was now seeping observably through her thick stocking, 'I should be glad to share with you.'

Ideas,
interviews
& features …

Unlived Lives

Louise Tucker talks to Salley Vickers

Miss Garnet and Elizabeth Cruikshank both love Italy and move to live there: have you ever done so, or considered doing so? And why is Italy more fascinating to you as a writer than, say, France or Spain?

For many years I spent one month a year in Venice, which is why *Miss Garnet* is, I hope, very accurate about Venice and I have also spent much time in Rome. It is certain Italian cities which have most drawn me, rather than Italy as a country. Venice, Rome, Ravenna, Siena are all places which affect my imagination and have made me think in different and creative ways. I have a particular love of the ancient world, too, so the Roman influence is also relevant. And Italian art is possibly my favourite art, though that is a very broad generalisation and I can at once think of exceptions: Rembrandt, Van Eyck, Velázquez, for example. But overall the Italians win for sheer breadth and range and style.

You have worked as an academic and a psychotherapist. What made you switch from one to the other and how does each career now feed into your writing?

I'm not sure I can answer that question accurately. I had always intended to be a child psychotherapist but having had children of my own I came to feel that there was nothing much wrong with children that wasn't being caused by the adults in their lives. Before I became a psychotherapist, I taught English literature which was something I did, really because it was all I was trained to do, while my children were young. I think the study of English literature and the literature of the ancient world maybe enhanced a natural love of language and gave me a foundation in mythology, both of which inform my novels. Working as a psychotherapist, having to find a place from which to understand those I was working with, gave me access to aspects of my self which were unlived. It is really from those unlived elements, which I have had to try to make conscious, that I found a way to realise my characters. None are taken from life, other than my own life, but it is not often that any aspect of my lived life gets into a character, if that makes sense?

Did your family background influence your different careers in any way?
My mother was a social worker and my father a trade union leader, and both were very committed socialists. In fact, rather unusually, I grew up in the Communist Party, though my parents left the party when I was comparatively young. But I did grow up with the notion of helping people being a sort of obligation. However, I don't know that my parents had much influence over my choice of career. My grandmother was a writer, rather an eccentric one. She wrote in secret because first her family and then her two husbands disapproved. She wrote some very acute, rather eerie short stories and plays, one of which, *The Man in the Case*, was ▶

6 Working as a psychotherapist, having to find a place from which to understand those I was working with, gave me access to aspects of my self which were unlived 9

LIFE
at a Glance

Born in Liverpool, lived in
the Potteries as a young
child and then moved to
London. Educated at St
Paul's Girls' School and
Cambridge. Worked as an
artist's model, a
schoolteacher, a university
tutor and lecturer in
literature, a Jungian
psychotherapist and is
now a full-time writer.
Two children. One
grandchild.

Unlived Lives (continued)

◀ censored. We were close, and I am
supposed to resemble her, so I suspect she
was the person who most shaped my
decision to write.

*The question that Gus poses, and which
David then mulls over throughout the rest of
the book, is 'how to live'. Do you have any
answers to it?*
Good heavens no! What an idea. My books
are about people trying to make sense of
living. I wouldn't dream of writing books
which purported to give answers to
anything.

*Suicide and accidental death are incredibly
difficult subjects for many to discuss. What
was the inspiration for writing about them?*
When I worked as a psychotherapist I had an
unusual number of patients who had been
close to death or had significant people in
their lives die. For reasons I won't go into, I
have always had an interest in and very little
fear of death myself, so it came naturally to
me to be able to talk to other people who
have had those close to them die. As many
people have pointed out, death features in all
my novels, though not, I would maintain, in
a gloomy or pessimistic way. Death can be
very illuminating and enlivening.

*Mental illness is frequently overlooked and
sometimes dismissed as less important than
physical problems. Why do you think such
misconceptions persist, particularly in
Britain?*
I think that, like death, most people are

frightened of mental illness, partly because they feel that they don't share a common language with those who suffer from it. Mental illness is still considered a stigma. Actually, very many people suffer, or have suffered, from some form of depression, and almost everyone suffers some sort of anxiety. But we are still a very repressed society and prefer to contend with bacteria and viruses rather than the much more human complaint of sorrow or chronic disappointment.

Thomas believes in 'hearth companions', devoted friends who look after you, and he is very unreserved, whereas David believes that it is rare to marry for joy, that decency often gets in the way. Are your feelings about relationships reflected by either character?
I must emphasise that my characters have their own views and opinions and that these are not imposed on them by their author and neither are they, for the most part, their author's opinions. It is a very common error to suppose that authors are reproducing their own thoughts and feelings via their characters. Any author worth his or her salt will allow their characters to choose what they think and feel. If things are going right, the character arrives and they tell you how they think and feel, if you know how to listen and pay attention to them, that is. I do, however, always have one character in each book who holds views close to my own. I shan't specify who they are except to say that they in no way resemble me, except in their philosophy and world view. ▶

Unlived Lives *(continued)*

◄ *When writing a book that is so embedded in art history, does the research invoke the story or vice versa?*

I do very little research. All but none. People might be shocked to know how little. This is because I believe that unless something is fully digested, already in your blood, so to speak, it will stick out like a sore thumb. I did some research on the Book of Tobit for *Miss Garnet*, as I was writing it, not before, because, like her, I became fascinated with the story and its origins (which are Zoroastrian) but that's about the size of it. So, no, unquestionably the story comes first and then with luck what I know, or enjoy, or care about and care for, feeds into it.

'Not much mattered. Which didn't mean that nothing mattered, either.' What matters to you, in your life and your writing?

Children, friends, art, music, literature, animals, the countryside. In writing, getting into words what lies at the back of my mind.

Writing has become almost as popular a career as pop stardom or football: do you think that this is simply a response to large advances or is it a sign of something more profound, that a story like Elizabeth's needs telling in order for a life to make sense now?

I can't say I've ever made the comparison between myself and a pop star or footballer. I write because I have something to say which I feel I would like to share with others, if they care to read it. When I no longer have anything to say I expect I shall do something else. I'm fairly good at moving on. And I

6 I do very little research. All but none. People might be shocked to know how little. This is because I believe that unless something is fully digested, already in your blood, so to speak, it will stick out like a sore thumb 9

would never write unless I felt that I had something to say and there were people who wanted to read me.

What is the process, or routine, of writing a book for you, if any?
Nothing planned. I write when I feel like it, stop when I don't, and my only rule is never to get dressed until I've finished what I want to write. When in full flow this can mean I never get dressed at all but spend all day, and even days, in my nightdress.

Do you think that fiction writing has a moral and/or educational purpose? Or can it simply be entertainment?
I think a good book must entertain. It's a great mistake, though not an uncommon one, to believe that good literature must be obscure and abstruse. With a very few exceptions, most great writers are highly readable. But 'entertain' is also a rich and serious word. We 'entertain' our guests. This includes, as a rule, giving them good food and drink. I believe a really good book will also have some moral purpose, which is not to say some moralistic purpose (the two are quite different). I don't believe a book should educate except in the sense of enlarging understanding, which, of course, is the best education. Books that set out with the purpose of educating or improving are dire.

What has been the most satisfying part of your career? And the most frustrating?
Without question, writing books. And, without question, writing books. ▶

⟨ I think a good book must entertain. With a very few exceptions, most great writers are highly readable. But "entertain" is also a rich and serious word ⟩

Unlived Lives *(continued)*

◄ *Do you have a favourite amongst your books and, if so, why?*

I think *The Other Side of You* must be my favourite. To my mind, it's the best book I've written so far, and it was the hardest to write, the one I dug deepest for. Of all the books it is the one I missed most when I had finished it. I missed the characters severely.

What are you writing now/next?

That is something I never disclose until it is finished (whatever I tell my publishers…). If I tell before it's ready then it disappears. ■

A Writing Life

When do you write?
If necessary, dawn till dusk. Or not at all.

Where do you write?
I have only certain places where I can write. I keep these secret. But they must have a view.

Why do you write?
God knows.

Pen or computer?
Pencil and computer. But mostly in my head before I start.

Silence or music?
Silence, or best of all, the sound of someone safe and trustworthy sleeping close by.

How do you start a book?
I never know.

And finish?
I don't know that either.

Do you have any writing rituals or superstitions?
I never look at my face in the mirror till I've finished work.

Which living writer do you most admire?
It was Penelope Fitzgerald until she died. Now I would say Shirley Hazzard.

What or who inspires you?
Anything can inspire me. A painting, a sentence in a book, a line of poetry, a ▶

A Writing Life *(continued)*

◄ landscape, a glimpse through a door, a conversation overheard on a bus, a sudden recollection.

If you weren't a writer what job would you do?
I'm unemployable so I would be on the dole.

What's your guilty reading pleasure or favourite trashy read?
I have no guilt about anything I read. The most un-grand reading I do, though, is the Flower Fairies series which I read with great delight to my granddaughter.

Rome in the Novel

by Salley Vickers

ROME, LIKE VENICE, is an emotionally charged city for me. I first encountered it not in person, but through my imagination, in two novels, which have become honoured intimates of mine, George Eliot's *Middlemarch* and *The Portrait of a Lady* by Henry James. Both writers lived for a period in Rome, as did Keats who came to Rome for his health and died there.

Keats, the house where he lived and died, by the Spanish Steps and the Protestant cemetery, just outside the old walls, where he is buried, with the pathetic epitaph 'Here lies One Whose Name was writ in Water', feature in *The Other Side of You* as does *The Portrait of a Lady*, which David is reading when he comes to Rome to give his lecture and has his crucial change of heart. I gave him this novel to read at this point for a reason: partly because it is a novel that has affected me deeply (James is perhaps the most important literary influence on me) but also to signal a shift in David, who until that moment we have only encountered reading Jane Austen. *The Portrait* is a sobering book, for it charts, in chillingly accurate detail, a grave life error made by its heroine, Isobel Archer. It is in Rome that we begin to grasp for the first time what she has done to herself, as we also do with Dorothea in *Middlemarch*, during her disastrous honeymoon in the same city. James's preoccupation with the darker strains of consciousness is relevant to David's own inner development and history. ▶

◄ Thomas, on the other hand, the man who represents the other side of both Elizabeth and David, and who finally, and tragically, dies, has a vivid engagement with life. The Pantheon, in his view, is 'the most perfect secular building in the world', which also reflects the view of his author. Built in 27 BC by Marcus Agrippa, as we are informed in a bold inscription over the entrance porch, it is a remarkable feat of Roman engineering, with the giant sphere, equal in height and diameter, giving the interior a peculiarly harmonious effect. It also has the occulus, the hole in the dome through which rain and, as Thomas reports, snow can sometimes be seen falling. Raphael the painter was buried here in glory, for the fiercely ambitious Raphael, unlike poor Keats, achieved a colossal reputation in his brief lifetime. Where Keats was so little known that his name doesn't even appear on his tombstone, Raphael's epitaph reads (in translation): 'Here lies Raphael, of whom nature was afraid while he lived and who, when he died, wished herself to die.' Outside the Pantheon, in the Piazza Minerva, close to the church of Santa Maria sopra Minerva, is Bernini's endearing statue of a baby elephant.

The Roman forum is where Thomas takes Elizabeth first and just beyond one end of it looms the grisly Colosseum, which I find repulsive and try not to look at. But this is tricky, as usually I do want to look at the Emperor Tiberius's arch, which, standing nearby, shows the Romans bringing home trophies from the sack of the Temple in Jerusalem in AD 70, including the sacred

Temple menorah. At the other end of the forum is the infamous Tarpinian Rock, from which those condemned to death were expected to jump (hard to understand today since the rock looks too undaunting to be an effective means of execution). At this end of the forum, too, is the Capitoline Museum, outside which stands a replica of the great bronze statue of the stoic emperor Marcus Aurelius, one of my best-loved philosophers. Inside the museum is my favourite bronze, a lean Etruscan wolf, apparently suckling Romulus and Remus – later, and rather crude and unsatisfying, additions, I'm afraid. The wolf needs nothing to augment her nobility.

In the Campo de'Fiori, where Thomas and Elizabeth go after viewing Rome from the Palatine Hill, stands the grim statue of Bruno, the burned man, whose stand against the prevailing Catholic dogma of the structure of the cosmos led ultimately, if indirectly, to his death. He was imprisoned for six years in Rome and finally tried and condemned to death, technically for his espousal of the heresy of docetism (the belief that Jesus didn't actually have a physical body) but it was tacitly recognised that it was his belief in the Copernican universe which brought about the death sentence. Unlike Galileo, Bruno refused to renounce his beliefs and insouciantly commented, as Elizabeth tells David, 'Perhaps you, my judges, pronounce this sentence against me with greater fear than I receive it.' It was perhaps this fearless speaking out which led to his being hustled to his death by night with his tongue in a gag (a horrible image ▶

◄ of being physically forced to shut up). His works were on the Papal Index as recently as 2003, when John Paul II made an expression of 'profound sorrow' at his execution.

Thomas's main preoccupation, as we know, was Caravaggio, but in the novel we observe some of the key paintings through David's more innocent and untrained eyes. At the church of Santa Maria del Popolo, one of the artist's two studies of St Paul can be seen. Thrown helpless from his horse, spread-eagled in what many now believe was an epileptic fit, blinded by the intensity of the inner vision he is experiencing, Paul is depicted throwing his arms wide in submission to the man whose followers he had persecuted and whose church he was soon to found and lead. At the San Luigi dei Francesci is the Caravaggio I respond to most: *The Calling of St Matthew*. Christ's level gaze and summoning arm are directed at the shocked tax collector, who feebly tries to guard his money with his right hand, while pointing with his left to himself, in disbelieving reluctance at being chosen as a disciple.

The Villa Borghese, set in lovely grounds, houses one of the two central paintings in the story, the other being *The Supper at Emmaus* in the National Gallery in London. The portrait of the young David, who has just killed his opponent, Goliath, hangs here. The young boy stands holding the head of his mighty victim, fragile in stature and mien, yet, as one can tell from the dark gaze of his eyes, gravely altered by his experience. The painting is one the narrator David has only heard of through his patient Elizabeth's account, and the moment when he sees it for himself, in her comprehending presence, is a moment of revelation for him. Each of these three figures, David, Elizabeth and the young David, has been the instrument, accidental or otherwise, of a death and in seeing this objectively executed in the painting of his namesake, with the deeper knowledge of his own story through Elizabeth's, David comes to some sort of shaky terms with his unwitting part in the death of his brother Johnny. It is this release, rather than a more obvious love affair, which his encounter with Elizabeth finally brings him and leads (fortunately for me!) to his writing my novel. Just as, by listening to her story, David enables Elizabeth to write the story of the Emmaus paintings of Caravaggio.

It was, therefore, with strange amazement that two days after *The Other Side of You* went to press I learned of the freshly discovered Caravaggios in Loche, France, of which one is another Emmaus painting. It was just such a painting with this same subject that Thomas was on the track of when his fatal heart attack occurs, which Elizabeth finally traces in her book. What made it even stranger was that I have Thomas trace the paintings through a French collection, a connection I could have had no knowledge of when I wrote the book. A piece of synchronicity of the kind which happens regularly when you write but which I could never have conjured artificially or dared to write as fiction.

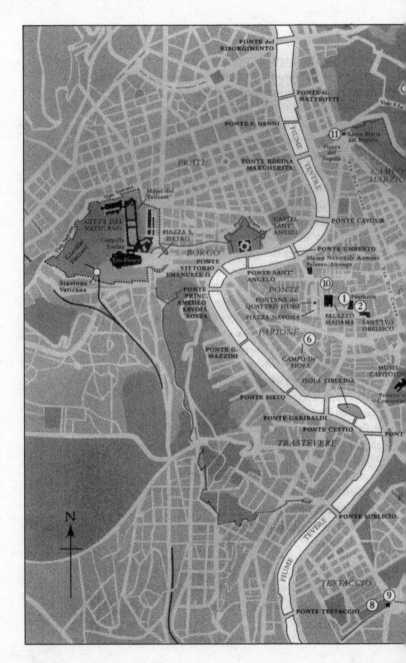

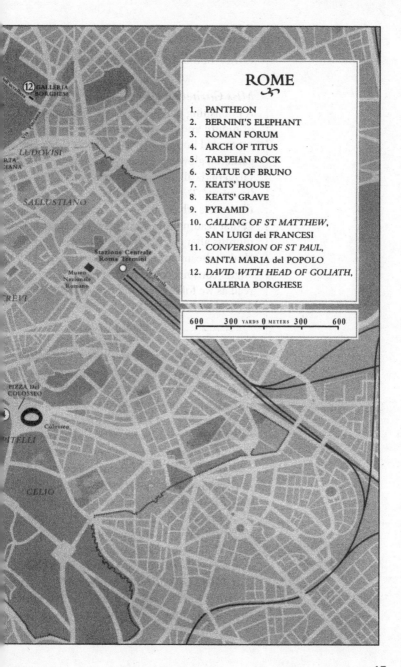

ROME

1. PANTHEON
2. BERNINI'S ELEPHANT
3. ROMAN FORUM
4. ARCH OF TITUS
5. TARPEIAN ROCK
6. STATUE OF BRUNO
7. KEATS' HOUSE
8. KEATS' GRAVE
9. PYRAMID
10. *CALLING OF ST MATTHEW*, SAN LUIGI dei FRANCESI
11. *CONVERSION OF ST PAUL*, SANTA MARIA del POPOLO
12. *DAVID WITH HEAD OF GOLIATH*, GALLERIA BORGHESE

600   300 YARDS 0 METERS 300   600

Have You Read?

Other books by Salley Vickers

Miss Garnet's Angel

A publishing phenomenon, driven by word of mouth and the spontaneous support of captivated booksellers, Salley Vickers's debut garnered glowing reviews. Penelope Fitzgerald called it 'subtle, unexpected and haunting'. *The Times* said that it was 'one of those tales which make such an impression at first reading that it haunts one's mind for months afterwards'. The atmosphere of Venice, the appeal of art and the lure of angels conspire to make an unforgettable read as we follow Miss Garnet in her quest for release from sorrow.

Mr Golightly's Holiday

Many years ago Mr Golightly wrote a work of dramatic fiction that grew to be an international bestseller. But his reputation is on the decline and he finds himself out of touch with the modern world. He decides to take a holiday and comes to the ancient village of Great Calne, hoping to use the opportunity to bring his great work up to date. He soon finds that events take over his plans and that the themes he has written about are being strangely replicated in the lives of the villagers he is staying with. And as the drama unfolds we begin to learn the true and extraordinary identity of Mr Golightly and the nature of the secret sorrow that haunts him.

Instances of the Number 3

Bridget Hansome and Frances Slater have only one thing in common, Peter Hansome, who has died in an accident. Without husband or lover, the two women find that before they can rebuild their lives they must look to themselves and in doing so they encounter a mysterious side to the man they have both loved which neither had suspected. So begins an unlikely alliance between wife and mistress and a voyage of discovery that is as comic as it is profound. *Instances of the Number 3* is a witty and beguiling exploration of love, bereavement, Shakespeare, illusion and the impossibility of escaping your past. ■

If You Loved This,
You Might Like...

The Beginning of Spring
Penelope Fitzgerald

The Transit of Venus
Shirley Hazzard

Gilead
Marilynne Robinson

Mr Fortune's Maggot
Sylvia Townsend Warner

The End of the Affair
Graham Greene

A Month in the Country
J. L. Carr

The Brothers Carburi
Petrie Harbouri

The Lost Painting:
The Quest for a Caravaggio Masterpiece
Jonathan Harr

Beyond Black
Hilary Mantel

The Vanishing of Esme Lennox
Maggie O'Farrell

Find Out More

www.salleyvickers.com
The author's own website has information on all of her books, as well as an events diary, sections for reading groups and booksellers, reviews and articles. You can email Salley directly from the website or join her mailing list.

The National Gallery, Trafalgar Square, London
www.nationalgallery.org.uk
You can visit *The Supper at Emmaus*, the painting that David discusses with Elizabeth either online (search for Caravaggio) or in the gallery itself.

Museo e Galleria Borghese
Piazzale del Museo Borghese, 5 Rome
www.galleriaborghese.it
As well as the Caravaggios mentioned in the book, the Borghese Gallery also has works by, amongst others, Titian, Raphael and Rubens. There is also a Caravaggio on show at its sister gallery, the National Gallery of Ancient Art at the Corsini Palace.

www.enjoyrome.com/walking/caravaggio.html
A novel way to visit the Caravaggio paintings on show in Rome. This tour takes in most of the major pieces as well as explaining more about the painter's life in the city.

Caravaggio (directed by Derek Jarman)
Jarman's films are often love or hate affairs but this biopic about the painter's life and sexuality was one of the director's most commercially successful and accessible projects. Stars Sean Bean, Robbie Coltrane and Tilda Swinton.